BROKEN HEARTS

REBECCA JENSHAK

www.rebeccajenshak.com

Cover Design by Emily Wittig Designs
Formatting by Jersey Girl Design
Editing by Edits in Blue and Ellie McLove at My Brother's Editor

ALSO BY REBECCA JENSHAK

Campus Nights Series

Secret Puck

Bad Crush

Broken Hearts

Smart Jocks Series

The Assist

The Fadeaway

The Tip-Off

The Fake

The Pass

Standalone Novels

Slapshot

Jilted Jock

Sweet Spot

Electric Blue Love

PLAYLIST

"Girl Like Me" by Black Eyed Peas feat. Shakira
"Memories" by David Guetta feat. Kid Cudi
"Paradise" by MEDUZA feat. Dermot Kennedy
"Don't Rush" by Young T & Bugsey feat. DaBaby
"Popstar" by DJ Khaled feat. Drake
"All My Favorite Songs" by Weezer
"Young" by GIRLI
"We're Good" by Dua Lipa
"Goosebumps Remix" by Travis Scott and HVME
"Higher" by Clean Bandit feat. iann dior
"Bed" by Joel Corry, RAYE, and David Guetta
"Safe With Me" by Gryffin feat. Audrey Mika
"Wildest Dreams" by Taylor Swift feat. R3HAB
"Obsessed" by Addison Rae
"Fly Away" (Jonas Blue Remix) by Tones And I
"Lovefool" by twocolors feat. Pia Mia
"Dandelion" by Galantis and JVKE
"Lifestyle" by Jason Derulo feat. Adam Levine and Maroon 5
"Nobody" by NOTD and Catello
"Lush Life" by Zara Larsson
"All I Want" by Olivia Rodrigo
"At My Worst" by Pink Sweat$ and Joel Corry
"Dancing in the Moonlight" by Jubël feat. NEIMY and Tiësto
"Arcade" by Duncan Laurence feat. Fletcher
"Iris" by Natalie Taylor
"This Feeling" by The Chainsmokers feat. Kelsea Ballerini
"Heaven" by Bryan Adams

Chapter One

RHETT

"Everybody in?" Liam glances into the rearview mirror for the all clear as we pile into the back seat of his truck. He's got the fun task of chauffeuring his drunk teammates home.

I start to tell him we're all set, but suddenly my mouth is occupied.

Is it weird to make out with a girl while your buddy is half sitting on your lap? Liam's truck isn't that roomy, and there are five of us smashed into the back seat. My hand is at Layla's waist but also touching Maverick's ass.

I concentrate on her soft lips and the faint taste of raspberries and liquor. She's soaking one side of me. The party we were at had a wet T-shirt contest, and Layla was an eager and enthusiastic participant. I thought she was into Jordan, who's jammed in on the other side of me next to Ketcham, but her lips don't lie.

My phone buzzes in my pocket, and Mav jumps. Or he tries to. There isn't really anywhere to go. "Woah there, buddy. Aim that thing the other way."

"It's my phone." That's all I get out before Layla starts kissing me again. Her fingers glide through my hair, and her tongue does laps around my mouth.

When the truck stops, I come up for air. Damn. That was unexpected. The doors open, and Maverick and Ketcham tumble out from either side. The rest of us follow.

"Thanks for the ride," I say to Liam. Layla is on my heels. I didn't realize she was coming with me. Though maybe I should have. Looks like the party has moved to our place. I head straight to my room while the rest of the guys grab beers and head out back on the deck where people are hanging. Layla is glued to my side.

I'm tired, but when she starts kissing me again, I don't protest.

"You're so hot. How have I never noticed you before?" she asks between kisses. Her hands make quick work of my button and zipper, and she pushes my jeans and boxers down enough that my dick pops out. We're not wasting any time here.

"You too," I say, ignoring the question altogether.

She giggles. "Oh my god, I love your accent."

"Thanks."

"Can you record my voice mail for me?" She takes off her shirt. Her bra is white and see-through and still wet.

Uhh, what?

"You know, like, *Layla isn't here right now. Leave a message, and she'll get back to you.*" Her head bounces side to side as she mocks my Minnesota accent.

"Maybe later," I say and motion toward my dick hanging out between us. He's starting to get shy and call this thing off.

"Oh, right." She sets her phone on my desk and then unhooks her bra revealing small, perky tits that jiggle as she lowers herself in front of me. Her lips graze the head of my cock, and I suck in a breath through my teeth.

Any reservations I have about doing this—and I have a few—fade to the background. She stands and pushes me onto the bed. While she works on tugging my jeans down over my thighs, not an easy feat, I kick off my shoes and lie back.

Fuck, it's been a long day. A long two days.

It isn't every day that a college hockey team makes it past the regular season. In fact, it's a first for Valley U hockey.

We started partying just after breakfast. No, let me back up. Celebrations for winning the hockey west quarterfinals really began the minute we got back to Valley late last night, but it's blurred into today. Breakfast and lunch were liquid only, and I'm starting to feel it. I need food and maybe a nap. I wonder if Layla's got any snacks on her. I want to ask, but my dick is in her mouth, and that seems rude. Plus, if she answers, she'll have to stop sucking me.

I close my eyes and focus. Food later. How long can this last anyway? I haven't had a blow job in… so long I'm embarrassed to count backward to find out. And Layla's mouth is warm and inviting. She keeps popping off and kissing my legs and stomach, and every time she switches the focus away from my dick, I groan.

"That feel good?" she asks as she runs her hands along my inner thighs and kisses my knees.

The correct answer is yes, and that's what I say, even though I really want her to bring her lips closer to my dick again. She's got a whole routine—kissing down my legs and then back up, a few quick sucks of my cock, and repeat.

It's all very sexy and frustrating, but I'll be honest, I'm starting to lose interest. I plan out what I'm going to eat. We don't have a lot of food in the apartment. I think there's some leftover pizza in the fridge. Or there was this morning. The likelihood that's still left is small. Maybe I can get something delivered or talk one of the guys into doing a taco run.

Yeah, *tacos*. Tacos will be good.

With that settled, I turn my attention back to Layla. My hands tangle in her hair, and I guide her back north.

"Uh-uh," she says and climbs up my body. Her hands wrap around my wrists, and she pins them to the bed above my head. Well, that's kinda hot. Her tits are in my face, and she's putting just the right amount of friction on my dick. I grind up into her.

"No hands." She's a bossy little thing.

Then she drops back between my legs and continues adoring my thighs. Is this a thing now? Did I miss the memo on foreplay involving a thorough kissing of my hairy legs? Do some guys really like having their calves kissed? I'm clearly not one of them. Or maybe I'm just too drunk to appreciate it.

My mind drifts again—tacos and maybe a Dr. Pepper. I hardly ever drink soda, but man, am I craving one right now.

I pull my hands behind my head and let out a long breath. Now Layla's massaging my legs, and I'm totally down for that. Hell yeah. Her hands are magic. My limbs relax. I guess I didn't realize how tightly strung I was. It's been quite a month.

The hockey season is coming to an end, which means do or die games at every turn. Plus, I just broke up with my girlfriend of six years. We'd been doing the long-distance thing since high school, and it just wasn't working. I was starting to dislike her, and that made me dislike myself for being with someone I didn't really like anymore. It's complicated. When you've known someone since kindergarten, you don't want to get to that point where you dislike them. We have history, and it wasn't all bad times. It just isn't right anymore. Still sucks.

Speaking of sucking… or not sucking, as is the current state. My poor underused dick gives up, and I just enjoy the free massage. Layla's hands are small, but man, she's got a firm grip, and all the tension slowly leaves my body until I'm putty.

Tacos are really going to hit the spot. That Dr. Pepper, too, because I'm fading. Food and caffeine will be the perfect pick-me-up.

That's my last thought before Layla's screech bounces off the walls of my room. "Oh my god!"

My head's heavy as I lift it from the mattress. She stands in front of me, naked from the waist up and fire in her gaze.

I'm about to ask what's wrong when my bedroom door flies open. Maverick and Jordan crowd into the doorway, taking in the scene. Their heads volley between us.

"What the hell, guys? Get out."

Jordan shields his eyes, but neither leaves.

"Is everything okay in here?" Mav asks. "Was that a happy scream, or someone call 911 scream?"

Happy. I think. I look to Layla since she's the one who screamed. She doesn't look happy.

"He fell asleep." She recoils in horror.

It takes me a second to realize she means me. I'm the *he* in that statement. Fuck. Did I?

They all look to me. I'm still freeballing it. I find my boxers and slip them on, then grab my jeans. I'm hopping around, trying to force them over my thighs as Maverick helps a now crying Layla find her T-shirt and tries to calm her down.

"I'm sorry," I offer. "I drank too much."

"Am I that ugly that he fell asleep?" she asks Maverick. His arms wrap around her back, and she buries her face in his chest. Mav gives me *what the fuck* eyes over her shoulder.

I move closer. "No. It isn't you. I fall asleep all the time."

"That's true," Jordan says. "Yeah. He passes out every single time we watch game film."

"You're comparing me to some boring game film?" She sobs harder. I'm not the only one who drank too much. Layla is drunk girl, ugly crying.

I'm speechless, but Jordan is quick with his words. "No way. You're awesome. You're gorgeous and fun. Rhett's the boring one."

I'd like to object, but if she needs to believe it's all on me, then I'm okay with that. Dammit. Did I really fall asleep while hooking up? Or almost hooking up? Or getting ready to hook up? I'll be honest; I have no idea where that was going. I was either getting the best massage of my life or the worst blow job.

She peeks out from under Maverick's arm to glance at Jordan. "You think I'm gorgeous?"

He nods. "Absolutely."

Mav eases the girl in my room toward the door. "Jordie, why don't you take Layla outside. Maybe the fresh air will help."

She goes willingly, snuggling into Jordan's side.

I run a hand through my hair and then give my face a few smacks to wake me the fuck up.

"Dude, seriously?" Mav asks, finally erupting into laughter that has him bending at the waist. "How does that happen?"

"I was tired and hungry." I lift one shoulder and shrug. Now that I'm clearly not having sex, I need food. "Taco run?"

"I FEEL BAD. SHOULD I TEXT HER?" I ASK, UNWRAPPING MY FOURTH taco.

"Nah, I took care of it," Jordan says, leaning back in the booth and lifting his glass. "The only thing she's going to remember about today is that she got the best orgasm of her life. You're welcome."

"Thank you, I guess." I can cross Layla off my list of potential hookups. "I'm bad at being single."

"It isn't something you can be bad at. Well, unless you fall asleep while a chick goes down on you." Jordan smirks.

"She was all over the place," I protest. "My dick was getting very little of the attention."

Jordan pauses with a taco up to his mouth. "Still. You were naked with a girl. A hot girl."

"Have you successfully hooked up with anyone since Carrie?" Mav asks.

"Define successfully."

His dark brows raise. "If I have to tell you what success means, then I don't think you've been doing it right."

"You need a sure thing," Jordan says. "And maybe an energy drink."

"We can stop on the way back to the apartment," Liam offers.

If these guys are trying to help, I really am in trouble. None of these guys are in a position to dole out advice.

"Nah, I don't want to go back to the apartment. Can you drop me at the rink?"

"Is that a good idea?" Liam asks. "You've been drinking since this morning."

Last night, technically.

"I'm good," I say. Whatever alcohol was in my system flushed itself out when Layla burst into tears with my flaccid penis hanging out.

Liam takes me to the arena when we're done eating.

"I'm gonna drop off Mav, then Jordan and I will come back," Liam says.

"We will?" his roommate asks, not looking pumped about the idea.

"Fun's over, buddy," he says. "We need to get to work."

Jordan drops his gaze and nods. He had a rough game last night, and we can't afford for anyone to be in a slump going into the semifinals.

"Later." I lift a hand as they pull away from the curb.

I shower and change at the rink. The figure skaters have the ice for another fifteen minutes, according to the schedule. With nothing to do, I sit back, close my eyes, and wait. At least no one here will care if I fall asleep.

Chapter Two

SIENNA

The chill of the ice nips at my skin as I skate around the rink. I pull my headband snugly over my ears and come to a stop in front of my friend Josie.

"We're going over to Olivia and Kate's house to watch *Dance Star,* and then we're going to hit up The Hideout for dinner. I bet the hockey team is there celebrating their big win. Are you coming?"

The rest of the team has finished practicing and exits the ice, and she steps off behind them. When she realizes I haven't followed, she glances back for an answer.

"No. I think I'll stay for a little while longer."

An amused smile pulls up the corners of my friend's mouth, and she frees her long, blue hair from the ponytail. "Does Coach know you're staying?"

"I'm fine." I check my heart rate on my watch. "I just want to work on the spin at the end of my short program."

"A girl can't live on skating alone." She combs through her hair with her fingers.

"There's half of a sandwich and some mini pretzels in my bag."

"I was talking about boys and alcohol. In excess. Come on, we have three weeks to prepare for the Desert Cup, and your spin is already perfect."

"See you in the morning," I call over my shoulder as I push off and glide away.

By the time I make it around the oval-shaped rink, she's left with the rest of the team. *Finally,* I'm all alone.

I leave out my earbuds and enjoy the sound of my skates moving along the ice. Closing my eyes briefly, I let all my senses absorb this moment. Even the echo throughout the arena as people go in and out of doors is a welcome sound.

College is a hard place to find any solitude. And ice time is difficult to come by. I'm soaking it up and really appreciating it when I realize I'm not completely alone.

Rhett Rauthruss, one of the Valley U hockey players, sits in the first row near the tunnel to the boy's locker room. Leaned back and slumped down in the seat, he's dressed in a gray T-shirt and black athletic pants instead of the full pads and gear the hockey team usually wears. One skate crossed over the other, eyes closed. The rest of the team is nowhere in sight. I skate around twice more before I stop in front of him.

His dark blond hair falls over one side of his face, and his chest lifts with deep, even breaths. I grab the hockey stick resting near his feet and poke him with it.

Nothing. Maybe he's dead.

"Are you alive?" I ask.

The rise and fall of his chest continues in a slow and steady rhythm. Okay, not dead.

While I contemplate how to handle the situation, I take in his features. Full, pouty lips, big, straight nose, and an angular jaw.

I've never been this close to him. While I often cross paths with the hockey team since we practice in the same building and share the ice, I've never met this particular hockey player. Some of his teammates, yes, but I don't know much about Rhett, aside from his name and now how handsome he is when he's sleeping.

"Hello?" I try again to get his attention. He's the only thing standing in the way of an hour of ice time with no one watching.

His brows pull together just a fraction, but otherwise, he doesn't move.

"Hey!" I shout and give him a harder poke with the stick still in my hands.

He startles. Piercing blue-gray eyes snap to mine, but he's slow to sit up. His shoulders hitch, and his back arches as he looks around the empty rink. "You're the second girl to wake me up today by screaming."

When he stands, I hand him his stick and skate backward. "I didn't scream. I raised my voice to get your attention." *To get you the hell out of my space.* Rarely do I get the ice to myself, and he's ruining it. Also, I resent the implication that somehow I'm at fault here. This is my time.

"Yeah, well, at least I wasn't naked this time." His lips fall into a thin line, and he looks embarrassed by his confession like maybe he didn't mean to share that with a stranger. He comes onto the ice. He's tall, and standing in front of me he seems much bigger than he did sitting down.

"I'm not done skating. I have the ice for another hour."

"You woke me up to tell me I can't skate?" He pulls one of

the hockey nets into place and drops a few pucks onto the ice. "I checked the schedule. There was nothing after four."

"Technically, that's correct, but no one ever comes in late on Sunday afternoons."

"*Technically*, that's not correct. I did today." He smiles like he knows he's got me. He does, but I'm still not ready to give up the fight.

I want all the voices to hush—external and internal. And for that, I need peace and quiet.

"I need to go through my routine without any distractions. I have a show in three weeks."

"And I have the most important game of my life in six days."

I purse my lips. I should have let him sleep.

"I won't say a word, and I'll stick to this half. That good?" He fires a puck into the net without looking at me.

"Yeah, okay." I give in. It isn't the solitude I was looking forward to, but at least he won't be paying me any attention. He seems even less interested in chatting with me than I am him. "Whatever."

He faces me, and those stormy eyes bore into me. I think he might cave or at least offer an apology. Instead, he nods once, drops his gaze back to the ice, and starts skating around and shooting more pucks into the net.

I find my earbuds and turn up the volume to drown out the sound of him, but it's incredibly hard to forget he's here. He got me all riled up when all I was looking for was calm.

And why is Rhett Rauthruss hanging out at the rink by himself on a Sunday afternoon anyway? Not just any Sunday afternoon. They won the quarterfinals just last night. He should be out celebrating with all his teammates, just like Josie assumed.

I've seen Rhett before. The same as I've seen most of the guys on the team around campus and the rink.

Even if we weren't sharing a practice facility, I'd probably be able to identify them. They're well known and liked on campus. Since the hiring of Coach Meyers four years ago, he's slowly built a team of insanely talented players. Several of them have already been drafted by NHL teams.

We often practice directly after the boy's hockey team, but they're usually in full practice gear, complete with helmet, and a lot harder to check out. And it turns out, Rhett is nice to check out. Not my type, like at all, but still undeniably hot.

The hockey guys are known on campus for two things—being fun to look at and hooking up nonstop. I guess three if you count the talent but honestly that gets a lot less chatter than the other two items.

I've never seen the appeal that other girls do. It isn't that I'm opposed to casual sex, but I like there to at least be the delusional hope of it being more. Hookups can lead to relationships if the situation is right. Right?

It never has for me, but I'm holding steady in my belief that it's possible, and I just haven't hooked up with the right person. I know one thing for sure—Rhett and his teammates are not the kind of guys you hook up with hoping for more. That would be dumb even for a semi-believer such as myself.

I practice my spin for a while and then go through my short program twice. I'm taking a break and watching Rhett (while trying to play it off like I'm not watching Rhett) when two more hockey players join him. They must be freshmen or transfers because I can't place their names. One has surfer blond hair styled so neatly

I never would have pegged him for a hockey player, and the other is his polar opposite with dark hair sticking out around a backward hat.

Where Rhett was quiet and attempted to be courteous, these new additions are loud. Even with my music turned up, I can't block out the noise.

Josie should have stuck around. It looks like the hockey team is celebrating here today. She'll be mad she missed this. Me? Not so much.

I turn on my favorite song and step back onto the ice. Rhett glances over with what might be an apologetic look. I can't decipher it through my frustration. The other two turn and blatantly stare. They speak to one another, but I can't make out their exact words thanks to the song blasting in my ears. As I skate, I do my best to push them out of my thoughts and focus.

In three weeks, I have my final collegiate competition. The last chance to skate, really. Sure, I could seek out local shows after graduation, but I know that once I get a real job this summer, the likelihood that I'll have the time to dedicate to practicing, as I do now, is slim.

So, Rhett and his hockey buddies cannot distract me. I won't allow it.

I finally find my flow again after a couple of angry girl songs put me in the right headspace. There are few things that Lady Gaga and Taylor Swift can't make better. I put on my program music to go through my routine once more. My legs are tired, and I'm beyond hungry, but I have to push through.

One of the guys yells loudly—really loudly. It's incessant, and he shouts the same thing over and over until I cannot ignore him.

Gritting my teeth, I stop so I can yell back when a hard body collides with mine. I bounce backward like I hit the wall and sprawl out on the ice. My left side takes the brunt of it, and while I think I'm okay, it freaking hurts.

When I open my eyes, Rhett is standing over me. His blue eyes are wide as he stares down at me. His mouth moves, but I can't hear him.

I sit up and take out my earbuds. "What the hell?"

"I'm so sorry," Rhett apologizes. His mouth moves in the same way it had moments ago.

"She okay?" One of the other guys asks. He and his buddy stand back a little way, watching but keeping their distance.

"*She's* fine." I stand and wobble. My heart races. Although, that may have more to do with my anger and the adrenaline still coursing through me.

Rhett takes my elbow to steady me. "Maybe you should sit for a minute."

I rip my arm away. "I told you I'm fine."

Except, I'm still wobbly and I almost eat it. Wordlessly, Rhett takes me by the arm and helps me off the ice.

"I think Jeff is here." The guy with neatly styled blond hair says. He comes to my other side, and the two of them all but carry me off the ice with tight grips on either elbow.

"Can you go let him know we're coming back?" Rhett asks him. He takes over, walking in front of me with his hands at my waist. His large palms span my ribs, and the heat of him seeps through the thin material of my tank. He guides me onto the bench just off the ice.

"Jordan, go with Liam. If Jeff isn't here, call the front desk and see who's around. We'll be right there."

"I said I was fine," I insist, although ouch, my hip throbs where I landed.

He crouches down in front of me and hands me my blade guards. "You hit pretty hard."

"Yeah, I know. I was there." The edge to my voice is lost in his concerned gaze and the pain shooting down my left side. Damn, that hurt.

"I'm so sorry."

I wince as I put on the guards and stretch out my legs in front of me. "So much for staying on your side."

"Do you feel like you can walk, or do you want me to carry you?"

"You can't be serious." A small, manic laugh slips from my lips. "You're not carrying me."

He nods once and stands tall. Ignoring the pain, I get up and walk ahead of him toward the trainer's office. Every step makes my hip ache.

Jordan and Liam are waiting for us, standing next to one of the trainers I don't know, but I recognize the blue polo shirt they all wear.

"Hey, I'm Jeff. Heard you took a spill on the ice."

A spill? I glance at Rhett, who looks down at his skates as he speaks, "I skated into her."

Jeff's brows raise. "That had to have hurt. There are guys on the team that couldn't collide with Rauthruss and walk back here on their own." He motions with his head for me to come back. "Hop up here and let me take a look."

Rhett and the guys linger as I awkwardly sit on the trainer's table.

"You three can go," Jeff says.

Jordan and Liam don't need any more encouragement, but Rhett is slower to leave.

"I'm going to wait just outside," Rhett says. I'm not sure if it's meant for my benefit or Jeff's.

I hope it's not mine. I want him here even less now than I did an hour ago. And that's saying something.

"Anything hurt?" the trainer asks once they're gone.

"My hip, mostly. Also, the left side of my face, but I'm okay, really. I've been hurt worse."

"Then there is no harm in taking a look. Lie back and roll onto your right side."

I do as he says, and he feels around, tenderly pressing on my hip and then raising and lifting my leg, asking if it hurts as he moves me at different angles.

"Well..." he says finally. "I think you're going to live, but I'm going to grab some ice packs and have you sit back here for fifteen or so."

"That's not necessary."

"It is necessary. You took a nasty hit. Ice it and hang around for a bit."

When he walks off, I lie back and press my fingertips to the tender skin under my eye. I can hear the guys out in the hallway. The door is open, and they aren't even attempting to whisper.

One of them says, "How many more girls are you going to make cry today?"

"She didn't cry," Rhett snaps back.

I try to follow their conversation as they continue to poke fun at Rhett. I don't have enough backstory to make complete sense of it, but I can understand enough to determine that Rhett is exactly the type of guy I pegged him for—a complete player. Not to mention an inconsiderate brute.

Pity. He really is nice to look at.

Chapter Three

RHETT

Adam and Maverick walk down the hallway toward Jordan, Liam, and me. We're still waiting outside of the trainer's room.

"What's going on?" Adam's worried expression darts between us.

I bypass his question to ask my own. "What are you guys doing here?"

"I texted them," Liam says. "I wasn't sure how serious it was."

"Having a real bang-up day, aren't you?" Mav asks, shaking his head with a grin.

"She's fine." I think. I hope. I've never seen someone fly through the air like that. She probably weighs a hundred pounds, and I hit her skating fast to reach a puck Jordan knocked toward her side of the rink. I was afraid it would hit her, or she'd trip over it. I should have let it go. Hindsight is a real bitch.

"Is she still in there?" Adam points toward the open doorway.

"Yeah."

"You two can take off," Adam tells Liam and Jordan. "Thanks

for the heads-up."

I push off the wall and slap hands with Jordan and then Liam. "Thanks for staying."

"Try not to make anyone else cry today," Jordan says and then juts his chin toward the trainer's room. "But, uh, if she needs consoling like Layla did, I'm wide open."

"Yeah, yeah, you're a real Prince Charming," Adam says and shoves at his shoulder. "How about you get some rest tonight so you can get your ass back here at six in the morning?"

Jordan salutes him with his middle finger. "Aye, aye, captain." He looks to me. "Later, lady-killer."

Adam keeps up his tough-guy act until they're gone. His serious expression melts into a wide smirk. "Tired? Sleeping okay?"

I glare at Maverick.

"I didn't tell him," he insists, raising his hands in front of him.

"Actually, it was Heath I overheard telling the story of your narcoleptic hookup." Adam leans against the wall, smiling at my expense.

"Does everyone already know?" It's rhetorical. Of course, they do.

Mav answers anyway. "Kind of hard to keep a story like that to yourself."

"Ah, relax," Adam says. "I'm impressed in a weird sort of way. At least you're getting back out there. And I'm glad we finally have some embarrassing stories to lord over you. God knows you have plenty on me."

"That's a fact."

Adam crosses both arms across his chest. "So, you fell asleep hooking up with one girl, and then you came here to blow off some steam and took out another chick?"

I rub my forehead with two fingers.

"Is that an accurate summary of your day, buddy?" Maverick asks.

"I fucking hate you guys."

Adam tosses his head back and laughs. "Who is she anyway? Liam just said a skater."

"I don't know."

Jeff sticks his head out, holding on to the doorframe. "We're done in here. You guys can see her if you want. Although maybe keep a foot of distance in case she feels like repaying you for the shiner she's going to have.

"You gave her a black eye?" Mav hoots with laughter as he and Adam walk in front of me.

My phone buzzes in my pocket. Carrie again. Just what I need. Another girl to yell at me today. Though, to be fair, at least two of them had good reasons.

"Sienna!" Mav calls, snapping my attention to the girl sitting on the trainer's table. He envelops her in a hug. "Rhett didn't say it was you, or I would have kicked his ass already."

"I'm fine. A little banged up." Her gaze finds mine. She's holding an ice pack up to her eye, and another rests on her left thigh.

"You know each other?" I ask. Duh, obviously they do.

"Yeah, of course." Mav takes a seat next to her on the table. "Sienna is my favorite yoga teacher."

"You do yoga?" Adam asks him.

He scoffs like he's offended. "You should see my plow pose."

"No thanks," Adam says.

Maverick nudges Sienna. "Are you okay?"

"Yeah, just a little sore."

"I could still kick his ass for you, if you want."

I glance between them trying to read the situation. Maverick is the friendliest guy I know. He's never met a stranger and chats up anyone. He also hits on everyone, making it hard to tell when he's really into a girl or just being his usual friendly self. For some reason, I'm hoping it's the second in Sienna's case.

My phone rings again. Damn, Carrie is getting persistent.

"That Carrie?" Adam asks as I silence it and put it back in my pocket.

"Yeah."

"Another one of the girls you've tortured today or one you plan to torture later?" Sienna smiles sweetly.

I balk. The guys laugh.

"I like her," Adam says.

"All right, closing up for the day. Get out of here so I can sleep easy knowing you knuckleheads aren't injuring yourselves or anyone else." Jeff turns off the lights on one side of the room.

Maverick stands and helps Sienna to her feet. She protests a lot less with him helping her, I notice.

"Did you drive or do you need a ride?" he asks her.

"I am fine. Honestly."

She hobbles, favoring her left side.

"We'll drop you at your dorm," Mav says.

And that's that. The four of us walk out to Adam's Jeep. I climb into the back with her, and Mav sits up front.

"I'm really sorry." I can't think of anything else to say. Her left eye is starting to turn colors, and I feel like a damn asshole.

"You mentioned that." She smiles ever so slightly. "I'll live."

I fall quiet. Mav peppers her with questions and fills us in on what a great yoga teacher she is and how she's his favorite. I mostly tune him out and scope her out for the first time since we met.

I must have still been drunk earlier because I hardly afforded her a second glance, and she's worthy of a second and third glance. Even the yellow and blue starting to streak her face doesn't take away from the bright green of her eyes. Her lashes are long and strikingly black against her skin. Her dark brown hair is pulled back into one of those messy buns girls wear and I can't tell if it's short or long.

"I'm Rhett," I say finally.

"Sienna."

"Nice to meet you."

She hums, and the smallest of smiles tips up the corners of her mouth. "Nice is not the word I would have used."

When Adam pulls up in front of her dorm, she opens the door. "Thanks for the ride."

"See you tomorrow in class," Mav says out his window.

I bolt across the back seat as the door closes on me.

"I'll be right back," I tell the guys.

I hustle after her, reaching her just inside of the main lobby of the dormitory.

"Hey, wait up." I fall into step beside her.

"Following me?" She continues walking toward the stairway.

"I feel terrible. Let me make it up to you somehow. Dinner? Coffee?"

Her brows lift. "Are you asking me out?"

"No," I say quickly. Not the worst idea, but it's clear she isn't on board. "Just an apology meal."

"I'm good."

"Then, yes, a date."

Abruptly, she stops walking, and I catch myself two steps ahead of her.

"A date?" Those green eyes pin me to my spot.

I shrug. "Or just coffee."

"With you? The guy who was hooking up with someone earlier today and made her cry?" She says it like it's a question.

"How do you..."

"Your buddies were talking pretty loudly. I didn't get the whole story, but I think I heard enough."

I open and close my mouth. What the hell do I say to that?

My phone rings. I ignore it, but Sienna glances to my pocket and laughs. "I think you've already got your hands full. See ya around, *lady-killer*."

She pushes past me, and I let her go. I take out my phone and power off the stupid thing as I walk back outside.

When I'm in the back seat, Mav turns around and regards me seriously. "She okay?"

"Seems fine." I bang my head against the window. What a fucking day.

"Leave it to you to hurt Sienna of all people." Mav's facing forward, so I can't see his face, but the back of his head shakes from side to side.

"I was chasing a loose puck. I was trying to keep it from hitting her."

"In this case, I think the puck would have done less damage.

"No fucking kidding." I sigh. "And what do you mean Sienna

of all people? I was feeling pretty fortunate I took down a tough chick with no heart. She didn't even cry. I cannot take another girl crying on me today."

Mav swivels around, and his jaw hangs open.

"What?" I look from him to Adam. The latter shrugs.

"You don't know?"

"Know what?"

"I don't know how anyone can put their foot in their mouth so well without even knowing what he's doing."

"What the hell are you talking about?"

"First of all, she has a heart. She's one of the nicest, most down-to-earth girls I've ever met."

"And secondly?"

"Sienna has a rare heart condition. I don't know all the details, but I think it's pretty serious."

An uneasy feeling washes over me. "How do you know all this?"

"We chat during yoga. Her heart stops, or she faints, or both, maybe. It happened at one of her competitions last year."

"Ooooh." Adam shakes a finger at him. "I heard about that. She has long QT." He whips around to stare at me with wide eyes. "You took out a girl with a bad heart?"

"You could have killed her," Mav says. "No heart." He huffs.

My stomach drops. Holy shit. I don't know what long QT is but it doesn't sound good. "How the hell was I supposed to know? And it isn't like I did it on purpose. It was an accident."

We pull up to the apartment and Mav jumps out. "I was just giving you shit on that last thing. I don't think you would have killed her, but it does seem very appropriate, considering your track record today."

Fuck my life.

"Hey," Heath says as I walk out of my room Monday morning. His eyes are barely open as he chugs a protein drink. His girlfriend, Ginny, sits on a stool next to him with her head on the counter.

"'Morning," she says.

I tug the end of her braid as I go by. Ginny is Adam's little sister, and since he and I've been rooming together for the past four years, Ginny's like a kid sister to me.

Adam appears next, slinking out of his room and shutting the door quietly behind him. Reagan stayed over last night, as she generally does now. Both my roommates are in serious relationships, which is bizarre since I was the only one in a serious relationship until a few months ago. Now I'm dodging phone calls from my ex and blundering my way through being single. Life is weird.

He grunts something that might be good morning as he heads to the kitchen to make oatmeal. I'm too tired to even think about eating. The sun isn't up yet, and we have a skills practice in thirty minutes.

I'm not complaining. I'm stoked we get to play hockey another week, but two days of celebrating looks like it's taken its toll on all of us.

My stomach growls. Obviously, it doesn't have the same issue with the time that I do. I'm grabbing orange juice from the fridge when Maverick walks through the front door.

"Goooood morning," he calls, sounding way more chipper than the rest of us. When I turn around, he laughs. "Nice shiner. You and Sienna match. Adorable."

I'm too tired to come up with a witty comeback. But it's a new day. And today can't possibly be any worse than yesterday.

Chapter Four

SIENNA

It looks like my three-year-old niece did your eye makeup." Josie watches me from the doorway of our shared bathroom while I dab concealer on the black and yellow under my eye.

"I can't tell if I'm making it better or worse."

"Less eye shadow. You aren't fooling anyone." She reaches around me for her toothbrush.

She's right. I look ridiculous. I wipe off my makeup and start over with just my usual basics of foundation and mascara.

"Does it hurt?" my roommate asks as we're leaving our dorm.

"Only if I touch it."

She moves her hand up like she's going to poke it, and I slap her hand away.

With a laugh, she asks, "Did he at least apologize?"

Last night when Josie got home, I was already asleep, so I gave her the short version of yesterday's events when she woke up and saw my black eye. I left out the part where he asked me out. Or sort of asked me out? An apology date where I'm limping and have a black eye does not sound super romantic.

"About a dozen times."

"I can think of worse ways to get a black eye. Rhett Rauthruss is some serious eye candy. I heard he's single now, too."

"Aren't they all?" I place a hand on my chest. "Commitment scares me. I'm just going to fuck everything that moves."

She laughs again. Josie has a great laugh. The kind that you can't help but smile when you hear it. "You sound like Elias. How is he?"

"Great," I say and prepare to fill her in on the latest of my best friend's shenanigans, but outside we meet up with more girls on the team headed to practice.

"Oh my gosh, Sienna! What happened to your eye?" Olivia asks when she sees me. I give a very abbreviated version as we jog the few blocks to the arena in the dark. My left hip and knee are both bruised and sore, but otherwise, I seem to have survived the collision without any injuries.

At the rink, I'm forced to retell the story again while we warm up in the hallway waiting for Coach. She arrives, coffee in hand and a clipboard in the other. "Before we get on the ice, take a look at the updated schedule." She holds up the clipboard. "I printed it out, but you'll find it in our shared calendar too."

I can tell by the grumbling of the girls closest to her that the changes aren't good.

"We're sharing the ice with the hockey team?" Josie finally squeaks when we make our way to the front. Her tone is skeptical and not altogether thrilled. Same, girl, same.

There's complaining all around. My teammates shout out questions to Coach, wondering how this will possibly work. Others are pouting that it isn't fair.

"We still get the same amount of ice time, but we'll need to share for our morning practice. And I've negotiated for an additional hour in the afternoons for those of you who want it. It's the first time in the school's history that the hockey team has gotten this far. We are going to support them the same way we want them to support us."

"Yeah, right," someone mumbles. None of us qualified for nationals this year which might make us a touch more bitter than we'd otherwise be.

Coach gives us a look that says, it is what it is, and we take the ice. "We'll make the best of it." She smiles. "And they're here, so let's get to work."

We turn and watch as the hockey team files out next to us. When Rhett spots me, his eyes widen, and a gloved hand goes to his eye. His black eye. He pulls on his helmet with a broody look, and I can't help but smile. I had no idea he got hurt in the fall too. I feel a tiny bit bad even though he was the one that ran me over.

"Sienna, a minute," Coach calls.

I skate over to the bench where she waits for me. "I heard you took a tumble on the ice last night. How are you feeling?"

"Fine. I'm bruised but no injuries."

"You really shouldn't be on the ice by yourself."

"Technically, I wasn't by myself," I mutter to myself.

"I don't want to put restrictions on you that I don't require of the other girls, but with your heart condition, I need you to make sure there is someone in the building that knows what to do any time you step on the ice. Okay?"

I nod, feeling guilty and resenting it. "Yes, ma'am."

"Good. Now, let's get you ready for the Desert Cup."

It's hard to concentrate with the hockey guys on the ice. And not just for me. Coach gives up on continually yelling "Focus" halfway through practice and divides us up into groups to work on skills. Coach Meyers is having the same issue. Jordan and another guy trip over each other while staring at Josie doing a flying camel spin.

"Well, this was a great idea," I say to Olivia.

"I am loving this. Really peps up my morning. Although, I wish I'd worn something less wrinkled." She holds the fabric up to her nose. "And smelly."

I lean forward. "It's a little musty," I admit. "But I guarantee you smell better than them."

We glance back down at the guys. Sweat drips off them.

"He's cute," she says.

"Who?" I play dumb, but I know exactly who she's talking about. Rhett skates toward the center of the ice and gets back into line, staring at me the entire time.

"Your twin, Rhett."

Sure, he's cute. And he knows it.

We work through skills, making the best of our time on the ice, even if it's only half of our usual space. After I complete my turn, I skate to the back of the line. Rhett's standing nearby, also at the back of his respective line.

"Hey," he says. "How's the eye? Does it hurt?" He winces.

"I'm guessing about as bad as yours does."

"I'm so sorry." The sincerity in his tone catches me off guard. I mean, he sounded sincere last night, but now there's something else behind his voice. Guilt?

I'm quiet as I study his face, trying to get a read on him. He's a tall guy, broad. Not too bulky, but solid. Makes sense considering it felt like I ran into a brick wall yesterday.

"I didn't know about your heart condition. If I had..." He trails off.

Well, now that makes sense. I don't hide my heart condition, but man, could I make a good case for it because this is just the type of reaction that frustrates me. Suddenly, he feels this greater sense of empathy like I'm some fragile damsel in distress.

"Don't worry about it," I clip and turn from him.

He skates beside me, moving up with my line. "You're okay, though, right?"

"Rauthruss!" Coach Meyers, the hockey team's head coach, voice booms over all the other noise in the rink. "Maybe you and your friend want to share what's so important that you're holding up two practices?"

"Sorry, Coach," Rhett responds.

Coach Meyers skates toward us. He looks from Rhett to me, and I see the second he puts it together.

He leans on the hockey stick in his hands. "You must be the unfortunate victim of Rauthruss' clumsiness."

I don't know how to answer that, so I just nod.

"Coach Brekke," he calls over us. "Mind if I borrow..." He looks to me for my name.

"Sienna."

"Mind if I borrow Sienna for a few minutes?"

My coach gives him a thumbs up.

Coach Meyers is probably my dad's age. He has dark hair that's graying at the temples and a few wrinkles around his eyes. It's easy to see that he has his team's total respect and attention as he blows the whistle and the action immediately stops.

"We're going to run an agility drill," he informs them.

The guys groan.

Coach skates, picking up cones as he goes, then placing four in a square. "Sienna, if you'll stand in the middle there."

I do as instructed.

Coach Meyers proceeds showing them what to do, moving and talking at the same time. "Skate around the first two cones with the puck, tight transitions, pivot, quick feet, pass, and then continue around. We'll do it for time. Anyone over six seconds owes me a suicide before they get back in line."

"What about her?" one of the guys asks.

"Glad you asked." Coach smiles.

"Automatic disqualification for touching her. Not even a hair on her head. Got it?"

"Yes, sir," they mumble.

Coach smiles at me. "Feel free to lean in."

They guys line up. Rhett's in the back.

"Rauthruss, why don't you show us how it's done."

The nervous expression on his face makes me giggle.

Coach passes him the puck when he's in position. "Go."

At his command, Rhett starts around the first cone. He's a good skater, smooth, and surprisingly light on his feet. I say surprisingly because he sure didn't feel light when he ran me over yesterday. I hold my breath as he moves around me the first time. It's sort of a weaving motion—around a corner cone, around me, another cone, and so on.

Rhett gives me a wide berth, not cutting as close to me as he is the cones. And I'm not the only one that notices.

“Tighter transitions in the center,” Coach barks, sending a pass right at me. Rhett pivots and stops the puck before it hits me, then skates backward around me. He doesn’t touch me, but I feel him. So close I could move a fraction of an inch and brush against him.

He finishes and stops, looking to coach for his time.

“Five and a half seconds.”

Rhett’s face relaxes. That is until his coach looks to me.

“What do you say, Sienna? Any contact? I couldn’t see from this angle.” He fights a grin. I doubt there’s much Coach Meyers misses.

I consider lying. It would be amusing to watch Rhett’s reaction if I did. His expressions play out so well on his face. I like that about him, actually.

“No contact,” I confirm.

“You’re sure?”

The guys laugh. I do too.

“All right. Thank you, Sienna.”

“Rauthruss, give me a suicide anyway.”

“What?” His mouth falls open, and he looks between his coach and me.

“Consider it an apology. Should I make it two?” Coach asks me.

I pretend to think about it, bringing my hand to my chin and making him sweat it out for a few seconds. “Nah, I think one should suffice.”

“Fair enough.” He nods to me. “Thanks for your help, Sienna. I think we can manage on our own from here.”

I skate toward my team, sneaking a peek at Rhett skating along the wall. He really is a good skater, and something about seeing him in the full gear after knowing what he looks like underneath really does it for me. Yeah, I'd say I like this apology a whole lot better than his others.

"All right, boys," Coach Meyers calls. "Keep it moving."

The rest of practice is far less eventful. Coach Meyers keeps the hockey guys on point, and we work on jumps in small groups. There is no time to look at Rhett. Okay, there's very little time. And the opportunities I do get, he's completely focused on hockey.

After morning practice, I have classes until lunchtime, and then I have to book it over to Ray Fieldhouse where I teach barre and then yoga.

My schedule is crazy busy, but I happen to like it that way. And the money I'm making teaching group fitness classes will help pay my rent for a while after graduation. I still don't have a job lined up, and with only two months until I say goodbye to college, it's starting to feel like I never will.

How do people choose a career? Trying to imagine myself working forty-plus hours sitting behind a desk, working my fingers to the bone doing anything is difficult. Or maybe I just haven't found the right thing. My dad thinks it's the first of those two. "You can't expect to love any job right away. Work hard and be loyal," he says, every chance he gets.

That has worked well for him. He started as an assistant and worked his way up to an executive at a software company. I'm proud of him, and I think it's amazing what he's done, but I'm not necessarily sold on his story being the right plan for me.

I have another interview next week, and I'm hoping that this time when I sit down across from the interviewer, I'll feel something akin to genuine excitement.

As people trickle into the classroom, I smile and start the music. Barre isn't my favorite class to teach, but it's popular and almost always filled to capacity. Today is no different.

For thirty minutes, I lead them through a brutal toning workout using my ballet training.

"Eight more," I call.

A collective groan sounds under the music. I know I'm an awful person because I love that groan. It means I've done my job. I glance up at the clock to make sure we're on track. A line has already formed for the yoga class that starts next. I love teaching yoga. It's not quite as popular as barre, but most of the students who attend are pretty advanced, so I can push them harder than if it were a class full of beginners.

"And you're done. Nice job today."

As my barre students leave and yoga students start to come in, I take a drink of water and switch the music.

I'm rolling my mat onto the floor when I notice Rhett standing outside of the door. A few girls from my last class are lingering, checking him out. I look around for Maverick. He's usually here by now, and the fact I even have to look for him should tell me he isn't here. Johnny Maverick doesn't enter a room without you noticing.

I still remember the first time he came into one of my classes. It was last year, about a month into his freshmen year. He was reluctant—not that I realized it at the time. But now, after getting to know his personality, I realize that was a much tamer, reserved person that walked into the studio.

Even reserved, I was intimidated. He's a tall guy, covered in tattoos, dark hair—your basic bad boy. That is until he opens his mouth. Once I got to know him, I realized how nice and funny he is. He's part of the reason I enjoy teaching this class so much. No matter how hard I push him, he manages to make it look easy.

But he's not here, and instead, it's another hockey player walking into the room. He approaches me at the front while others are finding places around the room to unroll their mats.

Dressed in athletic pants and a Valley U hockey T-shirt, he looks too hot to be real. He doesn't have the same bad-boy look like Maverick. He's more broody jock. Still, he has this appeal about him that is more than just his pretty face or his amazing arms, which I'm definitely not staring at.

"What are you doing here?" I'm pretty sure the question comes out like an accusation. He puts up all my defense modes like my brain is aware that letting him in would be oh so very bad for my heart.

"I want to apologize." He holds up a hand when I start to interrupt. "I know, I already have, but I keep getting it wrong. And I'm probably going to this time, too. You seem like a cool chick. Mav has nothing but good things to say, and I guess I just want to make sure we're good." He smiles and points to his eye. "I have a matching black eye, and I did a suicide apology this morning."

"Neither of those was by choice, but the second was pretty amusing."

"Being here was all me though." He grins, a boyish charm that I'm sure gets him whatever he wants.

"How'd you find me, anyway?"

"Maverick. Oh, and he wanted me to pass along a message that he has to miss yoga today because he's meeting with Coach, but he'll see you on Wednesday." He nudges me playfully with an elbow. Even that small touch makes my heart rate accelerate. "We good?"

"Grab a mat."

When my intentions are clear, his deep laughter spills out. The sound makes my stomach flip. "If I stay for class and do some downward dog and stretching shit, then we're good?"

I smirk. Stretching shit? Oh, this is going to be fun.

Chapter Five

RHETT

Lying flat on my back, I stare at the white ceiling and moan. She broke me.

The *she* in question peers down at me with a pleased smile. "Class is over. You can go now."

"If only my legs worked." I roll over onto one side and then push myself into a sitting position. I'm soaked in sweat—something I didn't realize was possible from yoga.

"Tell the truth," I start once I manage to get to my feet. "You made those poses up, right? There's no humble flamingo, half lotus, or full monkey. You were fucking with me."

"Half monkey." She smiles. "No, those are real poses. Well, not exactly the way you were doing them."

I hang my head. My hair falls into my face, sticking to my forehead. I need a shower. Maybe two. And a soak in the ice bath.

"Are we even now?" I hold my hands out to my sides, letting her revel in my embarrassment. I'm sweaty and gross, and I just made a complete ass out of myself for the better part of my lunch hour. My stomach growls. And I missed lunch.

"Yeah, we're even." She moves to the front of the class, turns off the music, and gathers her things while I mop up my sweat and wipe down the mat.

She glances down at her watch and presses two fingers to the pulse point on her neck, which reminds me what Maverick said about her heart and having to monitor it.

"Everything okay?"

"Yeah, I'm fine. I just like to keep an eye on my heart rate throughout the day. Habit, more than anything." She drops her arm to her side. "See you tomorrow, Rauthruss." She backs out of the studio. "I don't think yoga is your calling." She brings her hands together in front of her, a huge smile on her face. "Namaste."

OVER THE NEXT FEW DAYS, I DON'T HAVE ANY MORE RUN-INS with my new favorite skater. I see her at practice, but Coach keeps us focused on hockey with the threat of running us until we puke.

Thursday late afternoon, I'm in my room finishing econ homework when my phone rings on my desk. I don't have to look to know who it is, but I glance down anyway. My ex has been calling at least three times a day since last weekend. Yesterday and today, that number has increased dramatically. I feel like an ass for not answering, but we can't keep doing this.

The first week we were broken up (for the second time in a month), I answered every single time. She cried, begged me to take her back, and I sat on the other line feeling like an ass. I almost caved too. I don't like that she's hurting. We were together for nearly six years—that's a damn long time, and it isn't like I just stopped caring about her completely. She's a great girl. She's just not the right girl for me.

I thought I was doing the right thing by continuing to talk to her and being a shoulder she could cry on, but instead, I think I just gave her false hope. After a three-hour call last week where I heard her out, listening to all the really great reasons she thought we could make it work, I finally told her there was no way I was going to change my mind and asked her to stop calling so much.

She gave me the space I asked for, for a few days, but then the calls started up again after we won the quarterfinals. It sucks. I press silent as Adam fills my doorway.

"Hey." He leans against the doorjamb, taking up most of it. "You want to go to The Hideout and grab an early dinner?"

"I was just gonna eat a sandwich or something. I've gotta finish this and then study for a quiz."

My phone pings with a new voice message. Fuck, that's new. She doesn't usually leave messages.

"You know what, fuck it, I'm starving." I stand, abandoning my phone on my desk. I hope I'm doing the right thing by holding firm on my decision not to answer. I've never disliked having a cell phone more in my life.

It's just the two of us when we get to The Hideout. We put in our order, and the server brings us our beers while we wait.

"No Reagan?" I ask. It's a rare evening that Adam isn't with his new girlfriend, so I fully expected her to show up.

"She and Dakota are running together at the track."

"Things are good then?" I know they are. I can see it all over my buddy's face. He's totally gone for her. They recently had a falling out, and he walked around sulking like I've never seen from him. Adam was the king of breakups, moving on within the week or even sometimes the same day.

"They're great, yeah." He leans forward, both hands around the glass. His smile goes serious. "What about you? Talked to Carrie?" He tries to come off relaxed, but I know him well. We've been roommates and teammates for too long. I see right past his calm demeanor. The team is playing well—even better than people expected from us this season, and he's worried about me and how my breakup with Carrie will impact my time on the ice. He's captain, so I guess it's his job to worry.

It isn't completely unwarranted. There were a few games after we broke up the first time where I was a wreck. I might have been the one to end it, but it isn't like I stopped caring for her. We were together for so long and I really loved her. But when I made the decision to end things it wasn't without a lot of thought and soul searching. I know it's right and as the time has passed, I still feel solid in my decision. I've moved on even if she hasn't.

But, I get where Adam is coming from. We've got the record to beat and everyone is gunning for us. It's going to be a long grind over the next month to get to the Frozen Four.

"Things are good. I promise. Carrie is still calling, but I haven't spoken to her in a week."

"That's gotta take a toll. Why don't you block her number?"

"Nah," I say automatically. "You think?"

He shrugs. "I don't know. Sucky situation all around."

"Definitely. I think she'll stop on her own. It's probably just routine. We spent most of our relationship on the damn phone." It took me almost two weeks to stop reaching for it the second I woke up every morning.

Our food comes, and we fall quiet as we devour greasy burgers and fries.

"Had any other catastrophic run-ins with the opposite sex I should know about?" Adam tries and fails to keep a straight face.

"No," I grumble around a mouthful of food.

He leans back in his chair, smiling at my expense. "Don't worry. I'm sure you have plenty more opportunities in front of you."

"Not if word gets around that I fall asleep on chicks or give them black eyes."

Adam chuckles. "You just need a good wingman." He points at himself.

"What about Reagan?"

"The best wingmen are in relationships. It's what keeps them from swooping in and stealing the chicks for ourselves. Especially with your weak game."

"That and knowing Dakota would cut you if you hurt Reagan."

He nods. "That too. Come on. It'll be fun. Finish your food, and let's go to the bar. I recognize a friend of Ginny's I can introduce you to."

I'm not really interested in putting on a smile and making small talk, but ten minutes later, I'm following him to the half-circle bar along the back wall of The Hideout.

Adam never looks out of place or uncomfortable. I admire that about him. I don't know what to say or how to act with girls after being in a relationship for so long. No one expected much from me when I was with Carrie. I was off-limits. That made me more intriguing for some girls, but I just faded into the background for most. I'm good with fading into the background.

"Ava?" Adam approaches a girl with short, black hair at the bar.

She turns in her seat. "Adam, hey!"

She tucks her hair behind her ear and sits a little straighter. She's clearly surprised we've approached her, but Adam being Adam quickly puts her at ease.

"Good to see you. Have you met my buddy, Rhett?"

Her dark gaze slides to me. She smiles politely and raises a hand in a cute, shy wave. "I don't think so."

"Nice to meet you, Ava." I wave back.

"You too."

Adam shifts closer to me and mutters under his breath, "Ask to buy her a drink."

I'm pretty sure Ava heard him, but I ask her anyway. "Can I buy you a drink?"

"Umm..." she starts.

"Excuse me," a deep voice says behind me, and I sidestep to let the guy pass. He goes straight for the empty chair next to Ava and takes a seat. He swivels around so that his knees rest against Ava's.

Ava looks at her lap. "This is my boyfriend, Trent. He's visiting for the week."

Awesome. I'm hitting on girls while their boyfriend is in the shitter now. It's a new low.

Adam clears his throat, hiding a laugh. "That's great. Where are you from?"

"I go to school upstate." He's eyeing us up, trying to decide if we're a threat.

"Adam is Ginny's brother," Ava tells him, and immediately his expression shifts into something much friendlier.

"Oh, cool. You play hockey, right?" he asks Adam.

“That’s right. We both do.” Adam looks to me, and I nod.

“Really cool.” Trent places a hand on Ava’s thigh.

I get it, buddy. She’s yours. No need to pee on her.

“Well, we were just heading out, but it was good to finally put a face with the name.” He’s super handsy while leading his girl away from us.

Adam slumps into Ava’s empty chair after they exit and hangs his head, laughter spilling from his lips.

“Some wingman you are.” I take the other chair.

“I forgot she had a boyfriend.”

“Convenient.” I lift my near-empty beer bottle when the bartender looks my way, and she grabs me another.

“We’ll find you someone else. It’s early yet.”

The TV grabs my attention again. It’s figure skating, and I think of Sienna. A new skater is taking the ice. She poses, waiting for the music to begin.

“I think I’m good. And besides, I’ve been thinking about asking out Sienna.” Again. Maybe this time without stumbling all over myself.

“The chick you gave a black eye?”

I scratch my nose with my middle finger. “Drink your beer so we can get the hell out of here. I need to study.”

“Whatever you say, *lady-killer*.”

Chapter Six

SIENNA

I leave my dorm early Friday morning to get on the ice before anyone else.

"Didn't your coach tell you not to be on the ice by yourself? Also, you really shouldn't be walking in the dark across campus." Elias's brows pinch together on the screen of my phone.

"I cleared it with Coach, and that's why I'm talking to you."

"What exactly do you think I'm going to do if someone attacks you? Yell at them to please stop?"

"No, dummy. Hang up and call the police."

He chuckles. It's three hours later in Toronto, and Elias is already at the rink where he skates with his pairs partner Taylor.

"So, any plans tonight or are you spending another Friday night watching documentaries on serial killers." He shivers.

"If you don't like them, don't watch them."

"You misled me. You were all *'This one isn't that bad. You'll be fine. It's a great date night film'.*" He shoots me a glare. "That chick ghosted me after I woke up in the middle of the night screaming bloody murder."

Laughing, I swipe my card against the door reader and let myself in the arena. "I've gotta go. I'll call you later."

"No. Don't call me later. Go out and have fun. One of us has to."

"Bye, E. Don't die on me today."

He makes a cross over his heart before he ends the call.

I stop in Coach's office to let her know I'm here and then head out to the ice.

"You," I say when I spot Rhett at one end stretching out.

"Hey," he says tentatively.

I shake my head. "Seriously? Every time I think I have this place to myself."

He stands tall and skates toward me. "I could say the same thing about you. Plus, I was here first this time."

"Can't a girl get a little peace and quiet?"

He smiles but doesn't answer.

"I guess you can stay," I say like I'm the boss of this place. He smirks. "Just... promise not to run me over."

He grimaces. "You'd think that'd be an easy thing to promise, but I'll just say I'll do my best."

"I forgot my headphones, so I'm going to play music over the speakers," I say as I skate to the opposite side.

"Sure, yeah, whatever. Pretend I'm not here."

Which is exactly what he does to me. He doesn't spare another glance in my direction as he starts skating around his half. I put the music on and fall into my routine. I go through it twice—once without jumps and the second all out. When I finish, I grab a drink and check my heart rate before I forget about my routine and just skate for myself. The cool air hits my face as I move, whichever way the music takes me. Everything feels lighter here. My legs, my arms. It's like flying as I move across the ice. Freedom.

My gaze falls to Rhett. He skates around the net, and our eyes meet for just a moment. He gives me his back again and continues shooting pucks into the net, and I do another half circle before I skate toward him.

"Can I try?" I motion toward his stick.

He straightens and pulls his bottom lip behind his teeth, watching me. "This feels like a trap. You're not going to hit me with it again, are you?"

Rolling my eyes, I say, "No. It just looks sort of therapeutic the way you're firing shots at the net."

"I thought you wanted peace and quiet."

"So did I."

He hands over the stick. "Do you know what you're doing?"

I line up with the stick behind the puck. "How hard could it be?"

I eat my words as I hit the puck, and it glides slowly along the ice stopping less than three feet in front of us.

"Harder than it looks, eh?" He grins. "Try again. Put your ass into it." He squints, looks up. "I'm just realizing how that sounds when it's not Coach saying it to a bunch of guys."

"It sounds weird either way. I thought it was all in the wrist and shoulders."

His brows raise and he cocks his head to the side.

"My little sister plays hockey," I explain.

Nodding, he steps closer. His scent—a mixture of sweat and some masculine smelling soap wraps around me.

"Move your right hand down a little lower."

My fingers inch down the stick. I look to him for approval.

"That's it. Now turn your body at more of an angle."

This is one of those moments where he could totally put his hands on my hips and show me. He doesn't, sadly. I shoot again, and this time the puck makes it all the way. It doesn't go in, my aim is crap, but it slides past the goal line, so that's something.

I hand his stick back. "Not as therapeutic when it doesn't go in."

He lines up, shoots, and the puck sails down into the net and dings against the back pole. There's a twinkle in his eye as he looks to me. "There's nothing better than that sound."

"Can I ask you a question?"

"I guess so," he says slowly.

"What scenario leads a girl to wake you up screaming while naked? Wait, were you naked or was she?"

He chuckles softly, closes his eyes, and shakes his head. "You've been thinking about that since we met, haven't you?"

"Pretty much."

He sucks that bottom lip behind his teeth again before answering. "We were both naked."

"Okay, so why does that lead to screaming?" I'm doing a pretty good job of envisioning a naked Rhett. He's just over six feet by my best guess. He's filled out but not bulky. I can clearly see the muscles in his arms stretching the fabric of his shirt. My eyes drop to his crotch. Maybe he's not packing? But would that make me scream? Run away, maybe, but not scream.

He catches me checking him out, and my face heats, but he doesn't call me on it. "We were naked," he says slowly, then pauses. "And I fell asleep."

"Oh." My eyes widen. "Ohhhh."

"Yeah." He takes another shot. This one goes in but doesn't make that magical sound he mentioned.

"So, then what happened?"

"Then I came here and got yelled at for sleeping again." He winks and skates toward the net to collect the pucks.

"Oh, come on. That's all I get? Where are all the details?"

"You know, you're chatty for someone who wanted to be left alone."

"I can't help it. Your retelling of the story really sold me," I say, sarcasm dripping from my tone.

He stops in front of me and grins, then rests both hands at the top of his stick. "You're a good skater. You said you have a show coming up. When?"

"You're changing the subject."

"Yeah, because it's humiliating. You have enough dirt on me already."

"Yes, there's a competition coming up, but the truth is I just like being on the ice by myself."

"I get that," he says.

"Do you mean *all* the way naked?"

Shaking his head, his deep laughter echoes in the empty rink. "Naked enough."

"How does that happen? Logistically."

"Well, you see," he starts in a serious tone. "When two people are attracted to one another—"

"I know how *that* happens. I want to know how you fell asleep? Do you have some sort of sleeping disorder?"

He's still laughing and smiling at me in a way that makes

my heart rate climb. I skate to the wall and jump to sit, taking long, even breaths. He follows, and I share my water with him. He squirts it into his mouth and hands it back.

We're quiet, sitting together and staring out at the empty rink. This is the quiet I was looking for when I got up this morning and decided to head to the rink early, but I'm the first to break the silence.

"In third grade, I fell asleep on the bus home from school. The driver got all the way back to school before he realized I was still in my seat. My parents had to come get me. Super embarrassing."

"Only mildly embarrassing by comparison to the circumstances in which I fell asleep."

"Well, I wouldn't know since I haven't heard the whole story."

He drops his head and runs a hand along his jaw. "I was at a party. We started drinking as soon as the bus got back from the quarterfinals. I think I slept two hours that night, and then we got up for drivers and donuts, and by noon I was done. I caught a ride back to my apartment with some buddies. She followed. I actually thought she was into my friend, but then she started kissing me, and she came into my room. I was so tired."

I'm holding back a smile as he pushes his hair out of his face.

"She was on her knees in front of me, and I was sprawled back on my bed…" He lifts his legs dangling over the edge and waves his hand between them.

"Oh my god! You fell asleep during a blow job?!"

He glances around like someone might be hanging around eavesdropping.

"Sorry." I lower my voice. "But seriously?"

"If I'd known it was going to happen, I would have better

prepared. Maybe taken a cold shower first or, fuck, I don't know."

"What do you mean if you'd known it was going to happen? Doesn't that sort of thing happen a lot—girls following you around and dropping to their knees?" My face is lava hot. "And I mean, okay, prepared or not, I don't think falling asleep is the appropriate reaction to sex."

"No. I mean, yeah, I guess. It's sort of a new thing, and I haven't quite gotten used to it."

"Well, it's the opposite for me. I used to have boys following me around, and now they don't. It's better in your shoes, trust me."

"Guys don't hit on you?" His expression says he doesn't believe me.

"Girls hitting on you is a new thing?" I give him the same look back.

We're smiling at one another, and there's this electricity in the air between us. Rhett's different than I imagined. Easier to talk to. Nice. Funny.

Suddenly we're not alone. A couple of hockey guys come out at the same time Josie arrives.

"Guess it's time," I say and jump down onto the ice.

"Hey." He follows. "What are you doing tonight? Would you want to hang out maybe? A bunch of my teammates are going to this party at the basketball house. You know it?"

"I do."

"So, you want to go?"

"With you?" I ask, a little confused.

He looks around. "Yeah?"

"Sorry, it's just… I don't think I'm your type."

"Okay." His brows scrunch together. "Why aren't you my type?

Or better yet, what do you think my type is exactly?"

"Look, I am cool with an occasional casual hookup, but based on the number of girls you've been entangled with this week alone… I'm sorry." It turns out there is really no good way to tell a guy you aren't into being his next slam piece.

"Right." Rhett skates backward. "Got it. Well, I guess I'll see you around."

I'M IN THE LIBRARY STUDYING WHEN ELIAS CALLS. I PROP MY phone up against my backpack on the table and accept the video call.

"Hi." I keep my voice low.

"Why have you not called me back? And where are you?" His eyes scan the background, and I can tell the second he realizes my location. "Unless you're planning to make a fashionably late appearance at this party, you're going to need to get a serious move on. It's already after eight."

"I'm not going."

I knew I never should have told Elias about Rhett asking me out.

"Why not? Ronnie sounds like a fun guy. Go have fun." Even if I couldn't see his big smile, I could tell how excited he is by his tone.

"You know that isn't his name."

"He gave my girl a black eye. He doesn't deserve real first name usage yet. Plus, hockey boys are stupid. One too many hits." He raps his knuckles on his head.

"And still, you want me to go out with him."

"Not with *him* exactly. There are only two months of college left. Go out, drink a little too much, make bad decisions, let me live vicariously through you." He sticks his bottom lip out in a pout.

I hum a noncommittal response. "What are you doing?"

He's holding the phone close to his face, so I can't make out the background, but it's dark. Elias is from Massachusetts but lives with a host family in Toronto while he trains with his pairs partner, Taylor. They have a shot at going to the Olympics. They're really freaking good.

"I'm in bed. I have AcroYoga at five o'clock tomorrow morning." The shade of his dark brown eyes is hard to see in the dim lighting, but it's impossible to miss the giant eye roll he sends my way. "We could do all the yoga in the world, and it's not going to make a lick of difference unless Taylor decides to trust me."

"You did drop her."

"It was one time. My wrist was fractured. I was holding her with a broken wrist!" He gets heated, waving one hand around as if he's holding up an imaginary partner.

"Until you weren't." I grin at his playful jaw drop as if he's really shocked by my words. We always tell it to each other like it is. No bullshit. "All I'm saying is maybe doing AcroYoga together will help rebuild some of that trust. You have to start somewhere."

"And I'm just saying no one is bonding that early in the morning. Also, you're one to talk. What about you?" That's the thing about having a best friend that's a guy—a guy not at all interested in sleeping with you—they don't tiptoe over your feelings.

"What about me?" I play it off like I don't know where this is going.

"You need to enjoy what's left of college. If work is anything like what I'm doing, it's a real snooze fest centered around a continual lack of sleep and caffeine. I hate to think of you sitting in the library tonight. Eeeeew. Plus, I think you want to go."

"What gave you that idea?"

He tilts his head and studies me. "Are you wearing makeup? Hmmm. And is that a new shirt?"

I bat my fake lashes. "Point made."

He laughs, smiling at me. "My dating life makes yours look pathetic, and I'm training or sleeping twenty-two hours a day. If you won't do it for yourself, do it for me. I need some excitement in my life."

"You have plenty of excitement without even trying. What about the girl you met at the coffeehouse last week?"

"Well, we've been texting..."

And as quick as that, I've turned the topic of conversation back to Elias. He very much enjoys talking about himself, and I'm happy to think about anything but Rhett and the party he invited me to.

I had fun with him today. I felt something, and it seemed like he did too, but maybe I imagined it? I don't want to be a dumb girl who's reading more into the situation than what's there. But I also know that the indescribable chemistry and connection I had with him is something I haven't felt in a long time.

It was only an hour and I had to basically force him to talk to me. But once he did, I felt it. There was something else accelerating my heart rate and giving me butterflies deep in my belly. I don't put myself out there very often, and it will really sting if I put myself out there and I'm wrong.

I close my laptop as Elias chats my ear off and give up on getting any more schoolwork done tonight. I really came here to convince myself I didn't want to be at the basketball party.

Elias yawns as he finishes telling me every detail of the text exchange he's been having with the girl he picked up while grabbing coffee. He's handsome and charming, and even though I haven't met him in person, I can tell he's one of those people that are impossible to resist. But he's also super picky.

One date, sometimes less, and he convinces himself that it'll never work. She has a pet goldfish and those freak him out, or she's a flight attendant for an airline he doesn't like. One time he stopped texting a girl because she had the audacity to wear white pants after Labor Day. And he is not the picture of fashion. He wears socks with his sandals. He's not allowed to judge anyone.

"I should let you go," he says. "And you should change into something far more revealing, call Josie, and then go to that party."

"Tempting," I muse.

"I'm texting her now. Better think up a really good excuse or hide."

"How do you even have her number?"

"We exchanged after your accident last year. In case of emergency." He says it all so casually. Funny how a few near-death experiences can make a person so blasé about it all.

Elias and I have the same heart condition. That's actually how we met. I was scrolling YouTube one day and stumbled upon a video where he was talking about the condition and how it impacts his training. It seemed like fate to see another figure skater my age dealing with it. I reached out, we started messaging back and forth, and now he's stuck with me for life.

My phone pings with an incoming text.

"That was fast," I say as I read the message from Josie. **OMG. I'm jumping in the shower. I'll be ready in thirty minutes.**

"I knew I could count on Josie."

"I don't think this is a good idea. I told him no and basically implied that he was a slut. Won't I look like a bitch showing up now?"

"Please. If you show up looking hot, he's not going to remember anything you've ever said or done."

"I have too much going on right now." It's a last-ditch, bullshit excuse and he knows it. Of course, he calls me on it.

"You need to get laid," he says loudly.

I duck my head in embarrassment, even though no one can hear him, thanks to my ear pods. He's not wrong though. "Fine, but if this ends badly, I'm blaming you."

"I can take it. Call me tomorrow or later tonight if you're doing the walk of shame." He makes an X over the left side of his chest.

I do the same and then flip him off for good measure.

Oh, crap. What have I gotten myself into?

Chapter Seven

RHETT

Ha ha, very funny," I say when I see the mysterious gift left on my bed—a shopping bag filled with three different brands of energy drinks, condoms, and a box of Kleenex.

"What are the tissues for?" I ask, bringing the entire bag out into the hallway. Music blasts through our apartment as we get ready to go out. There are two bathrooms in this place, but the guys are all crowded into one fighting over the mirror.

"Those are for the girls you make cry," Heath says. Mav elbows him, and Heath rubs his arm as he adds, "I mean, that's what I assume."

"Please, I know this was all you two." I hold up the box of glow-in-the-dark condoms.

Mav cackles. "Those are fun. Makes your dick look like a lightsaber."

Adam meets my gaze in the mirror. "Maybe the glow will help keep you awake."

"I hate all of you." I take the bag back to my room and toss it all on the bed except the largest energy drink.

"That Carrie blowing up your phone earlier?" Adam calls across the hallway.

"Yeah."

"Everything good?" I know he's terrified I'm going to get back with her. Adam never liked Carrie. The feeling was mutual, actually. Carrie didn't really get along with any of my teammates.

"All good." I don't know if I manage to sound like I don't care, but that's the vibe I'm going with tonight. I don't give a fuck. About any of it. Not that my ex won't stop fucking calling or that every time I try to move on with someone else, it blows up spectacularly.

"Last night to get stupid," Adam says when we're all finally ready to go. "Tomorrow it's time to go to work."

"Hell yeah," we agree.

We get to the basketball house, known on campus as The White House, and within the hour, I'm already too drunk to walk a straight line. Last night to get stupid? Challenge accepted. I have finally reached the point of not caring about the disaster that is my dating life.

Here's a free party tip for you. If you want to have a good time at a party (or anywhere, really), stick with Maverick. He knows everyone, drinks like a damn fish, and nothing gets in his way of having fun.

We've been teammates for two years now, but we've only hung out just the two of us a few times and never like this where I'm ready to match him drink for drink. The longer we hang, and the drunker I get, the more I think how ridiculous I've been stressing over everything. Mav is single, and he's always happy. I don't know why I let my breakup drama get in the way of having fun for so long. But no more.

We're talking to a group of girls who immediately ghost us when some frat dudes arrive with a cooler of Jell-O shots. Mav doesn't seem fazed in the least.

"Who needs girls?!" I shout and raise my drink.

"Easy there, let's not talk crazy." Mav pushes my hand down.

"I'm jealous, man," I tell him. "Nothing gets to you. You're always the life of the party. I don't know how to do it," I admit. "I was a couple for so long. Now everything out of my mouth is a disaster. I fell asleep during a blow job."

He laughs and wraps an arm around my shoulders. "Yeah, also add that to the vault. Take another drink and forget it happened."

"She didn't want to go out with me because she thinks I'm a player." I laugh, a little slurred. "It's kind of funny, really."

"Who didn't want to go out with you?"

"Sienna. I asked her out." I managed to keep that to myself all day, but the liquor has loosened my lips.

"Well, what'd you say? What'd *she* say?"

"I asked her to hang out tonight, and she told me I wasn't her type."

"Ouch." He unscrews the cap on the Mad Dog 20/20 and hands it over.

"Yep." I tip back the bottle. I care a lot less than I did two hours ago. The truth is, maybe she isn't my type. Or maybe I don't have a type. She seems different than Carrie, and that's all I have to go by.

"Sienna's rad. I could see you two together but stop overthinking it. If it happens, it happens. If not." He shrugs.

"That's the most Maverick thing you've ever said." I mock his shrug, exaggerating it in my drunken state. "Whatever happens. If it's meant to be, it'll be. If not, I'll just bless the women of Valley with my six-pack and beer drinking skills."

He grins. His shirt is still on, but the night is young. "Now you've got it. Come on, let's get you on the dance floor."

I start to protest. I don't dance, but fuck it. Tonight I do. Not well, but whatever. Maverick moves straight to the middle, where a group of girls shakes their asses in rhythm to the music. They swallow him up, and… yep, there goes his shirt.

I hang back, but soon I'm pulled closer and sandwiched between two very enthusiastic chicks.

"I don't dance," I say.

One of the girls leans forward, and I think she asks me to repeat what I said, but I can't hear anything over the music.

Huh. The one place I can't put my foot in my mouth. Yeah, I can get down with this.

Chapter Eight

SIENNA

My stomach is in knots as we push through the party with drinks in our hands. Josie walks in front of me, holding my hand and pulling me along behind her. My roommate is a lot more social than I am. It isn't that I never go out, but most weekends, I prefer hanging with Josie or Olivia or, yes, watching true crime documentaries. I find it reassuring that terrible things happen to even really good people. Make out of that what you will.

My gaze darts around, looking for Rhett as we weave across the backyard of the basketball house. A huge pool takes up a large portion of it. People stand in groups in and around it. On one side of the yard, a DJ booth is set up, and there's a mass of bodies moving to the music. The other side of the yard has the keg, according to Josie, and that's the direction we head.

"Are you supposed to be meeting him somewhere?" she asks when we finally reach the line at the keg.

"Not exactly." I twist my hands in front of me. "He doesn't know I'm coming."

She laughs, fills us each a cup of beer, and then starts back toward the middle of the yard. I was perfectly content hanging on the side and out of the chaos.

I continually scan the party, but I don't see Rhett anywhere. I was so sure he'd be here. I didn't even consider the possibility that he made other plans.

"We're dancing," Josie announces and pulls me again, sloshing half of my beer on the ground.

"We are?" I ask, the question gets lost in the noise as we step closer to the source of the booming music. She drags me behind her and I squeeze her hand to work out some of my nerves.

She stops a few yards away from the people dancing. "What's up with you? You're acting like you're nervous, and you have no reason to be. Is it the dress? Are you uncomfortable? Because you look amazing."

"No. It isn't the dress. Looove the dress," I assure her, smoothing a hand down the skintight pink dress from her closet that she insisted I wear tonight. "It's Rhett. I think I like him." Damn him. "I don't even really know him, but I can't stop thinking about him. I'm all out of sorts."

"I hate it when that happens." She smiles at me. "Forget about Rhett for an hour. Let's just have a good time and then we'll ask around and see if he's here."

As she speaks, I spot him. I grab her arm, so she doesn't step any closer. There he is. The guy I stupidly can't stop thinking about. He's on the dance floor sandwiched between two girls. One plastered on his front with her hands on his chest and another at his back rubbing her boobs all over him.

A surge of annoyance and frustration blasts through me. Followed quickly with jealousy. The latter pisses me off the most.

Of course, he came anyway and is dancing with other girls. I said no. Which is why the jealousy I feel is particularly annoying.

Josie follows my gawking stare. "Guess he came."

"Yeah. Found him. Now can we go?"

"Sienna!" Maverick's voice manages to boom over the music. I glance back to the dance floor to see him in a similar position as his teammate.

I wave, and he untangles himself from two girls, who move on to someone else in his absence. Mav moves toward Rhett, who speaking of, still hasn't noticed me, but the two girls he's dancing with are inching up his shirt, and four hands move over his back, stomach, and pecs. The one in front squats down and licks his abs. That's as much as I see before I turn and walk away.

Josie jogs beside me to keep up. "Where are you going?"

"This was a mistake."

Maverick, half naked, tattoos rippling under his muscles, catches us. "Hey, no way, you came! Rhett's going to be so stoked."

"Right. He looks pretty stoked." I wave a hand of indifference toward him. He's finally spotted me and is attempting to squeeze out from between his dance partners. They are not letting him go without a fight. I can hardly blame them.

He looks sinful in a plain white T-shirt and jeans, staring at me with apologetic eyes. The thing is, I'm not even pissed at him. I'm pissed at myself for assuming he was going to be hanging off to the side, waiting and hoping that I'd come. I told him no because this is who he is, and I didn't want to get my feelings hurt, but then convinced myself otherwise because that's what I wanted to believe.

"Ah, don't be mad at him. I had to practically drag him out

there. Let's go save him." Mav wraps an arm around my shoulders and pulls me back toward the dance floor. Rhett's managed to get free and heads toward us.

"Hey," he says tentatively. "I didn't think you were coming."

"Surprise!" Sarcasm drips from the word.

Josie and Maverick look between us. An awkward silence falls over our small group.

"Dance?" Maverick asks my friend, holding his hand out to her.

"Absolutely." Josie slides her palm into his. She looks over her shoulder as they move into the center of the dancers.

Rhett shifts nervously in front of me. "You look nice. I've been wondering if your hair was short or long. I can never tell when it's all up."

"You have?"

"I like it." He lifts a hand and brushes his fingers along the ends of my hair. He sways and inadvertently pulls my hair as he does. "Oh shit, sorry."

He untangles his fingers with a sheepish grin.

Rhett is drunk and for some reason I find it a little charming.

"Do you want to dance?"

I shake my head. "No, I think I'm good."

I don't think I can live up to the threesome he had going earlier.

"Okay, uh, drink?"

I'm still carrying a mostly full cup of beer, but I nod.

We walk side by side. His arm brushes against mine, and neither of us pulls away. Now that I've found him, I have no idea what to say.

At the keg, he takes my cup, looks at how full it is, and laughs. "Do you actually want another beer?"

"I'm not much of a drinker."

He tops it off and takes a sip of it.

"I'm gonna level with you." He runs a hand through his messy hair. "I'm really drunk."

I can't help but laugh as he disarms me with a cocky grin.

"I didn't think you were coming, and I decided to say fuck it." He shakes his head. "Not fuck you, just *it*. You know girls, dating, life?"

"You realize *I'm* a girl, right?"

He closes one eye and pulls his bottom lip behind his teeth for a second. "I really suck at this. Like epic-levels of suckage." He waves his arm around dramatically, and the beer in his cup sloshes onto me, soaking the front of my dress.

It's cold. Really cold. I shriek and jump back. "Okay, well, this has been fun."

"Fuck. I'm sorry. Come on." Rhett takes over, gripping me by the arm and walking fast toward the house. He commands people out of the way, leading me inside and cutting to the front of the line for the bathroom. The door opens, and three girls stumble out.

"Excuse us."

Drunk, bossy Rhett is hot. Almost hot enough to ignore the stench of beer now coating my dress.

The next girl in line smiles at him. Her hand goes to her hair, and she curls a finger around a long, brunette strand. "No problem. Need any company?"

"Wha—" He fumbles, clearly trying to piece together why he'd need company in the bathroom. Before he can, I charge ahead. The beer is dripping down the front of me. Even my panties are wet.

To my surprise, he follows me in and shuts the door.

I find a towel, hope it isn't too used, and blot the front of my dress. Or Josie's dress.

"What can I do to help?"

I'm not making a lot of progress. With a sigh, I drop the towel to the vanity. "It'll dry."

A shiver wracks my body. The air conditioning vent in the bathroom has kept this small room cold, which probably feels nice if you aren't soaked.

"Here. Take my shirt." He pulls it over his head without a second thought and holds it out to me.

I stare. Not at the white ball of cotton in his hand, but at his chest. My mouth goes dry.

"Are you freaking kidding me?"

"Uhh…" His gaze drops from me to the shirt, back to me. "It's clean. I promise."

"You can't walk around like that." I fling a hand toward his abs. All eight of them.

The corners of his mouth tip up. "Like what?"

"Don't play dumb with me."

"Angel, around you, I don't have to play. You make me stupid. I can't get anything right."

"Looking like that, who needs a brain?" I mutter.

He stalks toward me, a cocky glint shining in his eyes. "Are you trying to say that you like what you see?"

"I mean, it's whatever." My gaze dips over his chest, though, and my nipples tighten. "Gah." I can't even pretend. "Your body is ridiculous."

"I'm glad you think so. I might never wear a shirt again if you keep looking at me like that." He gently places the T-shirt over my head and pulls it down. The heat of the fabric and the nearness of our bodies does funny things to my insides. My heart rate climbs, and my chest feels tight. I slow my breathing out of habit.

"Like what?" I reach out and slide my fingers over the ridges of muscle.

He inhales, and those blue eyes darken. He ignores my question. Not that it requires much of an answer. "Your hands are cold."

"Someone tossed a beer on me."

"I'm really sorry about that."

"You say that a lot."

"I've fucked up a lot. And I'm sorry for that too."

"The list keeps getting longer." My laugh dies when he places a calloused thumb at the corner of my mouth.

Staring at my lips, he traces along the bottom one with the pad of his thumb. "Add this to the list."

I'm in an alternate reality as he leans forward, still distracted by his body and the way mine feels when he's this close. It's only when his mouth slants over mine that my brain processes he's kissing me.

His hand on my face slides down to my neck in a possessive hold that contradicts the softness of his lips. My back is to the vanity, legs hitting against it, and Rhett crowds into my space as his tongue slides into my mouth.

My heart pounds in my chest. Somewhere in the very back of my mind, I'm aware that I'm doing a potentially very dumb thing. Kissing Rhett when I know it won't go anywhere beyond tonight. Still, I can see why he leaves a path of crying girls behind him. He kisses like a champ. He's sweet and tender and hard and demanding all at once, and my head is spinning.

He lifts me up and sets me on the vanity, then pushes between my legs. His fingers thread through my hair, and he tugs gently, exposing my neck. His nose grazes down the curve of my neck, and his mouth nips and kisses along the way.

My legs tremble as he moves those big hands of his to my legs. They inch up my bare skin and slide under the hem of my dress that's now hitched up very high on my thighs. My core aches, and I will him to move his fingers just a little higher.

His chest presses against mine, and I remember that I have a half-naked man in front of me. A half-naked man with a body built to make good girls want bad things. I slide my palms over his pecs and down his sides. My exploration encourages him, and one long finger finally touches my soaked panties.

"It's the beer," I say. It isn't, or at least not entirely.

We both groan as he circles my clit through the silky material.

I'm ready to let him fuck me here. Correction, I'm ready to *beg* him to fuck me here. And I'm not even the drunk one.

A knock at the door pulls us from the moment, reminding us there's a line of people waiting to get in here.

"We should probably go," I say, even as I spread my legs farther apart.

He pulls back, smug grin firmly in place, hand still rubbing me gently. "They can wait."

Unfortunately, they don't. The door opens, and the girl that asked if we needed company, walks in. She studies us for a beat before declaring, "Don't mind me. I just need to pee."

Rhett straightens, removes his hands from under my dress, and pulls the hem down to cover me.

"Ready, angel?" His voice is gruff with want, and no, I'm absolutely not ready.

He takes my hand and keeps me close as we exit the bathroom and head back outside. The cool night air hits me, and I take deep, steadying breaths.

Holy crap. I almost had sex with Rhett in the bathroom with a line of people outside. If I'm completely honest, I almost had sex with Rhett in the bathroom while a girl peed on the toilet. I'm not proud.

A group of hockey guys stands just outside of the doorway, girls intermixed with them. One of the guys, Jordan, I think, calls to Rhett, and we join the circle.

"Heard you were having a good time," the guy says, his gaze bouncing between Rhett and me. "Now I know why." He tips his head to me. "Jordan, we sorta met at the rink."

"Sienna," I say. "I remember you."

"That's Liam, Heath, Ginny, Dakota, Reagan, and you already met Adam," Rhett calls them out, pointing as he goes. I look at each and smile, offer a small wave.

"Did you and Maverick lose your shirts at the same time?" Adam grins as he tips back the beer in his hand.

"I spilled my beer on her."

I'd forgotten how drunk he is until he tries to wrap an arm around my waist and sways, which means *we* sway. I'm perfectly sober, but my legs are still shaking from what went down in the bathroom.

"Easy there," Adam says. "Let's not give her another black eye."

Rhett flips him off.

"Speaking of catastrophes, I'm still soaked. I should find Josie and see if she's ready to go."

His gaze trails down my body, and I'm pretty sure he's thinking about my panties. My body warms, cheeks flame.

"She's on the dance floor with Maverick," Adam says.

"Thanks." I wave again. "It was nice to meet you guys." Looking to Rhett, I say, "See ya later."

"Wait, you're really leaving?"

"Yeah, I'm wet and sticky, and I have to teach two fitness classes tomorrow morning anyway."

"Yeah, okay." His brows knit in confusion. "At least let me come with you to make sure you find Josie."

I nod, and we start across the lawn.

"We have the semifinals Monday night, so we're keeping it low-key the rest of the weekend, but can we hang again?"

"Uhh..." I decide to go with honesty since it's unlikely he'll remember asking me tomorrow anyway. "I don't usually do that type of thing, and I'm not judging you, or even me, casual hookups can be fun. I mean, that was fun. Really fun." I'm blathering on and talking in circles, and not really saying what I mean which is that I like him and hooking up will end with me getting hurt. "You're really drunk."

"Fair, but I wasn't drunk when I asked you to come tonight."

"This was a mistake. We both have a lot going on." I'm bullshitting. We both know it. Elias would call me out on it, but Rhett doesn't.

We reach the dance floor, and I spot Josie dancing with a group of girls, Maverick in the center of them. Josie sees us and waves.

The sight of Maverick without his shirt reminds me that I still have Rhett's.

"Oh, here." I start to take it off, but he stops me.

"Keep it. I'm going to head out soon too. Drinking makes me

tired."

"So I've heard." I take a step toward Josie, half hoping he'll stop me. He doesn't. "Later, Rauthruss."

THE NEXT DAY, I'M FINISHING UP WITH MY SECOND BARRE CLASS when Rhett appears in the hallway. He slips in as my students gather their things.

"Hey." Hands in pockets, he approaches me at the front of the room.

"You found me." I'm a little impressed he a) remembered I said I was teaching this morning and b) is awake this early.

"I looked at the group fitness schedule before I went to bed last night and set an alarm."

"Impressive."

He grins. "A first for everything. I didn't ruin your dress last night, did I?"

"No, it's fine. Your shirt is at my dorm. I'll bring it to the rink."

"Or you could bring it to my place later?"

I laugh. "Presumptuous much?"

"Not like that. To hang, watch TV, play Xbox or... whatever. I'd suggest something more exciting, but we have curfew at nine."

"Ouch."

"Yeah, Coach is pulling out all the stops to keep us distraction-free."

"And you thought inviting a girl over was the answer?"

"I'll be distracted by you either way."

My stomach flips. This freaking guy.

"What time?" I ask. I was prepared to say yes as soon as he asked—actually, as soon as I woke up this morning and wished I'd stayed at the party longer—but sober and charming Rhett is almost as impossible to resist as half-naked Rhett.

"Six." He hands me a piece of paper with the address and backs away. "And for the record, I don't usually do that type of thing either."

Chapter Nine

RHETT

I give Sienna a quick tour of the apartment, grab a beer, and offer her one. "I promise I won't spill it on you."

She smiles, but shakes her head. "No thanks."

"Right. You said you weren't much of a drinker. We also have water, orange juice, and a variety of energy drinks."

"I'm good, really. And I drink, sometimes, like last night. Just not very much or very often."

I grab a water and lead her to the couch. It's quiet for a change. Adam's at Reagan and Dakota's apartment across the breezeway, Ginny and Heath are in his room with the door shut, and Maverick is at his place. When I asked them not to bombard Sienna, I didn't think they'd listen. I'm pleasantly surprised.

"Because of your heart condition or just not your thing?"

She nods. "Mostly because of my heart."

"If you don't mind my asking, what kind of heart condition do you have?"

"It's called long QT syndrome. Basically, my heartbeat gets out of whack."

"But it's treatable?"

"I take medication, and I have an implant that monitors my heart, but no, not really. I just have to be careful and listen to my body."

"Skating isn't dangerous?"

"I have type one, which means both physical and emotional stress can trigger episodes. If I wanted to be completely safe, I'd have to avoid basically everything. Sometimes I can feel my heart get out of rhythm when I'm working out, other times I'm just sitting around doing nothing."

"Freaky. What's an episode like?"

"Usually it's just a fluttering in my chest or a lightheaded feeling." She shrugs and a small smile pulls at her lips. "I've gotten really good at listening to my body and knowing when to take breaks. I can do most things, in moderation. No roller coasters, though." She sticks out her bottom lip. "I haven't been to a carnival in forever. I miss cotton candy." She angles her legs toward mine. "Did you mean what you said about not usually doing that type of thing?"

I chuckle at the topic change. "Yeah, of course."

Her gaze narrows.

"You don't believe me?"

"Everything I know about you contradicts that. The day I met you, you hooked up with someone only hours before. Or tried to. Your phone was blowing up with different girls later that day." She laughs softly. "Then last night..." Her voice trails off, and I'm accosted with hazy visions of Sienna in the bathroom of the basketball house.

"I guess if you'd only known me the past week, I could see

where you might get the wrong idea, but that's not me. I got out of a relationship recently, and last weekend was... well, it was the result of a lot of things, but that's not something I do on the regular." I'd certainly like to, though, with her. I leave that part out. "And last night—"

"You were really drunk. I get it."

"Yes, but sober Rhett would have done the same thing. Minus drenching you in beer."

An amused smirk plays on her lips.

"Okay, fine, that might have happened anyway." I bump her knee. "Last night was fucking awesome. I'm only sorry we got interrupted."

"Just as well. You'd probably have fallen asleep on me," she teases, but her breathing changes, and tension hangs in the air between us.

"Not a chance."

Her grin makes my cock twitch. Taking her to my bedroom after I just claimed to not be that kind of guy seems like a bad plan, so I pick up an Xbox controller. "Wanna play?"

She lets out a slow breath and nods. "What do you have?"

I show her the options, including all the other gaming systems. Between my roommates and me, we have pretty much every system and game out there. Sienna picks Mario Kart, and my dick finally gets the idea that we're not getting any action today. He's had to accept that a lot. I'm pretty sure he's ready to remove himself from me and find a new host body.

I'm usually pretty competitive, but we're firing questions back and forth as we play, getting to know one another.

"Only the one sister?" I ask. I pass her on the game and toss a banana over my shoulder.

She moves her whole body with the controller as she swerves out of the way. "Yeah. What about you?"

"Younger brother."

"Are you close?"

"Nah. He's five."

"That's quite a gap."

"Yeah. No kidding. I was seventeen when Ryder was born, and I've basically been away for his entire life."

"I bet he looks up to you."

"Not really." I shake my head and focus on staying just ahead of her on the game. I want to win, but I don't want to blow her out of the water. "When he grows up, he wants to be Spider-Man."

"It's good that he's keeping his expectations reasonable." She glances over and catches my eye. It's hard to look away from her when she's smiling at me like that. She looks away first, but I keep staring.

"I win!" she shrieks.

I glance at the TV screen in time to see her cross the finish line. My dude has crashed into the wall going nowhere, and that feels pretty accurate for the scenario.

"It's the best of four races," I say.

I best her in the next three and manage to keep my undefeated record intact. We're finishing up when Heath and Ginny come out of his room.

"Rauthruss, your phone's been blowing up. Real mood killer," Heath says. His gaze lands on Sienna, and he smiles awkwardly. "Hey, Sienna."

"Hi." She waves back.

Heath goes to the kitchen and opens the fridge, but Ginny joins us in the living room.

"It's so good to see you again," she says as she sits in the armchair across from us.

"Ginny, right?" Sienna asks.

"That's right." Ginny's smile couldn't possibly get any bigger. "What are you guys playing?"

"Mario Kart. Do you want to play?" Sienna offers.

"Yeah." She reaches for the extra controllers. "Heath, you want in too?"

"Uhh..." My roommate looks to me. Since I don't know how to politely communicate that I'd really rather not have them join us, I nod. "Sure."

"I'm terrible," Sienna says. "I only beat him on one race."

"You beat him?" Ginny asks, her brown eyes widen with disbelief. "No one ever beats Rhett."

I avoid Sienna's stare and shrug. "I'm having an off day."

The four of us play a handful of games before Sienna calls it. "I can't take any more defeat. You guys keep playing. I'll watch."

"Same," Ginny says. "You boys can have it. I want a chance to talk to Sienna anyway." She moves over to the couch on the other side of Sienna, forcing Sienna to move closer to me. Her leg brushes against mine. I have no idea how such little contact can send so much adrenaline rushing through my veins.

Not having sex today. Not having sex today.

That's a fucking mantra I hope to never repeat.

"Call of Duty?" Heath asks.

"Yeah. One game," I say. Ginny's latched onto Sienna and is already peppering her with questions.

I relax my leg next to hers. She briefly looks over, hits me with a smile, and turns back to Ginny.

Listening in on their conversation as I play, I learn that Sienna is from Wisconsin. A town about six hours from where my family lives in Minnesota—something I interject into the conversation and then get killed by Heath.

"Fuck yeah. Finally." Heath holds the controller over his head in victory. I'll get him later. Right now, video games are a distraction to what I really want to be doing.

"Thanks for the game," I say.

"Need a rematch?"

He knows me well. "Later. I'm gonna hang with Sienna."

"Right." He stands. "Baby doll?"

"What?" Ginny asks, briefly looking up at him. Guess I'm not the only one enamored by Sienna.

He motions with his head toward his room.

"Ooooh. Okay." Ginny squeezes Sienna's hand. "Rhett is the greatest. I'm so glad you two are hanging out. Really, the best. He's—"

"That's enough," I cut her off. "Please don't embarrass me."

"So modest. Another great attribute," she says as she gets to her feet. "I'll see you later?" Ginny asks Sienna.

"Yeah, maybe."

"Hope so!" Ginny bounces to Heath and jumps on his back before they disappear down the hallway.

"Sorry about that."

"It's fine. They seem nice."

"Wanna watch a movie or something?" I've never invited a girl over to the apartment to hang out. Well, unless you count Carrie and the two times she visited. But that was different. We were already together.

"Sure."

While I flip through the channels, she leans back on the couch until her shoulder rests against my chest. I sink farther behind her, taking advantage of the position and getting closer.

We decide on Aquaman and settle in just as the front door opens. Mav walks through with his dog Charli in one arm, a bag of groceries in the other.

"Hey-o!" he calls, shutting the door behind him with a foot. "Sienna! What's up?"

"Just hanging out. You live here too?"

"Nah, downstairs."

The door opens again, this time Dakota steps through it. "All I have is apple cider vinegar," she says to Mav. Then she looks at the room and waves to Sienna and me.

"She and Reagan live across the breezeway," I explain, then ask them, "What are you guys doing here?"

"We're grilling," Mav says with a duh expression.

"Well, can you do it quieter? We're watching a movie."

"Oooh." Dakota's eyes light up. "I love this movie." She sets the vinegar on the kitchen counter and sits with us. "Rhett, that shirt looks great on you." Her gaze rakes over me which is super weird. I legit don't think Dakota has ever complimented me before.

"Uhh...." I glance down at my plain black T-shirt. "Thanks, I guess."

"It really brings out the gray in your eyes."

"You do have great eyes," Mav calls from the kitchen.

What the hell is going on? I realize now why my roommates

spend so much time in their bedrooms when their girlfriends are over. It's like a bus station in here with people coming and going, interrupting and acting fucking weird.

Mav stacks plates, meat, and seasoning into his arms. "Food will be ready in about forty minutes. Are you staying, Sienna?"

She looks to me.

"Maverick is a pretty good cook," I tell her.

"Pretty good?" He scoffs. Charli barks at his feet.

"I guess now I have to stay to find out."

Dakota stands and flips her red hair over one shoulder. "I better go supervise."

"Worried about me?" Mav asks her.

"Worried that you'll burn the place down and take my apartment with it."

The sliding glass door opens and closes, and their voices trail off.

Unfortunately, we only get about ten minutes further into the movie when Adam and Reagan arrive. Everyone's here now, so at least I can stop waiting for the damn door to open.

I love these guys, girls, too, but they keep smiling at me like I'm their little brother who's going out on a date for the first time. Fuck that noise. I'm the only one of the group that's had any semblance of a serious relationship. Ginny and Heath have been together the longest, but even that relationship is new compared to how long I was with Carrie.

I give up trying to keep her to myself, and Sienna doesn't seem to mind when we all go outside to eat dinner together. The guys keep bringing up random shit—an assist I had last game, that time I stepped in front of a chick about to get run over by a cyclist on campus—that fucking hurt. Adam somehow even remembers when I helped a girl in our freshmen dorm find her lost emotional support gerbil.

What exactly is it about me that screams desperation so loudly my friends feel like they need to sell me on Sienna? Okay, I know why but I'm not some sad case. I'm not them, and I definitely don't need them to convince some chick I'm good enough.

The girls seem particularly attached to Sienna, and she has to promise them they'll hang out again before I can steal her away after dinner.

I shut the door in my room and run a hand through my hair. "I'm sorry about that. That was painful. My friends were trying to sell me on you."

She laughs. "Well, they sold me on them anyway. They're great."

"Yeah, most of the time," I agree.

We sit on top of the comforter on my bed, backs against the headboard. I slide my hand over hers and intertwine our fingers.

"What are you doing after graduation?" I ask. "Going back to Wisconsin?"

She shrugs. "I haven't figured it out yet. I have an interview tomorrow, actually. Do you have a job yet?"

I nod. "Yeah, my family owns and operates a rink. We do skating lessons, camps, rentals. I'm going to help run it, expand the hockey side of it. Plus, I'll be closer to my brother as he grows up."

"Admit it. You want to be his hero instead of Spider-Man." She leans her shoulder against mine.

"I just want to know him, you know?"

"Yeah." She sighs. "I definitely get that. Allison, my sister, will be heading off to college in a couple of years, and then who knows where she'll end up. I miss seeing her, but we text and talk on the phone. My family does these super corny Zoom calls every Monday night."

"Sounds nice."

"Yeah, I guess it is."

I rub my thumb over hers. A simple movement that makes my cock press against the zipper of my jeans.

She tilts her arm, moving mine with it, to look at her watch.

"Do you need to be back at a certain time tonight? I thought we could watch a movie without my roommates interrupting us every two minutes or something else chill. The bus leaves tomorrow at six."

"No, I was checking my heart rate." She lets her arm fall slack. "I'm fine," she adds. "Sometimes, when I'm with you, my chest feels tight like I've been pushing my body too hard."

"Hanging out with me causes you physical pain. Got it."

Her laughter fills my room, and I lean forward to capture her lips.

My chest feels tight too. Shit. My *entire* body feels tight.

"Is kissing considered a chill activity?" The breathy words are spoken into my mouth.

Instead of answering, I cup the back of her head and deepen the kiss. Her hand reaches up and rests on my chest. She lightly fists the material in her palm.

Nah, there's absolutely nothing chill about kissing Sienna.

Chapter Ten

SIENNA

We've been kissing for the better part of an hour. Just kissing and OMG just kissing Rhett is *so* not just kissing. He toys with a strand of hair at my neck while he nips at my bottom lip.

"I should probably go," I say. Leaving is the last thing I want to do, but the longer we keep at this, the harder it's going to be to go. And I have to go. I'll hate myself tomorrow if I hook up with him and that turns out to be all he wanted from me.

"Okay." His hand slides back to lightly grasp my neck and he pulls me in for another scorching hot kiss.

So quickly I'm caught up in him again, and tossing good intentions out the window to keep sucking face. He's really, really good at it.

He pulls back before I do with a little groan deep in his throat. "Do you need a ride back to the dorm?"

"No, I borrowed Josie's car."

"Let me walk you out." He stands and pulls me with him. The apartment has quieted and none of his friendly roommates or their girlfriends are in the living room as we walk through.

The night is clear and there's a breeze that whips my hair around my shoulders and into my face.

"Can I see you again?" he asks, swinging our joined hands between us.

"Umm..." I start watching the ground in front of me. I know I'm going to say yes, but I need a few seconds to let all of my fears bounce around in my brain. "When?"

"Whenever you're free," he says so casually like he's willing to rearrange his whole schedule to see me again.

"Great. How about tomorrow night?" I bite back a smile as I glance at him.

He rubs at his jaw. "I've got a small conflict tomorrow night."

We both laugh.

"Are you nervous about the game?" I stop next to the driver's side door of Josie's car.

"Yes," he admits, then changes the topic back. "Go out with me Tuesday night?"

I'm hesitant to make plans with him. I like spending time together. I really like kissing him, but I'm still not sure I truly believe he isn't a player. Plus, there are only two months of school left. Where can this possibly go? It feels like spending more time with him is the equivalent of signing myself up for a mini life course in dating disasters.

"Text me when you get back to Valley." I lean forward and press my lips to his, then shift to open the car door before I attack his mouth and say screw the consequences.

He holds on to the top of the door while I get situated in the seat, then shuts me in.

I roll down the window and put it in reverse. "Good luck tomorrow night."

"Good luck at your interview."

"You remembered."

"I know it seems like my brain doesn't work when you're around, but I do remember the things you say."

He steps back and I ease off the brake, letting the car slowly roll backward. "Thanks for tonight. I had fun."

"Me too." He grins and stays in the same spot, watching as I pull away from the apartment.

And despite all my reservations, I smile like a fool the entire drive back to the dorms.

MONDAY AFTERNOON, I RESERVE A PRIVATE ROOM AT THE LIBRARY for my video call interview with Dalton Technologies. Kelsie, the HR woman conducting the interview, smiles brightly at me when I join the call.

"Hi, Sienna!"

"Hello." I wave and fidget with the collared dress shirt. I'm not nervous, but I really hate interviews. Does anyone like them? Kelsie sure seems like she does.

And she's good. Within two minutes, she's cut through the awkwardness and put me at ease. She tells me all about the company, then the job. It's an entry-level position that creates sales materials for the healthcare software the company sells. The company is big, with two locations, which they call campuses. And each campus has amenities like a cafeteria, game room, meditation space, and a gym that rivals the one here at Valley.

I knew a lot of these facts already. My dad has worked at Dalton for twenty-five years. In fact, the position I'm interviewing for is one he held early on in his career. He worked his way up to being an executive in the customer education department, where he works now, but over the years, he's held a lot of different jobs with Dalton, so at least some of what Kelsie tells me makes sense.

"Do you have any questions for me about the campus or the position?"

"No, I don't think so," I say. "I've been to both locations with my dad so I'm familiar with where they are and everything."

She smiles big again. I wonder if they teach that in HR classes. I try to mimic her. I'm not positive I want this job, but I know that I need to act like I do.

"Your dad is the best. Everyone loves him around here." Another huge smile. "Well, should we talk about next steps?"

"Umm, sure."

"I'm going to email over information packets with all the details I told you on the phone. Look over everything, and you can just email me back if you have questions. The healthcare benefits are incredible. I think you'll be really pleased with that. I know preexisting conditions can be difficult."

I blink a few times, trying to think what to say. Kelsie doesn't pick up on my hesitation, and I manage to compose myself.

"Thank you. I will look everything over."

"If you'd like to talk to one of our sales managers, I can set that up, but I've already been given the go-ahead to extend an offer to you, so I will also be emailing that over."

"Wow. Really?"

She nods enthusiastically. Big grin. "Congratulations."

"Thanks." I guess?

"It was really wonderful to meet you, Sienna. Please do not hesitate to reach out if you have any questions at all, and congratulations again."

We say our goodbyes, and Kelsie ends the meeting. With a *what the heck just happened* sigh, I sit back in the chair. I just got a job.

I pack up and head back to the dorm.

"Hey," Josie calls from her desk without looking up. "How was the interview?"

Her hair is piled up on her head with two pencils sticking out of it. Josie is an art major, and I know how deep she is in the creative zone by the number of colored pencils holding up her hair. Right now we're at a point she can still communicate. Four or more, and there's no talking to her. She might speak, but she won't remember it later.

"Good. I got the job."

She swivels in her chair. "Oh my gosh, Sienna. Congratulations!"

"Thanks."

She gets up to hug me. "Or not? You don't look very excited."

"I'm stunned. They just gave me the job. I thought I'd have to answer questions about my strengths and weaknesses, tell them all the really amazing attributes I have that make me the perfect candidate."

She snorts. "You were just grumbling about those questions last night."

"I know, but I spent two hours preparing. What a waste."

"What is your greatest strength, Sienna Hale?" she asks, crossing her arms over her chest.

"I am disciplined and focused, and action-oriented," I say, just as I rehearsed.

"That's three, wow."

"Right? And I can provide examples for all, mostly around skating."

"Which would be great if you were interviewing for skating jobs." She gives me the look—the one that says she disapproves of me giving up skating after college.

The thing is, very few people make it as a professional skater like Elias and Taylor. Far more take jobs with ice dancing shows. Those are great. Josie works for one every summer and plans to do it after she graduates next year, but those shows are high-performance. There are flashing lights and loud music and all sorts of drama and flair. That's what makes them super fun and exciting for an audience, and also dangerous for me. Even if my doctor signed off, most companies wouldn't hire me, knowing the risk.

If I just came right out and told Josie that, she'd stop giving me that look. I guess I don't want her to. Some part of me wants to let her believe I'm capable of that. Half the battle with my heart condition is keeping people from feeling sorry for me or treating me differently.

And, I'm okay with skating being a hobby from here on out. I love it, but I accept that it's not my destiny. The problem is nothing else interests me enough to be excited about doing it for the rest of my life. I like my business classes, and I'm sure once I settle into a job, everything will be fine. It just seems like everyone else is so excited about their plans after graduation, and I feel very meh.

I reach for one of the positives. "They have a really great fitness studio with yoga classes."

"The selling point is yoga?" She laughs. "You can do yoga anywhere."

"Thanks for ruining the selling point."

She sits on her bed. "Well, what are the other selling points then? Outside of yoga."

"It's close to my family, the health benefits are excellent, 401k match, and I know it's a great company that's treated my dad well. I just thought I'd feel more excited."

"I don't know if anyone takes an entry-level job thinking it feels great. You can work up to a better position, though. It takes time."

I don't point out that she's ecstatic every summer when she heads off for her job. Last year she was performing on a cruise ship, though, so her job definitely has more selling points than the one I was just offered.

"Thanks, Dad." I stick out my tongue at her. "That's exactly what he said when he recommended me for the job."

"Are you going to take it?"

"I don't know." I fall onto her bed and slump over so my head is in her lap. "I don't think I'm cut out for the real world. Maybe I'll get a bunch more degrees. What is women's studies anyway?"

She snorts and runs a hand over my hair. "You'll figure it out, and you'll be great at whatever you do."

My phone rings in my backpack.

"What's your weakness?" Josie asks as I get up to retrieve it. That'll be my family ready to Zoom.

I grin. "Limited experience."

She rolls her eyes. "That's everyone interviewing for their first job."

"I know, right? It's the perfect bullshit answer to a bullshit question."

Chapter Eleven

SIENNA

Hi!" I answer my phone and wave at the screen while Josie goes back to drawing at her desk. My parents are crammed together on our living room couch.

A second later, Mom moves the phone to show me Allison sitting in the armchair across from them.

"Congrats, Al." She plays on her high school junior varsity team, but got bumped to play varsity for the first time because one of their star players got injured.

"Thanks," she says, trying to play it cool. She breaks seconds later. "It was so awesome, Sie. They turned all the lights down, and the music was so loud that the announcer had to yell our names. I've never felt more important in my entire life."

She keeps rambling about her hockey game last night.

"Mom sent me the video," I say, when she takes a breath. "The only person yelling louder than that announcer was Dad."

She snorts. "Mom threatened to sit across the rink next time."

"I'm going to at least need to invest in earplugs," Mom says. She's smiling though and just as proud of Allison.

My chest tightens thinking about how I'm missing watching her play. Add that to the selling points of Dalton. I could actually see my sister play a few games. "Did your coach say whether or not this was going to be a permanent thing?"

"I hope so. Chelsea is out for the rest of the season."

"I'm so proud. My little sister is crushing other people's dreams to make her own happen," I joke with my hand held over my heart.

"Hey, it isn't like I injured her. And I'm sorry she's out, that royally sucks, but you have to take the opportunities given to you." She's all sass and fiery determination. We are alike in a lot of ways. We have the same dark hair and same green eyes. But at five foot eleven, she looks older than fifteen. In fact, by the time she was ten, she was already taller than me. I'm more quiet determination and Allison is unapologetically tenacious in everything she does.

"You're not wrong there. When's the next game?"

"This weekend. It's going to be a tough game." Her expression goes serious, and she gets quiet, presumably worrying about their next game.

My parents jump in to ask about skating and school. Dad hammers me with questions about the interview and congratulates me when I tell him they already sent over an offer.

"They're a great company," he adds. "Good benefits, nice office building."

"It would be so nice to have you living closer again," Mom says.

"You know I'll visit more no matter what," I tell her. "And Kelsie mentioned the great health benefits." I roll my eyes. "Doesn't it seem sketchy that they offered me a job without a proper interview. I don't even have any experience!" I don't want to tell people how to do their job, but maybe Kelsie should be fired for hiring someone without properly interviewing them.

He waves me off. "No one comes in with any useful experience. It's about character, and Bob knows you're a good egg."

"Bob?"

"I worked with him when I was overseeing the program managers, remember?"

"No."

"Handlebar mustache, wore flannel before it was trendy."

I huff a small laugh. "Vaguely sounds familiar."

"He'll be your boss. He's a great guy and has a good team. They're at the south location with the good cafeteria."

"Another selling point," I mumble.

My dad looks like he's two seconds away from giving me another lecture on working my way up, climbing the corporate ladder, when Olivia walks through the door.

"Game is in five," she says. "Are we watching it here or downstairs?"

There's a bigger TV downstairs in the lounge area, but Josie's already propped up her laptop and is finding the game.

"You're watching hockey?" Allison asks, brows raised.

"Of course. Valley is in the semifinals." And my new crush is playing. I run two fingers along my bottom lip thinking about Rhett and wondering if I should keep kissing him.

"If they win, they play the championship at Valley!" Allison says.

"I know." In the past I probably wouldn't have known but thanks to Rhett, I am well aware. "We're really excited." I move my phone so they can see Josie and Olivia.

"Hi girls," my mom says. Except they can't hear her because

I'm wearing my earbuds.

"My mom says hello," I tell them.

They wave and say their hellos.

"Here we go," Josie says. I glance over in time to see the camera zoom in on Valley U's hockey team warming up. If they win they'll move on to the championship this weekend. If they lose, their season is over.

As the game starts, Josie and Olivia settle on the floor to do homework, and I listen as my parents fill me in on everything happening there and periodically glance up at the screen to check the score, and okay, to see if Rhett is on the ice.

Allison and my dad are talking about her last game again, all things they've already told me, but they're both really excited so I let them chatter on. I'm tuning them out, anyway, watching the game. Number twenty-three comes onto the ice and I can't tear my eyes away from him. Valley has the puck and he speeds down the ice. Several guys take shots at the goalie, but nothing makes it in. Finally after three or more attempts, Rhett rebounds a blocked shot and passes to Adam on the other side of the net for the first goal of the game.

"Oh my gosh!" I yell. Josie and Olivia look up to see the Valley players huddling up, congratulating Rhett and Adam on the goal.

My family stops talking to see what the commotion is about.

"We scored." I can feel the blush creep up my neck. I don't think I've ever been so excited about a goal in a hockey game. "Valley is up by one with three minutes left in the second period."

"That's a lot of time," my sister says. "Is Luke Ketcham in the net?"

"Uhh..." I glance at the screen. I'm not about to tell them I only know the name and position of one Valley hockey player. The team is huddled up celebrating, but then it pans to the goalie and he turns so I can read the back of his jersey. "Yep."

"He's one of the best. The highest number of games won and most saves in a single game. I think he was drafted already." She looks to me like I might know. Yeah… nope, my hockey obsession is more a singular hockey player obsession.

The rest of the second period goes by scoreless, but when the third begins, Josie and Olivia abandon their schoolwork and I say goodbye to my family so I can sit and watch with my friends.

"Have you heard from him since they left?" Josie asks.

"We texted back and forth this morning, but just about the game."

"I hope they win. Can you imagine? It'll be nuts." Josie squeaks with happiness.

"There goes what's left of our ice time," Olivia says.

Josie laughs. "Hey, I think we should continue to share. It's some serious motivation to land a jump when a group of hot hockey players are watching. It's been the best week of practice ever for me."

I snort. "I doubt Coach is going to find your reasoning solid."

The final minute has us sitting shoulder to shoulder in front of Josie's laptop, holding hands. If they win, I have a great excuse to text Rhett later.

Prescott has the puck. They pass it around looking for opportunities. Valley uniforms are everywhere trying to cover every inch to block any shot attempt. Still, Prescott manages to get it within a foot of the net. There are too many bodies in front of the goal to keep track of the puck. They hack at it looking for an opening.

I hold my breath as another shot's fired. This one gets by everyone but the goalie. He keeps his pad down on the ice protecting it until the final buzzer sounds.

"They won!" Josie screeches and bounces up and down, still clutching my hand. "They did it. Oh my god."

We jump around our room and squeal with happiness. I send Rhett a text before I talk myself out of it. *Congratulations!!!*

"This is crazy," Olivia says. "I think I can hear people yelling outside." She moves to the window and we follow.

Sure enough, people are screaming and dancing around in the grassy area outside of our dorm.

"Let's go down there!" Josie rushes to the door. The hallway is filled with people who had the same idea.

Outside music is playing and one guy even has his face painted blue and yellow. People are hugging and high-fiving as if they'd been the ones to win tonight. It's insane and absolutely amazing.

I snap a couple of selfies with the chaos in the background and send those to Rhett too. The mood mellows, but people hang around. Olivia eventually leaves to finish studying and Josie and I take a seat on the grass with a hundred or more people wanting to enjoy this crazy moment together.

"This is incredible," I say, looking around the darkened campus. The glow of street lamps is the only light.

"It's a shame the hockey team missed this."

"I'm sure they went out to a bar or something. The bus doesn't come back until tomorrow morning." My stomach sinks as I imagine a drunk, charming Rhett pulling women into dirty, bar bathrooms to celebrate.

"Still. It isn't the same."

"Isn't it? Girls and booze are interchangeable." I check my phone to see if he's texted back yet. He hasn't.

"Do you really think that Rhett believes that?"

"I don't know," I admit. "It would be easier if I did."

"And way less fun." She pulls her hair back into a low ponytail. "I don't think he's this player you're making him out to be. Nothing I've heard about him backs it up. Seriously, I don't know a single person who has hooked up with him, and I've been asking around."

"You have?" A smile tugs at my lips, partly in relief and partly because it's just like Josie to dig for dirt without my asking.

"I might have been poking for my own purposes. There are some seriously cute guys on the team that I needed more information on, but, yes, I asked around." She shrugs. "If he's hooking up with an endless stream of chicks, they're not talking about it."

My phone pings and I glance down to see Rhett's face in a sweaty selfie with Maverick. They must have taken it just after the game because I can see lockers in the background and they're in a state of being half undressed. They're smiles are giant, though, and I feel a new surge of excitement for them. Laughing, I hold the screen out for Josie to see.

"Your smile is as big as his, friend. No matter your reservations, you like him."

"You're right. I like him. I do."

"But?"

"I just hope he doesn't crush me."

"I think you have to go for it. If you do and he breaks your heart, then you've got me to pet your hair and tell you how wonderful you are."

I snort laugh.

"I would! I would do whatever I had to until you were over him. But if you don't see where this could go, you'll regret it, and I can't fix that one so easily."

Chapter Twelve

SIENNA

After my Tuesday afternoon yoga class leaves, I turn on my own music to do some fun poses and basically just play around a little before I go back to my dorm room. I place my hands on the floor and go up into a handstand. I'm upside down when he walks into the studio.

I wobble and bring a leg down, then the other to stand upright. "Hey."

"You made that look too easy."

My stomach dips at the sight of Rhett. He's in his blue Valley hockey T-shirt and jeans, with a white Bruins hat low on his eyes.

"You're back."

"Got in about twenty minutes ago."

"You just missed yoga class."

"Thank god." He laughs softly. "Are you teaching another one this afternoon?"

"No, I was just messing around a little."

"Don't let me interrupt." He drops to the floor next to the wall and leans his back against it.

"Oh no, you have to participate or I'll feel awkward."

He kicks off his shoes and goes up into a handstand. His shirt rides up giving me a view of his chest and abs. He walks around the room on his hands, circling the entire perimeter before jumping back to his feet in front of me.

"Not bad." I think for a second. "What about this one?"

I go into crow's pose and hold it for a few seconds.

He looks apprehensive, so I come out of it. "It isn't that hard."

"Oh no, I'm not making that mistake again. I ate my words last time I had that thought about yoga."

"Squat on the mat."

Reluctantly, he moves onto the mat and does as I requested.

"Little lower."

His lips twist into a smirk, but he does it.

"Now put your hands onto the mat in front of you under your shoulders and spread out your fingers." I walk around him, checking out his form. "Your knees should rest on your arms. Good."

I crouch down beside him. "Come up onto your toes and shift your weight."

His forearms and biceps flex. "Now what?"

"If you can, shift your weight forward until your feet come off the floor. Don't jump or hop. It'll throw you off balance." I move in front of him and place my hands on his upper shoulders in case he falls forward.

He gets up and holds it for a second. He lets out a whoop of excitement and then loses his balance and drops back into a squat.

"That was good for your first try. Give it another shot."

"I think I better keep my day job." He rests on the mat. "Speaking of jobs, how'd your interview go?"

I sit in front of him and cross my legs. "Good. Really good, actually. They sent an offer over this morning."

"No way." His mouth pulls into a wide smile. "Congratulations. I missed so much in a day. Tell me everything."

I chuckle. "Umm well, it's the same company my dad works for in Appleton. It's a software company in the healthcare sector."

"Nice."

"I would be writing and editing sales materials, I think. The interview was kind of a blur. It's a good company, though."

"That's really awesome. Congratulations."

"Thanks. I haven't decided if I'm going to accept it. I probably will. I don't know. I haven't lined up any more interviews so I most likely should."

"You don't sound very excited. Is there something else you'd rather do?"

"No, that's kind of my problem. I keep waiting for something to come along that makes me as excited as I thought I would be when I was interviewing for jobs. They're all fine and I think I'll be happy wherever I end up, but I don't feel that glee that everyone else seems to when they talk about their jobs after college. Are you excited about working for your parents?"

"Yeah." He shrugs and leans back on his hands. "I've worked there every summer since I was sixteen though."

We're quiet for a beat and I realize I haven't congratulated him on the game in person.

"Oh my gosh, I'm the worst Valley fan ever. Congrats on the win and your assist." I move forward to hug him. He's warm and smells like laundry soap and my pulse quickens being so close.

"Thanks." He smiles. "I still can't believe it. Totally surreal."

"Campus was nuts last night. Everyone is so excited that the championship game is here."

"Us too. Adam and I stayed up half the night talking about it. We're so freaking pumped."

"Did you guys get to go out somewhere last night to celebrate?"

"Coach took us out to dinner and I think a few of the guys might have went down to the hotel bar when we got back, but most of us were to amped up thinking about the next game."

"I had this mental picture of you in some bar, shirtless, slopping beer around on unsuspecting women who then pulled you into the bathroom."

He lifts a brow and then slowly sits forward until his face is inches from mine. "You're the only girl I want to slop beer on," he replies playfully and winks.

"Wow, I feel so special." I say the words sarcastically, but my stomach is filled with butterflies.

"What are you doing later?"

"I'm not sure. Why?"

"We're watching game film at five, but I was hoping we could hang out after."

"What did you have in mind?"

"Anything you want? You could come over or... anything." Come over. Translation, spend the night kissing and possibly more.

"Anything, huh?"

"Uh-oh. Why do I feel like I just unwillingly signed myself up for more brutal yoga or something equally humiliating?"

"That all depends. How's your voice?"

"WHY ARE YOU TORTURING THIS POOR MAN?" JOSIE ASKS AS WE walk around Prickly Pear, looking for a table. As soon as we walked in, Rhett went to grab drinks. He looks back and smiles at me from across the bar and my body tingles.

"I'm not torturing him. We haven't done this in ages. It'll be fun." We squeeze through another large group of people searching for somewhere to sit. "I don't remember karaoke night being so packed."

"Uh, Sienna." Josie nudges me with an elbow and points to a sign that says, *Speed Dating Event. Sign in at the bar.*

"Oh no!"

Rhett joins us with the drinks and an amused smirk. "Is this your way of telling me you want to see other people?"

"I thought it was karaoke night. I'm so sorry. We don't have to stay."

"Yes, we do," Josie says. "Look at them." She waves a hand toward a large group of guys with nametags on their shirts. "One of those guys could be my next boyfriend."

Josie and I take our drinks from Rhett and thank him.

"Nametags are in my back pocket." He turns so I can see them sticking out of his denim-clad ass.

He filled them out for us and I admire his small, neat penmanship as I pull the sticky label off and attach it to my shirt.

"You're cool with this? Really?" I move closer to him and drop my hand to his forearm.

"Yeah, it'll be fun." He cocks his head to the side. "Or really awful, but either way we'll have stories."

There are more guys than girls at the event. They sit the women in a line of chairs with about two feet of distance between us and a chair directly across where the guys take turns sitting with each of us for fifteen minutes before the timer goes off and they move to the left. Because we're at a bar, they also have special add-ons. If a guy wants to keep talking to you, he can buy you a drink and earn an extra fifteen minutes. And you have the chance to do a question and answer game where every correct answer about your partner, earns even more time.

I'm as nervous as I would be if it were a real first date when the first guy sits down in front of me. I glance down the line until I find Rhett a few chairs away. It occurs to me for the first time that while I might not be interested in chatting to these other guys, he might not be as opposed to getting to know some different girls. Ones that don't drag him out for a night of karaoke turned speed dating because they're terrified of hooking up and having their heart smashed into tiny pieces.

He's the hottest guy here by a mile. He ditched the hat tonight, but still went with his usual jeans and a gray T-shirt. He flashes a smile in my direction and then the first timer goes off for us to begin.

Will, my first date, tells me about his job working for a small advertising firm. He's nice and sort of cute, but I'm only half listening. I keep letting my gaze slide to the left to see Rhett. He's paired up with a pretty blonde. She's sitting on the edge of her chair so their knees touch and has his hand in her lap.

"What was that?" I ask Will. I'm pretty sure he asked me a question.

He glances in the direction I was staring. "I asked if you were seeing someone, but I think I got my answer."

"It's new. What about you?"

"A couple of girls. Nothing serious."

How charming.

"How do you feel about threesomes?"

I giggle because I think he's joking. He isn't. After that I stop pretending to be interested in Will and I watch Rhett to see what's happening with his date. They're both laughing and talking so I guess better than mine.

Needless to say, Will does not buy me a drink or ask me to play the game so we can spend more time together.

My next suitor is a graduate student at Valley named Chad. He's nice and doesn't ask me about threesomes. Who knew the bar was so low? I'm not feeling any sparks of attraction between us, but we're able to chat about classes and professors to kill the time.

I'm antsy for my chance with Rhett. If chatting with other guys and seeing him with other girls has shown me anything, it's that I want to spend time with him. I don't know how far I'm willing to put myself out there, but I'm not ready to walk away.

The next couple between me and Rhett opts for more time and the guy I walked into the bar with finally sits in front of me. He blows out a breath that makes his cheeks puff like a chipmunk.

"Having fun?"

He leans forward. "I don't want to alarm you but the woman sitting two chairs away from you is on house arrest awaiting trial for a crime in which she cannot speak about. She lives next door."

"And the one who was cradling your hand?"

"A palm reader. I'm going to live a long, healthy life."

"So you've had about the same luck I have then."

He reaches into his pocket and pulls out two crumpled pieces of paper.

"You got their numbers?" I ask too loudly and we get some side glances our direction.

"They weren't winners, but I am."

I shake my head. Of course he got numbers.

"This is a fun date." He leans back and stretches out one of his legs, hooking his foot under my chair.

"You're just saying that because you got a pocketful of numbers as backup."

"Wait, you really think I'm going to call the lady who read my palm or the one who can't go more than a hundred and fifty feet from her home for the next three months?"

"If not them, then maybe one of the others waiting to toss their digits at you."

"You're cute when you're jealous." He moves my chair closer to him with his foot. "What's your go-to karaoke song?"

"'Like a Prayer'."

He closes one eye and tips his head up to the ceiling like he's thinking.

"Madonna," I add. "Do you have a karaoke song?"

"No. When I sing, dogs howl."

"And still you came."

"I'll sing badly for you any time. What do you want to hear?"

"I was looking forward to hearing you belt out a love ballad. Maybe some Bryan Adams."

He smiles so big at me and he has a fabulous smile. The kind that makes a girl want to hand out her phone number. "Bryan

Adams? All right. Good to know. I might need to study up on my nineties ballads. Ever brought a date to karaoke before?"

"No, actually. You?"

"I've been on a date that involved karaoke but I'm pretty sure it was coincidental." He lifts a hand to get the moderator's attention.

"Everything going okay?" she asks tentatively. So tentatively I wonder what kind of interesting stories she might be able to tell about these speed dating events.

"I'd like to buy her a drink. Whatever she wants."

When she looks to me, I smile. "Can I get a vodka and Sprite?"

"Sure."

"And can we also do the question game?" Rhett asks.

Again our moderator looks to me for confirmation so I nod my agreement.

She brings my drink and then hands us each a pad of paper and pencil.

"I'm going to ask you three questions about each other. I hope you were asking lots of good questions and getting to know one another because these are tricky. After each one, I'll ask you to show each other what you wrote. Each correct answer earns you one minute which between the two of you could add up to a grand total of six."

Rhett chuckles quietly.

"Ready?" She looks to each of us.

I sit tall in my seat like a good pupil. "Ready."

"What is your date's favorite color?"

I laugh. "Favorite color, seriously?"

"It's the most frequently asked first date question," she assures me, then adds, "Take a guess."

Rhett holds the pad of paper up and scribbles something. I take a guess, blue, and we show our answers.

"Did either of you guess correctly?"

Rhett nods enthusiastically. "Yep, love blue. It's my most favorite color ever."

"And pink is… also my most favorite color." We share a secret smile.

"Two minutes," she says without looking at us. "Next question, how many sexual partners has your date had?"

"That cannot be a question people ask on a first date," I say.

She looks down at me. "It isn't, but it makes for really good bar conversation."

I hesitate, but finally decide on a number. Rhett seems to have a lot easier time deciding what to write.

"Okay, let's see those answers."

My stomach is in knots. I'm not sure I want to know the answer to this one.

Before we can share, our moderator gets called to help someone else.

"I'll be right back," she says before hurrying off.

"Let's see," Rhett says, sitting forward.

I turn the paper around and watch his expression as he sees the number. I went with ten because it felt like a good round number, but I have no idea. "Am I close? I don't need to know the real number, just let me know if I've got the right number of digits."

He barks a laugh. "You think it's possible my number has *three* digits? Like one hundred or more?"

"Yes?" Heat creeps up my neck and face. "What did you guess?"

"Five." He shows me.

The timer goes off and people move. Except neither of us do.

"Do you want to go sit at the bar?"

"What about the speed dates?"

"I think when you find the person you want to spend the rest of the night with, you're supposed to stop." He stands and holds out his hand.

When we get to the bar, I set my drink down and Rhett orders another beer. "And can I get a scrap of paper and a pen?"

"Sure thing." The bartender gets the paper and pen first.

Rhett scribbles something down and folds the paper and slides it to me. "That's my real number. Look at it or don't, but I can't have you believing I've slept with a hundred chicks." He shakes his head. "Where would I find the time?"

I steel myself for what I'm about to see, then unfold it and gasp. "Really?"

He grins. "Really."

"I... wow. Really? You're not fucking with me?"

His chest shakes with laughter. "I'm one-hundred-percent serious."

"But only one?" I'm shocked. How is that possible?

"What about you? Do I get the real number?"

I tear off a piece of paper and write my number on it. Like he did, I slide it to him, but when his fingers reach for it, I don't let go.

"I don't care what the number is, angel."

I let go and bring my thumbnail between my teeth while he looks.

"I was close." He grasps my wrist and pulls it away from my mouth. "Relax. Three is nothing to be embarrassed about."

"I'm not embarrassed. Not about my number, anyway."

He takes a drink from his beer and waits for me to continue.

"It's just this whole time I've been worried that you're some big player and I had it all wrong."

"Who's the player now?" he teases.

"I'm sorry."

"You're forgiven."

"Just like that?"

"Should I have made you sing me a love ballad?"

I relax, really relax, for maybe the first time I've ever been with him. Then his large palm stretches out on my thigh and all the nerves and butterflies are back. Because if he isn't a player, there isn't anything stopping me from letting him kiss me again.

And maybe more.

Chapter Thirteen

RHETT

Adam knocks on my open bedroom door. "House meeting in five."

I look up from my phone. "All right, but I'm not taking a shot every time I want to talk."

House meetings around here tend to end with us solving very little and getting drunk instead.

He snorts. "I already warned Maverick the apartment is dry until after Friday's game." He lingers, leaning on the doorframe. "Carrie?"

"Nah." Though she's texted plenty, too. "I'm texting Sienna."

"What's she up to?"

"I don't know. I haven't sent anything yet." Since we went out Tuesday night, I've been struggling to figure out what the next move is.

Adam clicks his tongue. "Maybe say 'hi, how are you doing?'"

"What if she responds with 'K'? Then what? It's been a couple of days and I think I might have waited too long."

"Bring your phone," he says, pushing up to his full height.

"We'll tackle that after the meeting."

We gather in the living room. Maverick always attends our house meetings even though he doesn't live here. He's here as much as the rest of us, so it makes sense even if it doesn't make sense. He's on the couch with Charli next to him and a metal water bottle in his lap.

"That better be water," Adam says, sitting in the worn leather chair.

I grab a chair from the dining room table and pull it into the living room.

"What's on the agenda, Cap?" Heath asks. He and Mav bump fists. They give Adam a lot of shit for these house meetings, but they're usually—no, always—the cause of them.

"I want to make sure the guys are keeping straight until after tomorrow's game. I know everyone wants to party and celebrate, but we can't have anyone fucking around and getting hurt or showing up to practice hungover."

"Pretty sure Ketch was still drunk this morning," Heath says.

A few of the younger guys went out again last night and practice this morning was shit. You'd think it wouldn't be such a struggle to stay sober for three freaking days. But it's exciting and unlike us, the younger guys don't appreciate just how fucking rare it is to get this far.

The vein in my buddy's head is popping. A sure sign he's stressed. "Exactly. That shit can't fly."

"He still managed to block most of what we threw at him," Mav pipes up.

"Most," Adam emphasizes.

"He lives in the dorms. How are we supposed to make sure he

doesn't drink?" I ask.

"Glad you asked," Adam says. "I am inviting all the guys to stay here tonight."

"Here?" Heath points with both hands to the floor.

"Mhmmm."

"You wanna have a fucking sleepover?" Mav barks a laugh. "I apologize for my language. Please strike the f-word from the minutes."

Heath pretends like he's scratching it out from an imaginary pad of paper. "So noted."

"You're serious?" I ask, trying to bring us back to the topic. The thought of our place sleeping even half the team makes my brain hurt.

"Some of the guys aren't going to like you fucking with their routines," Heath says. "And we can't exactly enforce it."

"Like hell I can't. Nothing is getting in the way of us going to the Frozen Four. Nothing."

None of us have spoken the phrase Frozen Four since we won the semifinal game Monday night. The Frozen Four is this end goal that we've all been silently working toward but don't talk about because we don't want to jinx it.

"Okay." I'm the first to agree. I trust Adam's instincts as our captain and if he thinks this is the best thing, I'll support him. "Where are we going to fit everyone?"

"We have three apartments if you include the girls." He nods toward Dakota and Reagan's apartment across the breezeway. "I'll sleep there with a few other guys. They said we could use their living room. The rest will be here and at Maverick's." He shrugs. "It'll be tight, but we'll make it work for a night."

"Fine, but Ginny's staying over tonight. It's my routine on home games."

"It's your routine every night," I add. Our rooms share a wall so I'm well aware of his ritual of banging his girlfriend every night. She's his lucky rabbit's foot and he rubs that shit every night.

"Just..." Adam sighs. "Sneak her in before the guys get here. I don't want to hear them all bitching about how unfair it is that you get to shack up with your girlfriend and they don't."

Heath smiles, fighting back a huge grin. "Anyone else find it funny that this guy is telling me to sneak his sister into my room?" He looks around to us. "No one? Well, I think it's fucking hilarious."

"Or she could stay at her dorm if you prefer." Adam scowls.

"No, no. I'll sneak her in." He chuckles. "This is turning out to be more fun than I thought already."

"Anything else?" Mav asks.

"Uhh yeah." Adam glances to me. "Rhett needs our help texting Sienna. He's overthinking it."

I glare at him. When he said we'd tackle it, I thought he meant the two of us.

"Shouldn't you have loads of experience in the art of sexting after dating Carrie for six years, most of that long distance?"

"This is different," Adam answers before I can. "This is new relationship stuff."

"So dick pics?" Heath asks.

I put my face in my hands. Fuck my life. "No, not a dick pic. I just want to say hey and make plans with her sometime."

"I'd go with a dick pic. That says it all. Trust me." Heath grins. I think he enjoys saying shit like that just to get a rise out of Adam. But I wouldn't be surprised at all to learn Heath is sending photos of his junk to Ginny on the regular.

Carrie wasn't into that, and I've thankfully never had to try to take a compelling picture of my dick to send a girl.

"Nah, nah, I've got you, bro." Maverick stands, holding Charli in his arms. He drops his dog on my lap. "Hand me your phone."

Charli is a cool dog. Super chill and pretty damn cute, too, but I'm not sure what he's going for when he says, "Say Charli's the best dog in the whole world."

"Charli's the best dog in the whole world," I repeat, and give his French bulldog a little rub behind her ears.

"Okay, never mind. That one didn't turn out. Just smile."

Maverick stands in front of me for a solid minute taking photos until I can't smile any longer.

"Okay, what the fuck are we doing here?"

His thumb swipes across the screen. "No, no, no, maybe, no. Ha! Charli looks scared of you in this one. No, no, no. Ooooh. What do we think?" He shows the phone to Adam.

My buddy shrugs. "What's the plan?"

"Send that to Sienna. Dog pics are far superior to dick pics."

Well, I was feeling hopeful he had some master plan, but seriously?

"She isn't even my dog."

"So?" He takes Charli and tosses me the phone. "I've tracked it. You're three times more likely to get laid sending that picture than one of your dick. Or, I am anyway."

"Maybe your dick is ugly," Heath says.

"Fuck off, my dick is beautiful, and don't pretend like you haven't seen it."

"Well, I haven't, so please, don't show us." Adam holds up a hand. Then he looks to me. "It's worth a shot. Charli's a really fucking cute dog."

"I just send the pic? No explanation?"

Mav groans, takes my phone, taps something out and hands it back. "I didn't realize you needed me to do it all for you, Rauthruss. You're welcome."

Oh fuck. A pit forms in my stomach as I read the text he sent.

Meet Charli (Mav's dog). She likes to cuddle with me.

And along with the text, he sent one of the pics.

"That's it? That's the magic? You didn't say anything about me wanting to hang out."

My phone pings and the guys all wait for me to read it.

"Awww! She's adorable. What are you doing later?"

Mav pumps his fist in the air. "And that's how it's done, boys."

THE TEAM IS LESS RESISTANT THAN I EXPECTED ABOUT SPENDING a night sleeping on our living room floor. Adam and Maverick go to the store to get groceries. Ginny showed up not long after our house meeting and she and Heath haven't come out of his room since.

I walk to the front door, phone to my ear.

"I'm here," she says. "I think. All of these apartments look the same."

I open the door as Sienna gets to the top of the landing.

"Coast still clear?" she whispers.

"The team should be here in the next thirty minutes or so." I open my arms and she wraps hers around my waist. She's still in her workout gear from teaching yoga. "Missed you."

She laughs softly against my chest. "Good. I sort of missed you too."

My grin is wide and can't be helped. "Sure you're up for this?"

"Are you kidding? A night with the entire hockey team. I'd be stupid to pass that up." She winks and walks into the apartment.

Who knew sneaking a girl in could be so much fun? We don't really need to sneak. Not until the team gets here, but we head straight back to my room.

There's something about trying to keep quiet that makes us both giggle as I shut my door and kiss her.

"I thought you said you needed to study. I brought my books."

"Later," I promise.

I frame her face with my hands and back her up to the bed. She falls onto the mattress and I cover her.

At this point we've spent hours kissing, and it's been awesome, but tonight I'm hoping she's ready for more. My dick kicks against my jeans. Every movement she makes below me makes me harder.

Her hands slip under my T-shirt and roam over my back, pulling me down harder against her. Looks like we're of one mind—remove clothes, get closer.

I rear back and remove my T-shirt. Her green eyes darken as she checks me out. Taking her hands, I pull her up to a sitting position, take her mouth again, and inch her tank top up. She raises her arms letting me bring it over her head. She smiles shyly as my gaze lowers.

Her bra is hot pink with a little bow right between her cleavage. I finger the delicate knot.

"I like this." I lean forward and press a kiss to her stomach, then hook my fingers around the clasp in the back. She shrugs out of it and tosses it to the floor. "Like it even better now."

I capture her mouth, swallowing the light laughter, and bringing us back down to the mattress. I try not to rush this, savoring the top half of her before taking it to the next level, but Sienna grinds into my dick while she kisses me like she's been able to think of nothing else since we last saw each other. That would make two of us.

No time like the present. I scoot down, trailing kisses along her stomach. Her leggings mold to her lean hips and stomach, I inch them down, adding more kisses along the top of her panties.

Her hips lift as I settle between her legs. I slide one finger under the material leaving goose bumps behind.

Fuck, I don't think I've ever been so turned on in all my life as she threads her fingers through my hair, encouraging me to move lower.

"Hey," Adam's deep voice sounds as he walks into my room.

Sienna yelps. I jump up in front of her shielding her with my body, and Adam takes in the scene in front of him, then quickly turns to face the other direction, closing the door with him still inside.

"Don't worry. I didn't see anything."

"Get the hell out, man."

"Nice to see you again, Sienna." He's covering his eyes with a hand even as he faces the opposite way.

"Hey, Adam." Her voice is tight but filled with amusement.

"Dude," I say again.

"See you took it upon yourself to sneak in a girl as well."

"Apparently not well enough when people walk in my damn room without knocking."

"Yeah, trust me, I'm as sorry as you, but uh, we need you. Team meeting on the deck."

He fumbles for the door, still covering his eyes, and exits.

Sienna giggles and then slaps a hand over her mouth.

"I'm glad you find this funny," I say. "My roommate may or may not have seen your boobs."

She lifts a shoulder and lets it fall. "That was my master plan. A whole house of hockey players and me." She grins. "Should I go out there with you like this?"

"Uh-uh, player." I crawl back on top of her. "You're just mine tonight."

Chapter Fourteen

SIENNA

"Isn't the team suspicious that you aren't out there with them?" I ask Rhett later.

He came back right after the team meeting and hasn't left since. We have a little picnic laid out on his bedroom floor with the food he managed to steal from the kitchen and the emergency snacks I keep in my purse.

"No, they won't even miss me."

We've stopped bothering to whisper. The noise coming from the living room is so loud, there's no point.

"What's a typical Thursday night look like for you?" I ask, crossing my legs and leaning forward.

"Not that different."

"Half-naked girls picnicking on your bedroom floor is the norm?"

"Oh yeah." He smiles and tosses an almond in his mouth, continuing while he chews, "But usually they bring better food."

"Hey, if you don't appreciate my snacks, don't eat them." I swipe the bag of almonds from the middle and hold them close to my chest.

His blue eyes twinkle as he smiles at me. "What's a typical Thursday night for you?"

"Not that different," I mock him. "Picnicking half naked with hockey boys."

My phone lays at my feet, close enough Rhett can see the screen when it rings. Elias' name and face displays.

I wave a hand toward it as if to say, *See? I'm a wanted woman.*

Rhett chuckles. "Don't let me keep you from setting up plans for tomorrow."

I'm sure he doesn't expect me to answer, but I do just that, bringing the phone close to my face and smiling sweetly. "Hey there, honey."

"Honey?" Elias' face twists in confusion. "Okay, sugar bottom."

"What?" I burst into laughter. "Please don't tell me you call girls sugar bottom."

"Not any worse than honey." He grimaces. "What's up? Where are you?"

"I am with a boy." I turn the phone so Elias can see Rhett. The latter waves, looking uncertain. "Rhett, this is my friend Elias."

"Ooooh," Elias coos and waves back, "Hey, man." He lowers his voice. "Why are you answering your phone? Go, have sex." He shoos me with a hand.

Rhett chuckles. My face warms. "We're just hanging out, having a picnic."

"An all you can eat buffet kind of thing?" He raises his brows seductively.

"What? Eww. Gross, Elias." I point the phone toward our snacks. "No, real food."

"Mine sounds more fun."

"Well, I'm very sorry I answered now, thanks a lot." I shake my head, sneak a look at Rhett who's grinning. "What's up? You've got one minute."

"Nothing. I was just calling to check in."

Which means he was calling to tell me the latest in his disastrous dating life.

"All good here. You?"

"Fine, fine. Have fun and text me in the morning to let me know you're good."

"Okay."

"Now, hand the phone to Rick."

"Elias," I warn.

"Hand the phone over, sugar bottom, or I'll keep calling all night long."

Reluctantly, I do because Elias isn't one to threaten without following through.

"Hey, man," Rhett says casually like this is a totally normal occurrence.

"Hey, what's up?" Elias says in his smooth, charming voice. "Listen, I'm going to need your address and phone number. Consider it a security deposit for hanging out with my girl."

Rhett's brows lift and he looks to me. I bury my face in my hands.

"Not like that," Elias says. "She is into some sick, twisted shit."

Oh my god.

"But she is my favorite person in the entire world, so please don't be offended when I tell you that if you hurt her, I will break you."

I stifle a laugh as Rhett nods slowly. Elias is right around six feet and I know he has to be strong for the lifts he does with Taylor, but Rhett probably has twenty pounds on him. Up close, though, I doubt Rhett can tell that.

"Got it," Rhett says. "I'll have Sienna text you my number and address."

"Great. Thanks a lot, Ron."

Rhett hands me the phone with a huge smirk on his face.

"Are you serious?" I ask Elias.

"Absolutely, sugar bottom. Now go have some fun and don't die on me." He makes an X over his heart, winks, and then disappears as he hangs up.

"Seems nice," Rhett says with a laugh.

"He isn't, but I love him anyway."

"Does he go to Valley?"

"No." I text Elias Rhett's address because I know he'll follow up if I don't. I leave off his phone number. He can call me. I don't need him having Rhett's number. God, I can't even imagine. "He lives in Toronto right now training. He's a skater too, pairs. I've actually never met him in person, but he's my best friend."

"Really you've never met him in person?"

I shake my head.

"So you just know him through skating stuff online?"

"Yeah. I've known him going on five years now, I think?" It isn't the whole truth, but I don't want to get into another conversation about my heart condition. "He's really talented and a total pain in my ass." I hold up my phone. "And now he has your address. Sorry, but he really would have kept calling."

"It's cool. I've got backup." He motions toward the wall where on the other side an entire team of hockey players is laughing and shouting. They are awfully loud for being sober.

His phone rings and we both laugh at another interruption. He doesn't make any move to get it.

"You can answer it, if you need to."

"Nah, everyone I need to talk to is here. What did he mean by sick and twisted?"

I chuckle. "I like to watch true crime documentaries. Elias is a big ole scaredy-cat."

One side of Rhett's mouth pulls up into a smile.

"I have a question." I cross my legs in front of me.

"Shoot."

"How is it possible that you've only slept with one girl?"

"Still not convinced?"

"No. I believe you, but, come on. You're hot and I see the way girls are around you." And the way he kisses… goose bumps dot my arm just thinking about it.

"I was in a relationship. Plus hockey and school take up a lot of time. What about you? Boyfriends?"

"Two." I hold up the coordinating number of fingers on my right hand. "Both lasted only a few months and like you, skating and school is where I focused."

"Look at us, we have something in common." He grins and straightens out his legs in front of him. "My foot is asleep."

I get to my feet and offer him both hands. Tugging, I manage to get him upright. "I have bad news."

"What's that?" He crowds my space, wrapping his arms around my lower back and pulling me flush against him.

"I have to pee."

While Rhett stands in the hallway being my lookout, I dart across into the bathroom. I hurry and then open the door a crack when I'm done to let Rhett know I'm ready to run back across.

Unfortunately, someone else needs to use the bathroom at that moment.

"You can't go in there," Rhett tells him.

"Why not? I gotta take a piss," the guy says. "I'll be quick."

"Sorry, I called it." Rhett pushes into the bathroom and closes it behind him.

"Now what?" I whisper.

He shrugs. "He'll give up and use the other one."

"Dude, you better not be taking a shit in there," the guy calls from outside the door.

"Are you sure about that?"

Rhett chuckles, his laughter tickles my neck as his mouth descends to my skin. "Gonna be a while. Use the other one."

"What is it with you and bathrooms?" I ask as he lifts me onto the vanity and steps between my legs.

"You're the one that ran in here."

I start to defend myself, but when his mouth covers mine, the words die on my lips. His hands grip my legs and his hard bulge presses into my sensitive core. He works my leggings down and tosses them to the floor.

I break the kiss, moaning as he rubs against me in a slow rhythm that has me not caring where we are. "Did you lock the door this time?"

I don't open my eyes but hear the click of the lock.

"Nothing is stopping me from getting you off." Long fingers slip under the satin material covering me and one digit slips inside of me while the pad of his thumb circles my clit. His fingers stop, but before I can protest, he pulls me to the edge of the vanity, removes my panties, and lowers between my legs.

The stone vanity is cold beneath my ass but the heat of his mouth starts a fire inside of me.

Someone knocks and instead of answering, Rhett kicks the door and growls. I fling a hand against the mirror behind me, the other I run through his messy hair while his mouth devours me. I let out a moan as the orgasm builds.

"You're so fucking tight. So fucking perfect," he rasps as I come. "So fucking perfect."

Chapter Fifteen

RHETT

Sienna holds on to my arm as I stick my head out of the bathroom to make sure no one is in the hallway. Dragging her behind me, I shoot across to my room.

We collapse onto my bed. Her hair hangs down past her shoulders and her cheeks are pink from the orgasm I just delivered. I can still taste her on my tongue.

"That was fun," she muses.

Fucking right it was.

She climbs on top of me and I think I see Jesus.

"There seems to be a problem." She wiggles her perky ass, grinding her lower body against mine.

A strangled sound gets trapped in my throat. She slides off me and undoes my jeans. Her fingers move down under my boxers and brush against the head of my cock.

I'm going to last all of a nanosecond. She wets her lips like she might be considering using that luscious mouth on my cock. The thought alone is too much. I encourage her to use her hand by pumping up into her.

A pleased smile touches her lips, and she wraps her hand around the base of my dick. I lean over and capture her mouth while she jerks me.

Hand jobs… not something I usually fantasize about. No offense to the women of the world offering them up, but if I want a handie, I can do it myself. Obviously, I won't turn one down. I'm not an idiot. But no one does it better than me. I've got years of on-the-job experience.

Or so I thought. Sienna's got a tight hold on my cock and rubs against me all while letting me mouth fuck her, and holy shit, it's a full-body handie and I relinquish my hard-earned participation trophy to her as fireworks go off behind my eyelids and I shoot all over my stomach.

I stare up at my ceiling, chest heaving. "I'm not usually that quick on the draw."

"Mhmmm. That's what they all say."

I sit up and run a hand through my hair. "Give me five and I'll prove it."

She grins at me. Perfect pink lips that curve up split to show her teeth. "Oh no. You told me you needed to study, and it's getting late."

I groan. "I did say that, didn't I?"

She bounds off my bed to get her backpack. Her ass mocks me in those tight leggings. I clean myself up and then join her. With all the traveling for hockey, school has been a struggle this semester. And it's not going to get easier.

Seems pointless when I already have a job.

"Want me to quiz you or something?" she offers when I flip open my textbook.

"Maybe. What's in it for me?"

"A good grade."

"Eh." I run my hand along the delicate line of her neck. "How about every question I get right, you remove an article of clothing?"

Her pulse thrums under my touch, and she nods. "Okay."

Seems a lot less pointless now.

THE NEXT MORNING I WAKE UP WITH AN ANGEL WRAPPED AROUND me and the bells from Hell trying to pull me from sleep.

Sienna nudges me. "Your alarm is going off."

I tighten my grip around her. "I know. Shh... five more minutes."

Laughing, she tries to pull away, but I've got a death grip on her. Last night was amazing and I don't want it to end. The basketball shorts I'm wearing are doing little to conceal that.

"How much time do we have?" She presses her tits into my chest. She really likes rubbing up on my chest and I am into it.

"Not enough, sadly."

I can already hear the guys out in the living room waking and moving around. We have a light skate this morning and Sienna has practice. We both have to get going.

Reluctantly, I reach over to grab my phone and silence the alarm.

We're in a post-awesome-night-together haze until the screen comes to life showing I've missed thirteen calls from Carrie. Thirteen?! What the fuck?

Sienna is silent, but she buries her head in my chest and I know she's seen it.

"Everything okay?" she asks tentatively.

I toss the phone to the end of the bed. "Everything's great."

We get up and get dressed without another word. Fuck. I don't know what to do about Carrie, but more importantly I really don't want things between me and Sienna to end on an awkward note.

Once we're ready to go, I pick her up, pin her against the wall, and kiss her until she's breathless and giggling and there isn't any weird tension between us.

"What was that for?"

"For luck. Are you coming to the game tonight?"

"Yeah, definitely."

"Hang after we win?"

She nods.

"Cool." I pick up my bag and then take hers, too. "Ready?"

"Don't I need to wait until everyone leaves?"

"Nah, no reason to sneak out. It's too late for them to do anything about it now."

Heath was right. Sneaking around is fun, but watching my teammates glare at me with jealous eyes—that's fucking awesome.

THE CROWD AT OUR HOME ARENA IS PUMPED. WITH THIS MANY people watching, it puts a little extra juice in every movement I make. So does spotting Sienna in the student section wearing blue and yellow with a little roadrunner painted on one side of her face.

I wink as I skate by. She smiles big and keeps clapping with the rest of the arena.

Adam makes his rounds during warmups getting us all in the right headspace. When he falls in beside me, I'm already there.

"Has this place ever been this loud?" I do another quick scan, taking in all the filled seats. I can't believe we made it here. The championship game. So close to the Frozen Four I can taste it.

"Definitely not."

We each take a shot on goal and skate back toward the bench.

"You good?" he asks.

I knew that was coming. He's asked me so many times in the past month it's laughable. This time before I can answer he adds, "You look good."

"I'm fucking fantastic." I glance once more at Sienna before I step off the ice. "Let's do this."

The adrenaline of playing in front of our hometown crowd gets us an early lead, but even up by two, the threat of being knocked out keeps us working hard to prevent Southern U from scoring.

Coming onto the ice for the start of the third period, we're tired, but the entire arena gets to their feet and it's easy to push it aside with so many people cheering us on. We're so close.

I look to Adam before the puck drops. Like me, this is it for him. We lose and our hockey careers are over. The hard set of his jaw tells me he doesn't want to go out like that. Especially not here in front of our home crowd.

Southern is physical in the final period. Desperation makes them meaner and tougher.

"I think that motherfucker bit me," Heath says after a SU jersey gets a penalty for holding.

"They know they're done. Let's put the nail in the coffin," Maverick says as we set for the power play.

Everyone in the arena is back on their feet. It's so loud I can't even hear Coach yelling from the bench. Doesn't matter. We've got this.

It's a game of cat and mouse as we pass the puck around firing shots, grabbing rebounds, and taking turns hacking away at their goalie.

They aren't going down easily, I'll give Southern that. But they're worried about Heath scoring on them and giving me room to work. Maverick moves toward Heath just like they expect. His eyes never leave Heath as he shoots the puck to me and I get a clear look through the five-hole as SU's goalie shifts to reposition himself.

The goal post lights up seconds before the final buzzer sounds.

"THREE-BEER LIMIT, BOYS," ADAM SAYS, TOSSING COLD CANS FROM a cooler in the back of his Jeep.

In two days we travel to Icarus State for regionals, but we couldn't not celebrate our win tonight.

The basement of Sigma is jam-packed. It feels like everyone from the arena followed us. Sienna's supposed to meet me here, but I can't see shit over the crowd of people.

Ginny, Reagan, and Dakota are with us as we push through the dark room. So are a few other girls that came with Jordan and Liam. I didn't catch their names, but for some reason they all have a vested interest in helping me find Sienna.

"Is that her?" one of them asks, standing on her tiptoes and pointing to a girl that looks nothing like Sienna. Which is what I tell them.

"Brown hair and green eyes aren't a lot to go on." She holds on to Jordan's arm and tries to make herself taller.

"You forgot gorgeous," Maverick says, elbowing me and mocking my earlier description. I could give two fucks less. I stand by my description.

"There she is." Adam, the tallest of the group, points to the far right side of the basement where a group of people are playing flip cup. Sienna and Josie stand off to the side.

I start toward her, circling around the middle where people are dancing.

She doesn't see me until I get within spitting distance.

"Hey!" Her smile widens and she steps forward, tossing her arms around my neck. "You won! Congratulations!"

"Thanks."

She pulls back and I slip a finger through one of the loops on her denim shorts. They're really fucking short and her toned legs are going to be a real welcome distraction.

She has a mixed drink in her hand and takes a sip, smiling. I think it's the first time I've ever seen her cup half empty.

"Getting lit tonight?"

"You scored the game-winning goal. We have to celebrate!"

"I know. I was there."

Josie steps forward to speak over the music. "Congratulations!"

"Thanks."

My friends step up behind me, finally making their way through the party. I introduce everyone and we make one big circle.

Huh. I think this is the first time ever I've been out with my friends at a party with a girl. When Carrie visited, we usually kept to ourselves. This is nice.

Since we're taking it easy, we mostly stick to our circle, talking, hanging out, enjoying the night.

My buddy's girls are all about Sienna and her friends. Two more skaters have joined us, and they're all talking and laughing.

"Stealing her," Dakota says to me. "We need her more than you."

I highly doubt that.

Sienna winks as they tug her away from me.

"I found the downside of your girlfriends," I say when it's just the guys.

"Yeah, they tend to move in a pack. Don't worry." Adam tosses an arm around my shoulder. "They'll be back."

And come back she does, fifteen minutes later, arm in arm with Dakota and Josie, Sienna's laughing and her cheeks are flushed. I'm still milking my first beer.

Giggling, she shimmies in front of me. Her phone in the front pocket of her shorts falls out onto the ground.

I pick it up and inspect for damage before I hand it back. "You are the biggest lightweight."

"My pockets are so small. It keeps falling out."

"I've got you." I tuck it into my pocket.

"Thank you." She kisses me on the mouth, tasting like beer and wintergreen gum.

I don't think she's drunk, but she's definitely feeling it.

A new song comes on and she tosses her hands over her head.

"Oh my gosh, I love this song."

Maverick bounces in place. "Hell yeah."

"Come on, let's dance." Sienna takes my hand and pulls.

Ginny and Heath are already moving that direction and Adam and Reagan are sort of sway-hugging to the beat.

I stay glued to the spot. "I don't dance."

"Lies! You were dancing the other night."

"Would we call that dancing?" Mav asks with a grin.

We wouldn't, actually. I was standing there, and girls were dancing around me, not exactly the same thing. I say as much.

She closes the space between us, pressing her body to mine. "All you have to do is stand there and I'll make you look good."

Chapter Sixteen

SIENNA

There's a long list of things I rarely do because of my heart condition. It isn't that I can't drink, or do those other things on the list, but with so many things out of my control, I do the things I can to take care of myself.

So Rhett is correct when he calls me a lightweight for the second time as we make our way to the dance floor and I stumble over my own feet. I've had three beers and I'm definitely feeling it.

He holds me upright as we join his friends in the middle of Sigma's basement. Looking uncertain, he keeps his hands at my waist as I dance in front of him. He's just standing in place, but he makes it look good. Ripped jeans and a plain black T-shirt set off the blond of his hair and those steely blue eyes.

I took a lot of dance lessons growing up, but those mostly only get showcased on the ice. Without my skates, I've never felt that same confidence. But the way he stares at me like I'm this amazing, beautiful creature he can't believe he's with, gives me the boost I need to cut loose. The alcohol is also probably helping.

Olivia and Josie are still with us, squealing as they get right in the middle of the circle we've formed. Rhett's friends are nice, and they've been so welcoming to me and my friends.

Speaking of his friends, Ginny dances behind me, rubbing her butt against me playfully. I turn so my back is to Rhett while I dance with her.

"You're a good dancer," she yells over the music.

Rhett's hands rest low on my hips.

"Thanks! You too." I smile at her. I like Ginny. She's sweet. Her blonde hair whips around her shoulders as she moves. Her boyfriend Heath is like Rhett—standing behind her, not really dancing.

Dakota, the only single one, I think, moves between us all as she dances, hands over her head. She has the kind of confidence that makes her fun to watch on the dance floor regardless of if she had any skill or not. She does, though. Her cropped shirt lifts with each movement, grazing the bottom of her bra. Red, the same color as her hair.

Josie joins her and they are the center of attention. Rightfully so, she is a great dancer and she's stunning with her light blue hair. Their ability to let go and live in the moment pushes me to be bolder.

I swivel around and smile at Rhett, then dance backward toward Josie and Dakota. They welcome me by opening up to let me move between them. They grin and cheer me on as I dance in the middle of the circle, giving it everything I have and just having fun.

When the music changes and I glance over at Rhett, his eyes flash with heat that makes my already accelerated heart rate speed up and my chest tighten.

"Holy shit, Sienna." Dakota steps in front of me, blocking Rhett from my view. "You're amazing."

"Thanks." I gulp in air. This basement is hot and the alcohol and dance workout I did makes my skin sticky. I lift my hair and fan my neck. "I'm gonna sit the next one out."

"She's going to sit several out." Rhett appears beside me, his strong arms circle my waist and he lifts me up, carrying me away from the group.

"What are you doing?" I squeak and giggle in surprise as he moves through the basement toward the stairs.

He doesn't answer or set me down until we're upstairs. Pinning me against the wall, one hand at my waist, the other on the wall above my head, he captures my mouth in a bruising kiss. I forget I asked him a question until he pulls back and says, "I needed to do that. You ready to go? We can stay longer, of course, if you want to keep dancing, but I have all kinds of things I want to do to you right now."

"Like?" I ask, breathless and my sex clenching at his words.

His mouth opens, he pauses, and then shakes his head. "I can't come up with a nice way to say I want to fuck you into next week." He holds his hand out to me. "What'll it be, angel?"

Who needs nice? "I think I've had enough dancing."

WE CATCH A SOBER RIDE TO RHETT'S APARTMENT. IT'S QUIET, everyone else is still at the party, but we don't turn on a single light as we kiss our way through the living room, down the hallway, and finally into his bedroom.

His phone rings. The screen lights up his pocket in the darkness.

"You're ringing," I say, not removing my lips from his.

"No, you are."

He takes my phone out of his pocket and hands it to me.

"It's Elias." Shit, I know he's checking in on me. I texted him a picture of me drinking with the girls and like the overprotective brother-type he is, he's going to worry until I assure him I'm fine. "Just give me one second."

I answer, not moving away from Rhett. "Hey."

"Hey, I'm headed to bed. Everything okay?"

"Yes, I'm fine."

"With Roy?"

"Mhmm." I press my lips to the man in front of me.

"Okay. Be good-ish. Call me tomorrow."

"Bye." I slip the phone into my pocket. "Sorry about that. He worries."

Rhett's brow furrows. "About you being with me?"

"No, it isn't that." I shake my head. "He knew I was out drinking."

He waits for me to elaborate.

"Elias has the same heart condition I do, so when one of us does something that puts us more at risk, we get a little protective."

He nods slowly like he's finally piecing it together. His hands slide under my shirt and lazily stroke my skin.

Now that we're not in a frenzied lip lock, I'm nervous. I like Rhett. He's different than I expected. Nice, fun, stupid hot. Speaking of stupid, hooking up with him might be just that. I no longer think he's a player, but that doesn't mean this won't still end in heartbreak.

We messed around a bunch last night, but tonight feels different. Sex is imminent, and I know myself well enough to know that taking it to the next level will only increase my feelings for him.

"And are you okay?" he asks, sliding one of those hands up my back, sending a shiver up my spine.

"I'm perfect." Wrapping my arms around his neck, I jump into his strong arms and kiss him to show him just how okay I am. Josie is right. The regret of not knowing would be worse than any disaster that's heading my way.

He lays me down on his bed, kicks off his shoes, and pulls his T-shirt over his head. I move to kneel on the mattress in front of him and undo his jeans. God, he has a great body.

Anticipation and excitement make my fingers move fast, but Rhett's jeans are a real challenge to get over his legs.

He chuckles, helping me, and then I'm eye level with a serious bulge covered only by black boxer briefs. He stands there, unmoving, as I inch them down. His dick springs free.

I hesitate, swallowing. He's long and thick. A bead of precum leaks from the tip.

"It's so pretty."

His chest puffs out before the sound of his laugh fills the room. "Pretty?"

"Mhmm." I run a hand along the V of his hip. "Are you going to tell me it's handsome or some other masculine term?"

"Hell no." His voice is gruff and his ab muscles contract as I glide my hand south. "You keep staring at it like that and you can use whatever adjective you like. Besides, girls like pretty things."

That we do.

As I bring my mouth to the head of his cock, I suddenly wish I were more of a drinker because some liquid courage would be great about now. I'm all sobered up and second-guessing every movement.

"Ah fuck." His words are deep and throaty. His fingers thread through my hair and then one hand grips my neck, pulling me off his dick and guiding my face up until he slams his mouth down over mine in another crushing kiss.

Guiding me with that big hand at my neck and another snaked around my waist, he forces me onto my back.

He's muscular, but lean and watching his body move over me is the sexiest thing. His hand stays at my neck as he kisses his way up my stomach, stopping to bite each nipple, and then slanting his mouth over mine in the most tender way that I'm not expecting.

I shift my hips under him, grinding up into his dick. He groans and the grip on my neck tightens.

"One second." He shifts to open a drawer on his nightstand, grabs a condom, and covers himself.

At first I think it's light from the window shining in, but when he positions himself at my entrance, I giggle at the neon yellow color of his dick.

"It looks like a banana."

"Glow in the dark, baby."

"Afraid I wouldn't be able to find it?" I tease.

The thick head of his cock pushes in an inch and I suck in a breath.

A wicked grin pulls at his lips as he pulls out that delicious inch. Sitting on the bed, he pulls me up and onto his lap. He lowers me slowly down onto him. His penetrating gaze is millimeters from mine and he catches every whimper and moan as he fucks me.

His fingers tangle in my hair, pulling my head back so he can suck on my neck. All while he pumps my body down onto his over and over.

When my breaths come quicker, he grips both of my hips to increase the pace and angles my body backward so he can kiss and suck my boobs. I detonate in his arms. He's doing all the work anyway, but I'm a rag doll as my climax goes on so long it blends with his moments later.

My heart flutters and I lean forward and rest my head on his shoulder. He's still buried inside of me and he wraps his arms around my waist and brushes my hair away from my face so he can place a kiss on my forehead. And his heart hammers against me in perfect rhythm.

I fight a yawn as we get ready for bed. I finger-brush my hair and Rhett gives me a T-shirt to sleep in.

"Green," he says as he snuggles up behind me.

"What?" I fight my eyes to keep them open.

"At the bar, you guessed my favorite color was blue, but it's green."

"Mine is blue."

"I wonder what the third question was."

"I don't know."

"I wanna know you," he says quietly. "All the things."

I'm smiling when I fall asleep. It doesn't take long. Exhaustion pulls me under and I can't remember ever being so content. I'm woken by a phone ringing. My first instinct is something is wrong with Elias, but this time it's Rhett's phone ringing.

I nudge him. "Your phone's ringing."

"Hmmm?"

I nudge him again.

Without opening his eyes, he feels around for his phone and then brings it to his ear. "Hello?"

A feminine voice replies, zapping me from my happy, sleepy place. His eyes open and he sits up. He brings the phone away to look at the screen, then jams it back to his ear. "What the hell, Carrie? It's three o'clock in the morning."

I roll onto my back while he continues to talk to *Carrie* on the other end. My brain buzzes with possibilities—none of them good. Thirteen missed calls last night and now this? I've zoned out, stewing in awful thoughts, until his deep voice, still thick with sleep, mutters a string of curses.

"I'm so sorry. I was half asleep and I didn't realize who it was."

"Is everything okay?"

"Yeah, it was nothing."

I wait for him to say more, but like this morning, he doesn't seem to want to talk about it. He pulls me into his arms with a heavy sigh, and neither of us speaks again.

I don't sleep well the rest of the night. When it's finally light outside, I creep from the bed and get dressed, then request an Uber.

"You're leaving?" He sits up and runs a hand through his bed head.

"Yeah. I have practice this morning."

He glances at the window to the early morning sky and then raises a brow.

Pulling on my shirt, I kneel on the end of the bed.

"I didn't sleep," I admit. "What's going on with the phone calls?"

He sits up. "It's my ex, Carrie. She won't stop calling."

I have a thousand questions. "Why? What does she want?"

"I'm not even sure anymore. It's been almost a month since we broke up and she's blowing up my phone at the most inopportune times."

"Oh." I don't know why I assumed he'd been single longer, but knowing he was with someone just a month ago—someone who cares so much for him she still calls in the middle of the night—makes me uneasy.

"It's over," he says. "And I'm sorry that I answered. I wasn't thinking." His arms circle my waist. "Don't leave."

"I really do need to practice."

He bobs his head slowly. "Okay. Hang later?"

I hesitate. "I'll text you."

Chapter Seventeen

RHETT

"Look who it is!" Adam smirks from the kitchen when I finally get out of bed. Sienna had to leave for practice, but I went back to bed after she left to catch up on the sleep I didn't get last night.

I grab a Powerade from the fridge and fall onto a stool at the counter.

"Heard you had a good time last night."

"I did." I take a long drink. "Wait, who did you hear that from?"

"You. I literally heard it. We all did." He waves the spoon in his hand around and points to a giant box of condoms I somehow didn't see when I sat down. "Mav dropped that off for you."

Fucking nosy roommates. I shake my head and chuckle as I pick up the box of glow-in-the-dark condoms.

"Does Mav just have these in bulk or what? Never mind, I don't want to know. Not sure I'm going to need them, though." I run a hand through my hair, pushing the long strands out of my face.

"What happened?"

"Carrie," I grumble. "She called a dozen times last night." Nothing ruins the moment quite like your ex obsessively blowing up your phone at three o'clock in the morning.

"Chick is relentless."

"No kidding. I don't know what to do. Talking didn't work. Ignoring obviously isn't working either. Sienna took off as soon as it was daylight."

"That sucks. I'm sorry. Still no to the blocking her number?"

"That just feels… wrong."

"You could always change your number." He smirks and goes back to stirring his oatmeal.

"Yeah, maybe." I stand, taking the Powerade and condoms to my room.

We have the day off practice, but a meeting with Coach to talk about our next game. We play the Ice Bombers at regionals. Another do-or-die game.

Saturday night when we get back to the apartment and Sienna still hasn't texted, I know she's avoiding me.

Fuck. How did things with Carrie get so out of control? We've talked so many times about the breakup, hashing it out again seems pointless.

I call Carrie and while I wait for her to answer, I pace my room. Part of me hopes she doesn't answer, but if she doesn't then I'm just delaying the conversation. Something has to give. I can't keep going like this. I want to move on. I want *her* to move on.

"Rhett!" She answers after the third ring with a chipper tone that I didn't hear a lot of the last few months we were together.

"Hey, Carrie. You have a few minutes to talk?"

"I answered the phone, didn't I?" She laughs softly. "Congrats on your game! I'm sorry I called so late. I went out with some friends and didn't realize what time it was when we got in."

"It isn't just that you called so late." I screw my eyes closed. "You can't keep calling."

She's quiet and I feel like an asshole.

"We broke up," I add. "This isn't healthy for either of us."

"I miss you." Her voice softens. "Don't you miss me?"

I miss the routine of it sometimes, but do I miss her? No, at least not the same way she misses me. It brings me no pleasure to be the one shutting her down.

"We can't keep doing this. We agreed that it was best to give each other space."

"Well, I don't agree anymore. I want to talk to you and tell you about my day. You were my best friend." She's crying and fuck, that guts me. "I think we should get back together."

"You don't mean that. You were miserable. We both were."

"Things were busy. I got overwhelmed. I took you for granted. I won't do that again."

"Carrie, I'm always going to care about you, but that isn't what I want. I don't think it's really what you want either."

She sniffles.

"Neither of us can move on if we're holding on to the past."

"I know."

I sit on my bed and hang my head. "Are we good?"

"I will try to call less, but I'm not giving up on us."

I let out an exasperated sigh away from the phone. We talk a few minutes longer and I get off the phone not feeling any better about the situation than I did when I called her, but at least I've said what I needed to.

I GIVE SIENNA THE REST OF SATURDAY BUT SHE DOESN'T TEXT. First thing Sunday morning, I head to the rink. If I know Sienna, she is already here even though their practice isn't for a few hours. I'm not the least bit surprised when I spot her, skating around the ice looking graceful and strong. I change into my skates and then hang off to the side, watching her as she runs through her program.

Chin held high, cheeks red from the chill of the ice, resolve and confidence radiates from her. She's stunning. This can't be over.

I step onto the ice as she's coming around. She slows and stops in front of me.

"What are you doing here?" she asks, smiling, chest rising and falling as she catches her breath. She glances down at her watch, something I've noticed she does a lot to check her heart rate.

I shrug a shoulder. "Might have missed you."

"In the twenty-four hours since I saw you last?"

"Absolutely."

She laughs lightly and skates over to grab her water.

"I'm sorry about yesterday."

"Rhett, I'm not mad at you. I get it."

"But you ran off at the ass crack of dawn with some vague bullshit about texting me later. Then you didn't. You don't want to keep hanging out?"

"I like you. I've had so much fun this past week, but I don't think I'm capable of being a rebound."

I push off and go to her. "You're not a rebound. Carrie and I are over. We've been over. It's been a long time since I've felt the way

I do right now."

"Which is?" She smirks. She's fishing, but that's fine. About to get yourself a whale, girl.

"I like you." I tip her chin up with a hand and lean in, lower my voice. "A lot."

She lets me brush my mouth over hers, but then she shoves off from my chest skating backward. "Prove it."

I arch a brow up and follow her to the center of the ice. "Here?"

"Yep. I'll skate you for it."

"How exactly is that going to prove I like you?"

"Don't tell me you're scared?"

Is she serious? "Maybe you weren't paying attention at the game the other night, but I'm pretty fast."

"Oh, I was paying attention." She runs a hand up my chest seductively and then circles around me. "You in?"

"Absolutely, angel." Few things I wouldn't agree to right now.

We go to the goal line and I yawn, egging her on. In reality, blood is pumping through my veins. I love competing and if it means winning more time with her? Sign me up.

"Are you sure you don't want to warm up?"

"I'll be fine." I roll my head side to side and lean forward slightly. "Say when, angel."

She huffs a laugh, adjusts her headband and focuses forward. "When."

I let her push off first. I have no intention of letting her beat me, but she's a damn sight as she speeds off from me. She glances over her shoulder, brown ponytail blowing around her face, to see why I haven't moved yet. That's my cue.

She's fast, but I'm faster. I reach her in a flash, then slow down so we're skating side by side. Her tongue peeks out and she pumps her arms faster. I pull ahead as we reach the goal line at the opposite end and stop, ice spraying from my skates.

"Again," she says before she's even stopped.

"You think that was beginners' luck?"

"Backward this time." She turns, arches a brow, silently daring me.

"I have a better idea." I cross my arms over my chest.

"I'm listening." She stands tall. Goddamn, she's beautiful all determined and competitive.

"I'll skate your routine."

She laughs. When I don't join her, she says, "You're serious?"

"Completely."

"You don't know my routine."

"If you're so sure of that, then it should be an easy bet for you to take."

She cocks her head to the side and narrows her gaze.

"If I can skate your entire short program, then you have to give us a real chance. Deal?"

I can see her contemplating it and the second she gives in. "Okay."

I grin.

"But, if you fall on any of the jumps, then it's an automatic disqualification."

"I won't fall."

"So sure of yourself. This should be entertaining." She skates away from me, steps off the ice, and leans against the wall. "Want music?"

"Yeah, turn it up." That way she can't hear the swear words I'll likely be muttering as I do jumps and leaps I haven't attempted in years. Now that this is happening, my nerves kick in. I've watched her skate a lot. Little glances while we're practicing and a couple of times we've gone early together and she's let me be her personal cheering section.

I'm perfectly capable of skating her routine. Not well, mind you, but I'm ninety-five percent sure I can stay on my feet. You don't grow up with parents who teach figure skating and not think to yourself, *hey I'm gonna try that shit*. Or, I didn't anyway. Sometimes out of boredom and sometimes trying to impress girls. It didn't work then, at least on the impressing girls part, but I'm hoping to change that today.

Her routine starts staring down at the ice and then a whip of the head as the music starts. I glance over at a smug-looking Sienna when the music begins and then it's go-time. She's graceful, which I'm not, and her program includes a lot of waving arms and fancy footwork that I'm sure look ridiculous with my choppy movements, but I can only focus on remembering the choreography and not acing it. And staying upright. I almost bite it on the first jump, catching myself in the nick of time.

The next jump is the one I'm worried about and it's coming up fast. I say a silent prayer to anyone who might be listening, then give it my best. I chuckle as I magically land it. I throw my hands overhead and then go into the spin.

After that, it's cake. The only thing I can't manage is grabbing my skate behind my head, but I hold one foot up, imitating it the best I can and then fist-bump to the roaring applause I'm expecting.

When I glance back at Sienna, she's not alone.

My buddies, dressed in their workout gear, watch with

expressions ranging from amusement to confusion.

"What the fuck was that?" Jordan asks, brows raised.

"That shit's going viral," Maverick says, holding his phone up, probably recording me.

I ignore all of them and focus on Sienna. Her expression gives nothing away as she skates out to me.

"You jacked up the choreography and your jumps are shit, but that was damn impressive."

That thrill of success shoots through me. "My parents own a skating camp, remember?"

"Mhmmm." She's still staring at me through a narrowed gaze. "How do you know my routine so well?"

"The same reason I'm sure this isn't a rebound."

"You're delusional?" A hint of a smile appears, and I know I've won her over. This isn't over. Not by a long shot.

"Yeah, probably that too." I grip her waist hard enough she can't skate away from me like she's so prone to do. "You're under my skin."

She doesn't comment, but relents by leaning into me.

"Rauthruss, ready to watch some hockey or are you switching sports?" Heath calls.

"Coming," I yell, not looking away from Sienna. "Now, what time are you coming over later?" I wink, drop a kiss to her mouth, and skate backward away from her slowly, waiting for an answer.

"Seven. I have to finish slides for a presentation next week and take a nap."

"Awesome." A grin tugs up the corners of my mouth. I'm cheesing hard and I'm never going to live this down from the guys, but I don't even care.

Chapter Eighteen

SIENNA

Thursday evening, I go to Rhett's apartment. It's a busy week for the both of us trying to manage classes, practice, and spending every free second together. Tonight is the last night we'll be able to hang for a few days.

Tomorrow I head off to Phoenix for a competition and before I get back, he leaves for regionals.

"I have news," I say while we work on school stuff. He's sprawled out on his side studying management policies and I'm sitting in the middle of the bed with my laptop rereading the acceptance email I just sent. "I accepted the job with Dalton."

"Really? Congrats! So you'll be in Appleton?"

"Yeah." It doesn't feel real. I'm not as excited as I thought I'd be, but I know it's a good job and it's the best starting salary that I've been offered, by far.

"Awesome. We'll only be a few hours apart."

Five. Yes, I already checked.

His bedroom door is open and Maverick steps in. "Sardines?"

I make a face of disgust. Yuck. "No thank you."

"Not the food, the game," Rhett clarifies. "It's like hide and seek but you have to squeeze into the space once you find people."

"Oh yeah. I've played."

"We do it on campus and it's awe-some," Mav singsongs the last word.

"We don't have to play," Rhett says, but his knee bounces and he's already got one foot on the floor.

"It's fine. I could use some fresh air anyway."

On the walk to campus, Dakota slips her arm through mine and tugs me toward her.

"We're stealing her," she says.

"Get your own." Rhett tries to yank me back, but Dakota's quicker and she's strong, too.

She whips me away, leaving Rhett gawking after us. "No. This isn't happening. You guys have forced me to hang out with you and your boyfriends and girlfriends. Hell, I even had to pair up with those two—" He points to Adam and Reagan. "I finally brought a girl and I want to hide with her."

"Correction. He wants to make out with her in the dark," Heath says.

"That too." Rhett gives me puppy dog eyes.

"You kept her in your room all evening, and now it's our turn." Dakota smiles smugly at him. "Boys against girls. Go hide. We'll even give you a few extra minutes." She's biting back that smile now and mutters, "You're going to need it."

The guys perk up at that.

"We get to hide?" Rhett asks.

"Unless you're worried?" Dakota challenges.

Mav scoffs. Rhett rubs his hands together. They start off,

already scheming where to hide.

"Remember the rules," Ginny calls after them. "No going inside or on top of buildings."

They don't answer, but she laughs and shakes her head. "What are the odds that someone gets hurt?"

"Adam will guarantee that doesn't happen," Reagan says. "He's done nothing but stress over it all week."

"Sounds like my brother." She tilts her head and her hand goes to the end of one blonde braid. "You know, he's a pretty decent human sometimes."

"How long until we go find them?" I ask. They've wandered off far enough I can no longer hear them talking.

"We usually wait around five minutes," Reagan says. She's nice, beautiful too. She has these dimples that I can't stop staring at.

"I have no intention of finding them." Dakota lowers herself to the ground and sits with her legs crossed.

"What?" Ginny's laughter tinkles out into the night, but she sits beside her friend.

Reagan shrugs, and we join them, sitting on the grass in the middle of campus.

Dakota pulls out her phone and starts some music before answering. "It was the only way I could get you three away from your men. They've been very clingy this week."

Reagan sticks out her lower lip and leans her head on Dakota's shoulder.

"It's true," Ginny says. "Heath sat in the bathroom today while I shaved my legs because he wanted to—" She raises her hands and makes quotes. "Spend more time together."

"Anything not to think about the game," Dakota says.

"Not Adam. It's all he's thinking about," Reagan says. "He watched game film all night long. *All* night. When I woke up for classes this morning, his laptop was sitting on his stomach and he was passed out."

Dakota snorts. "They are all acting so crazy. The only one that seems normal this week is Maverick. He's his same ridiculous self."

Reagan looks to me. "How's Rhett handling it?"

"Oh…" I glance around the circle. "He seems fine. I don't think I know him well enough to know the difference yet."

"He's the most competitive one out of all of them," Ginny says. "So it doesn't surprise me that he's handling the pressure well."

"And he's distracted by this one." Dakota nudges my foot with hers. "I've never seen him smile so much."

"What?" I can feel my face getting warm. "No. That can't be right."

Ginny nods. "It's true."

"I mean, things are great and we're spending a lot of time together, but it's still new."

"I'm happy for him," Reagan says. "After the way Carrie treated him, he deserves someone amazing like you."

"Why? How did Carrie treat him? Aside from calling Rhett constantly, I don't know much about her."

None of them speaks at first.

"We don't really know anything about her either," Reagan says. "She only visited a couple of times and she didn't make any attempt to get to know us. It was more of the way he was with her. Rhett spent ninety-nine percent of his time on the phone with her, he always had to check in even if we were out doing things. I've never done the long-distance thing so maybe that's normal."

"He was a really good boyfriend," Ginny speaks up for him with a reassuring smile like she's trying to convince me.

"You don't need to sell me on him. He's great." Trying to take the heat off me and Rhett, I look to the single one of the group, Dakota. "So, Ginny and Heath, Reagan and Adam, and you and Maverick?"

"No." Dakota's red hair catches the moonlight as she shakes her head. "I'm forever single."

"Why forever?"

Reagan leans forward and holds a hand up to her face, then whispers loud enough for everyone to hear, "This one is super picky."

Dakota smacks her arm playfully. "They're called standards."

Reagan laughs and sits back. "What about you? Have you dated a lot of people before Rhett?"

"No, not really. A couple of guys, but nothing serious."

"Why not?" Ginny asks with a disbelieving arch to her brow.

"What she means is, you're hot and amazing. How are you possibly still unattached?" Dakota asks. "Fear of commitment? Long lost love?"

I giggle. "No, neither."

They're all looking at me waiting for me to elaborate.

"I guess between the heart thing scaring people off and skating taking up so much of my time, it just hasn't happened. I'm not a big drinker so I usually leave the party before people start pairing off and going home together."

"You were waiting for Rhett." When Ginny smiles at me like she's doing right now, I feel about a hundred years older than her and super jaded. My default would be to make some sarcastic comment, but instead I smile back at her. Maybe I was.

Ginny's phone lights up in her hand, breaking the moment.

"Heath?" Reagan asks.

"Yeah, he told me where they are and said to hurry up."

"Clingy," Dakota says with a snort.

"Adorable." Ginny sticks up for her man.

The four of us stand to go find the guys. Even if we didn't know where they were hiding, they're loud. I can tell they're trying to whisper but the deep baritone of Maverick's laugh is impossible to mistake.

When we reach them, all of them except Heath grumbles.

"I knew this spot was too easy," Rhett says. He's pretty cute all competitive and frustrated.

"Well, that was fun." Heath jumps to his feet and walks to Ginny, takes her hand, and drops a kiss to her mouth. "We're out of here. Ginny has an eight o'clock class tomorrow."

"Oh right, blame Ginny," Maverick calls after him, but Heath and Ginny are already headed back.

"He told you where we were, didn't he?" Rhett asks me once we've all started walking to the apartment.

Lips pressed together, I glance at him, deciding if I should tell.

"I knew it!"

"I didn't say anything!"

"You didn't have to. I can read your face like a book, angel."

"Oh yeah?" I lift a brow. "What am I thinking now?"

His eyes darken and do a sweep of my entire body. "That we need to hurry the fuck back."

LATER, WE'RE GETTING READY TO SLEEP WHEN I NOTICE RHETT turn off his phone.

"You don't have to do that."

"What's that?" He places it face down on his nightstand and gets under the blanket.

I motion toward his phone.

"No, it's fine. It isn't fair to you."

I turn, sitting on his bed, to face him. "What does she want?"

"Do you really want to talk about this?" he asks with a sheepish grin. "I promise, it's over. We broke up over a month ago. I've only talked to her to ask her to stop calling."

"It's been like this every day for a month?"

"Not every day, but pretty close."

"If you say that it's over, I believe you, but help me understand. You must have some idea what she wants."

"Me, I guess." He sets a hand on my knee, thumb absently stroking my bare skin as he speaks. "We dated for a long time."

"How long is a long time?"

"Six years."

"*Six years?!*"

He nods. "We grew up together in Minnesota. I've known her since kindergarten, and we started dating in high school. She went to college in Nebraska and I came here. We stayed together, but it was hard. We built lives separately and over the years we had less and less in common. Things deteriorated slowly. We hardly ever got to visit each other."

"Wow. So all of college you've been dating someone halfway across the country?" Now the only sleeping with one person makes so much more sense.

"I should have ended things sooner. Honestly, the last few months, maybe longer, were pretty awful. But we were friends before and I wanted it to work because I cared about her. I'm always going to care about her, but I don't want to be with her." He leans forward and presses a kiss to my lips. "I want to be with you, angel."

"I don't know what to say." And I really don't.

"Carrie is struggling to accept something I already have, but she will. I mean, I know I'm pretty bomb, but she'll find someone new."

THE NEXT AFTERNOON, I JOIN RHETT AND HIS FRIENDS AT THE dining hall for lunch.

"Is it on TV?" Rhett asks about the competition tomorrow. We leave this afternoon to make the two hour drive to Phoenix.

"No. Sometimes people will stream it online, just depends."

"Bummer we can't come," Mav says, propping an elbow on the table.

The guys are heading to Icarus State for regionals. After a week of hanging out nonstop, I'm going to miss the crap out of Rhett this weekend. I'll get back just as he's leaving.

His hand finds my leg under the table and squeezes. I think he feels the same.

"Do you have time to come over and hang before our practice?"

His thumb strokes my bare thigh and tingles spread through my body.

"No, I have to meet with my doctor before we leave."

"Everything okay?" His blue eyes search mine.

"Yeah, it's just a precaution before every competition." I check my watch. "Speaking of, I should get going."

He stands with me and pulls me against his chest. "Good luck this weekend."

"You too." I glance at his friends. They're watching with big grins on their faces. Laughing, I press my lips to his. "I'll text you later. Bye guys! Take care of him."

Chapter Nineteen

RHETT

"Did you find it?" Adam asks, taking a seat next to me in the living room.

"No, nothing." I've been searching for Sienna's competition all morning. Someone, somewhere has to be streaming it.

"What time does she skate?"

"Two o'clock."

"Here's something." Mav sits up on the couch. "NAU is live."

I move to sit beside him and look at his screen. "They're showing their own girls. That makes sense."

"Maybe they'll keep it going all day," Adam says.

I hum in my throat. I doubt they're going to keep sharing video of the competition all day long.

"Sucks you couldn't go," Mav says. "Are you freaking out?"

"Freaking out? Why would I freak out?"

"Yeah, you know, her heart condition."

"Oh, yeah, she's fine. She saw the doctor yesterday before she left. Standard thing. No, I just really want to watch. She's been so great about Carrie and she came to our game." And I really freaking like her.

Mav drops his phone between his legs. "What do you mean, she's fine?"

"Just what I said. The doctor cleared her to skate."

"Rhett, buddy, he might have cleared her, but she's not *fine*. Have you seen the video of her fall last year?"

"No. What fall?"

Mav blows out a breath and raises his dark eyebrows. He positions his phone so I can see it again, and this time he pulls up a video of Sienna skating at some competition last season. She's in a red outfit that sparkles as she moves along the ice.

She has such a smooth, graceful way about her. Even if I weren't super into her, she'd be hard not to watch.

"Here it is. Here it is," Mav says, reminding me that we're watching this for a purpose.

Adam comes over and crowds in to see.

I'm expecting her to jump and not clear the landing, but she's just gliding across the ice when her body crumbles. She goes down hard on the ice and the audience lets out a collective *"Oooo"*.

I stop breathing and my pulse speeds up while I watch the medical staff rush out, and then the video cuts off.

"Holy shit." Adam stands.

"I don't understand." My ears ring. "Sienna said she's fine. This was last year?"

"Yeah, early in the season, I think. She was in the hospital for a few days."

"How do you know all this?" My tone is accusatory. What I really mean is, *Why don't I?*

"She was gone from yoga for about a month. We had this awful teacher instead who—"

"Focus." I raise my voice. "What else do you know about her heart condition?"

"Woah, dude. I don't think I've ever heard you raise your voice before." He makes a face at Adam that shows his shock. "That's pretty much all I know."

"How could you not tell me? How could *she* not tell me?" I stand and pace the living room.

It's quiet. Too quiet. I look to Adam. He's mostly reasonable.

"That may not be the type of thing that's so easy to bring up. Have you talked about her heart condition at all?" he asks.

I think back on all our conversations. "Yeah. Kind of. Fuck. I guess not. She told me she takes medication and that she has to be careful and listen to her body. She said she has episodes, but this…" I wave my hand toward Maverick's phone. "She didn't tell me that."

I sit back down. My mind is spinning. "Now what? She's about to skate. Can that happen again? She has the monitor now, right?"

I feel sick. The image of her slamming into the ice replays over and over. Holy shit.

"I'm going to call her." I do just that as I walk to my room, slamming the door behind me.

"Pick up. Pick up. Pick up," I mutter quietly.

She does on the third ring. The background noise of the competition is so loud, I can just barely make out her voice. "Hello?"

"Hey, it's me. It's Rhett."

"I know, silly."

"Right." Her happy, bubbly tone is such a contradiction to the picture of her lifeless face in the video that's now frozen in my head. "You're okay then?"

"What?"

"You saw the doctor and he cleared you to skate?"

She doesn't respond right away, but the background noise dims. "Sorry. I moved somewhere quieter so I can hear you. I only have a minute. Olivia is up next. What's up?"

"I was just calling to make sure you were okay."

"Yeah, I'm actually not that nervous. It usually doesn't hit me until right before I step on the ice. Then BAM!"

I flinch and squeeze my eyes shut. There it is again. The image of her slamming into the ice. *Fuck*.

"How's the heart? Doctor said it'd be fine, yeah?"

"Yeah, he cleared me. I'm good."

"You're sure?"

She laughs. "As sure as I can be, I guess."

That is not inspiring.

"Oh, they just called Olivia. I have to go. I'll call you later," her cheery voice chirps in my ear. I should feel better. She's fine. The doctor cleared her. He wouldn't do that if something could happen, right?

"Okay. Stay safe." Yeah, like that isn't an awkward send-off.

I hang up and stare at the wall. "Stay safe?"

Real smooth.

THE BUS LEAVES SUNDAY AFTERNOON. I TALKED TO SIENNA LONG enough last night to hear about her day, but she was tired and I still hadn't figured out what to say about the incident which shall never be watched again. Even still, it's replaying in my mind every time I think I'm past it.

Uneasy and restless, I oversleep, and then in a rush to get out the door, forget my Nintendo Switch for the ride. I can't even distract myself with video games while I worry about Sienna skating. She's taking the ice any time now.

I'm agitated and don't feel like making small talk. Silent and broody is the general mood on the bus, though, so I fit right in. Regionals is four teams, single elimination. Today we play Icarus State and then, hockey gods willing, the winner of Troy and Stonewell.

Heath is in the seat next to me. "Are you going to bounce your leg like that the whole ride?"

I still. "Sorry, man."

"It's cool. Everything all right?"

I stare down at the phone in my hand. "Waiting to hear how Sienna's final skate went today."

"I have cards. Wanna play?"

"Definitely." I'm still kicking myself for not asking more questions about her heart condition. She's waved it off like it was no big deal, but I should have known. A doctor has to clear her for every competition—that should have been a major red flag. Not to mention all the small ones along the way—checking her heart rate, Elias calling to check in on her every day.

The bus stops at the hotel where we check in and drop our overnight bags.

"Home sweet home," Adam says, tossing his duffel on the floor.

The adjoining door between our room and Heath and Mav's

opens.

"Hey, neighbors," Mav says.

My phone buzzes in my pocket and it's the first time in as long as I can remember, that I rush to answer it. *Sienna.* "Oh, thank fuck," I say before I accept the call. "Hey, angel."

"I'll go…" Adam tips his head toward the other room.

I hit the video button. I need to see her.

"I'm a mess," she says when her face fills the screen. She isn't. Her green eyes are highlighted with more makeup than usual. Dark lashes and a fuck-hot red mouth.

"I haven't changed yet. I was too tired."

"You look beautiful. How'd your long program go?"

"Good. Really good. My best score of the season. It moved me into second, but there are still two more senior skaters."

"Wow. That's amazing. Congrats. What are you doing now?"

"Hanging in the hallway trying to rest. Josie's with me. She's going to get us food across the street." She tilts the screen and her friend waves.

"Hey, Josie."

"Turkey, no cheese, light mayo?" she asks Sienna.

"And chips. Oooh, and a cookie."

I can no longer see Josie, but I hear her laugh. "All right. Back in a few."

When she leaves, Sienna brings the phone closer to her face.

"You could go with her and call me later. I know it's crazy there. Here too. We just got to the hotel. The bus is leaving for the arena in thirty minutes."

"No, I offered to go with her. She wanted to be alone. She's pissed at herself for falling on a jump today."

"That sucks."

She hums. "It happens. I hope we're back to Valley before your game starts. Signal on the way here was crappy."

"Oh, that reminds me, Dakota wanted me to invite you to their apartment to watch with them. If you're back in time."

"That was nice." She stretches her slim neck. "I'm probably going to crash as soon as the game is over though. Better to be in my bed when that happens."

"Are you okay?" The niggling worry is back.

"Yeah, I'm just tired. I never sleep well in hotels. I can't wait to crash in my own bed."

"I can sleep anywhere."

She smiles. "Oh, I've heard."

A chuckle shakes my chest. Two minutes ago I wouldn't have thought I was capable of laughing. All day I've been worrying about her, but here I am smiling and feeling calmer. That's just what it's like with Sienna. She makes bad days better. She makes everything better.

Chapter Twenty

SIENNA

I take Rhett with me to the locker room so I can grab my bag. It looks like we're going to take third overall and I am going to take second in the senior division. Not a bad way to hang up my skates. Metaphorically, of course. We still have the Valley Classic, but it's more of a showcase with just one other university. This is the last competitive show of the season and I'm happy with what I've accomplished.

"Did you watch it?" I ask. I sent him a video that Josie took of my short program yesterday.

"About a hundred times," he says, lighting up my insides. "Did someone take video for me today?"

"Yes. I'll send it to you."

He grins so big like I'm sending him nudes. His gaze drops. "Can't wait. Green today, huh? I like it."

"Oh, thanks." It's an emerald green that Josie says makes my eyes pop. I step in front of the large mirror in the locker room and turn my camera to show him the full outfit—sans skates.

"I like it a lot. Wish I could have been there to see you skate."

"You see me skate all the time."

"Yeah, but this is different." He sits on the bed and leans against the headboard. "Hey, I have a question for you."

"Shoot," I say, flipping the camera back around, then grabbing my stuff and heading back upstairs.

"How come you never told me about your accident last year?"

I still even before I've processed the words.

Rhett continues, "When we were looking for your competition online yesterday, Mav found some old videos from last year."

"I told you about my heart condition," I say defensively.

"Yeah, but I didn't realize it was like that. Besides, knowing it and seeing it happen..." He tilts his head and gives me a tight smile. "I can't stop seeing it."

I steel my expression and feel myself withdrawing from him. He isn't the first guy to get freaked out and decide it's more than they can handle. I was dating Mike, the more recent of my two boyfriends, when I fainted on the ice. He was great while I recovered and then peaced out as soon as I was feeling better. It's hard to blame him. Who wants to date the chick who could drop dead at any minute?

"Why didn't you tell me more?" he asks.

"Because." I wave a hand in front of the screen. "This happens. I'm fine. I have a heart condition and sometimes it stops me. Literally stops me. I didn't want to scare you off with details that aren't important."

"It's pretty important."

"I get it. It's a lot to deal with and you already have enough on your plate." My eyes burn with tears that I will absolutely not cry. Not now. "You should go and get ready for your game. No need to worry about me."

"Trying to shoo me away, angel?"

"I'm letting you off the hook. I promise I won't even bad-mouth you to my friends. Not much anyway."

"Back up about twenty steps, angel. I'm not ending this."

"You're not? But you're freaked out?" I can see it all over his face even if he hadn't said it. I didn't put it together yesterday when he was acting strange, but now it all makes sense.

"Yeah, of course I'm freaked out. I don't feel like I know anything about your heart condition and I was caught off guard. I want to know those kinds of things. I'm tough. I can handle it." He flashes a sheepish smile.

"What do you want to know?"

"Do you have to get cleared by the doctor every time you skate? Was he there today?"

"No. He's in Valley. I just see him the week before a competition."

"Has he ever not cleared you?"

"I had to take some time off last fall."

He nods and looks to me thoughtfully. "You are inspiring, angel."

"Inspiring?"

"Yeah, that's the one thing I've said today that I'm standing by. The rest is probably garbage and I'm sorry if I said it all wrong. I like you and I'm not going anywhere. Did I already say that?"

"You did."

"Good. Don't forget it." He glances up and I hear some of the guys talking. "I've gotta get ready for the game. Call you later?"

"Sure." I know he said he's not going anywhere, but I try not to get too hopeful just in case.

"Good luck."

He winks. "Later, angel."

MONDAY MORNING, I GO TO THE YOGA STUDIO. I'M NOT TEACHING any fitness classes today, but Coach gave us the next two days off practice and with Rhett still gone, all my homework done, and my friends busy, I'm bored.

The hockey team won their first game and tonight they play again. It's the last game standing in the way of them going to the Frozen Four. I talked to Rhett when they were heading to the arena for their morning skate and he was so excited and talking so fast. It was adorable.

I'm taking a break and sitting on my mat when the door creaks open.

"Hello?"

The door swings open and Dakota and Reagan appear.

"I thought that was you," Dakota says. "What are you doing?"

"Hey!" I smile as they walk into the room. "Messing around, mostly. What are you two doing here?"

"She made me do a spin class." Reagan sits beside me and drinks from her water bottle.

"Made is a strong word," Dakota says and joins us. "We missed you last night. What time did you get back?"

"After eight," I say. "I watched the end of the game in bed and then crashed. Thanks for the invite though. Me and Josie were planning to watch at The Hideout tonight." From what I've heard, that's where everyone will be. I look to the girls. "Do you want to come with us?"

They look to each other and then me.

"We're going to the game. You have to come with us," Dakota says.

"To Troy?"

Reagan nods and smiles and her dimples appear. "We're surprising the guys."

Dakota leans forward. "We're leaving this afternoon and staying overnight. You have to come. Rhett will be so excited to see you."

"Yeah, you absolutely have to come with us," Regan says.

"I don't know. I have…" All my excuses die on my tongue. I'm caught up in all my classes and I already have the day off practice. "You know what, I'm in."

Chapter Twenty-One

RHETT

"Dude!" Mav skates toward me after the final buzzer. His arms spread out, smile so big. "Dude!"

My buddy is speechless. Guess so am I. We won. We're going to the Frozen Four. Something I've dreamed of since I was a kid. It doesn't seem real.

The rest of the team joins us and we're one big huddle on the ice, screaming our heads off.

The noise inside the arena could lift off the roof. So many Valley U fans made the drive. Including my very favorite fan.

As we skate toward the bench, I see her. Decked out in blue and yellow, jumping up and down with Dakota, Reagan, and Ginny. It feels sweeter having her here.

Coach tries to keep his smile small, but the crinkles along his eyes and mouth give him away.

"Great job tonight, boys." He bows his head and gives it a shake. "Damn proud of you all, but let's not get too carried away. We've still got more work to do. Enjoy tonight. When we get back to Valley tomorrow afternoon, your lives belong to me for the next week."

There's a chorus of agreement. He won't hear any arguing from us about buckling down. Not this week.

"Party in our suite," Mav says. "Pass it on."

Well, not after tonight, anyway.

Sienna and the girls meet up with us at the hotel. They're staying at the same one. Thank fuck. I missed the shit out of her.

"Congratulations!" She throws herself at me, yelling in my ear. "You're going to the Frozen Four!"

I lift her and turn us in a circle. She squeals happily.

When I put her down, she's got a goofy smile on her lips. "Ready to celebrate?"

My gaze rakes over her body.

Laughing, she swats at my chest. "That is not what I meant."

"Damn. Because that sounds like a way better way to celebrate."

"Later." She grabs a handful of my T-shirt.

Maverick and Heath's room connects to mine and Adam's so we open the door to make enough room for everyone to congregate between the two.

"Do you want something to drink?" I ask Sienna. We're sitting on my bed, which has my mind going to all sorts of fun places. Unfortunately, the five other people also sitting here with us is really ruining the moment.

"No, I'm good. I feel drunk I'm so happy."

"Same." I raise my hand to catch a beer Adam tosses my way.

She eyes the can with a smirk.

"Still have to celly with the boys." I lean in to whisper in her ear. "Don't worry. Only a couple and then we can sneak away."

She turns in my lap to better face me. "It's your night. Have as many as you want. We can celebrate after you win the next two games."

My dick perks right up. Not sure if it's the mention of sex or winning the Frozen Four. I take her mouth. I haven't been alone with her in two days and I suddenly need to be. Immediately, if not sooner.

"Be right back." I pull back and drop a kiss to her shoulder, then get up from the bed. Jordan and Liam are standing in the doorway between the two rooms.

"Hey." I tip up my head as I approach. "Can I borrow your room for twenty?"

Jordan lifts a dark brow. "Seriously?"

"No," Liam answers without consideration.

"Don't act like the two of you haven't hooked up with chicks on my couch."

"And in your room," Jordan mutters around his cup as he takes a drink.

"I don't even want to know," I tell him.

"Okay," Jordan gives in.

"What? No." Liam punches his arm.

"Not on the beds," Jordan instructs me, ignoring his roommate. He hands over his room key.

"Got it." I back away before they change their mind.

Taking Sienna's hand, I pull her to her feet and weave back through people to get to the hallway.

"Where are we going?" she asks, giggling as I practically drag her toward the room on the other side of mine.

I wave the key card in front of the lock and push the door open.

"Whose room is this?"

"Does it matter?"

"No." She smiles at me. "Not unless your coach is going to walk in on us."

"No more talking about my coach." I sweep her hair away from her neck and seal my mouth to her sensitive skin.

I scoop her up and look for somewhere to set her that isn't my teammate's bed. I settle for the desk, dropping her to it and stepping between her legs.

She fists my hair and presses her tits against my chest as I devour her mouth. My heart pounds in my chest, and if the way she's meeting me pant for pant is any indication, so is hers.

"You okay?"

"So okay." She pulls me to her and goes for the button of my jeans, then pushes them down until my dick springs free.

I'm frozen, watching as she hops down and pushes her skirt to the ground, leaving her in the smallest black piece of material I've ever seen.

She hops back onto the desk, but the height's all wrong.

"Bed?" she suggests.

"I have a better idea." I hoist her up and carry her to the bathroom. The vanity is covered in products, but I sweep a hand to clear it and set her on the stone top.

"What is it with you and bathrooms?" She giggles through the question while I push her panties to the side and circle her clit with my thumb.

"It's you. I can't seem to bring myself to care where we are. I just need to be inside you."

Her hands are braced on the edge of the vanity showing me the front of her watch. It's some sort of sport watch she wears all the time to view her heart rate as well as the time. I glance at it, noting the numbers steadily increasing. That's normal, right? Mine is definitely thrumming faster.

I try to go slow, but it's been several days without her and I need her in every sense of the word. Also, my stomach growls.

"Was that your stomach?" she asks with a laugh, but then moans as I push two fingers inside of her.

"I haven't eaten since the game," I admit.

"Maybe we should stop and feed you."

"I'm not that hungry," I protest but my stomach makes another gurgling noise.

Laughing, she pushes at my chest with a sigh. "I saw a vending machine by the elevator. Let's feed you." She hops down from the counter and starts getting dressed.

"But, but…" I motion to my dick.

"We'll come right back."

"Or we could keep going and then eat."

"Are you hungry?"

"Yes, I admit."

She tosses me my pants. "What my baby wants, my baby gets."

I put them on, with attitude, and she holds the door open for me.

"Then we're going the wrong direction," I mutter under my breath.

She laughs. "Come on, Rauthruss."

We find the vending machine at the end of the long hallway.

"What are you feeling?"

"Don't care." I run my hands over her hips.

She feeds money into the machine and presses buttons. I'm

not paying a lot of attention. Particularly when she leans over to retrieve her selections.

I follow her back to the room.

"Key?" She holds out her palm.

"Oh shit, I think I left it in there."

Laughing, she drops to the floor and sits with her legs stretched out in front of her, ankles crossed. "Joining me?"

I take a seat beside her and she tosses a bag of chips in my direction. The noise from the party on the other side of the wall drifts out—laughter and loud voices.

"Your parents couldn't make it?"

"No, but they'll be in Kansas City for the Frozen Four. You could meet them if you come." I bump my shoulder against hers.

"Really?"

I shrug. "If you want. You're going, right?"

"Yeah, I want. That sounds nice. Ginny's dad offered to drive us."

"It won't interfere with your practice?"

"No, I don't think so, but I should check with Coach when I get back tomorrow. My last competition is the week after."

"Where is it?"

"At Valley. It's a small competition, just one other college, but it'll be nice to compete one more time."

"Yeah, I get that."

"At least you'll be able to skate every day after college. I don't know what my life will be like without waking up early every day and going to the ice."

"Have you found an apartment yet in Appleton?"

"No. I guess I should get on that or I'm going to be crashing with my parents."

My phone buzzes in my pocket. "Speaking of my parents, that's probably them."

I dig it out of my pocket. Carrie's name flashes on the screen. "Or not."

"Still calling, huh?"

"First time in a few days actually. She probably wants to say congratulations."

Sienna nods. "You can answer if you want."

"Nah." I slide it back in my front pocket. "She can tell it to my voice mail."

"What was the final straw with you two?"

"What do you mean?"

"You said things slowly deteriorated, but obviously not for her. What made you walk away?"

I take my time, chewing the Doritos way longer than necessary. "She cheated on me."

"What?" Sienna's back comes off the wall, and her eyes widen.

"She kissed some dude at a party. She came clean immediately, and I was pissed, of course, but mostly, I guess, I was just upset that I didn't care more than I did. She was adamant that we could fix things between us, so I decided after six years, another few months trying to work on things wasn't much to ask. Needless to say, things didn't improve. So, I ended things."

"Wow. I was not expecting that."

"No more talking about my ex." I crumple the empty chip bag in my hand.

"Sorry."

She pulls a pretzel from the bag in her hand, and I snatch it with my mouth.

"Kind of stale," I say as I chew.

"Fine cuisine, it isn't."

"Company's good, though."

"Should we go back to the party? I don't want you to miss out on it. Tonight's a big deal."

"It is. And I'm exactly where I want to be."

"Or just outside of it anyway." She nods her head toward Jordan and Liam's room.

Laughing, I pull her onto my lap. "This isn't so bad either."

I slide my hand between her legs and underneath her skirt. Her panties are soaked and her green eyes darken when my fingers brush against the silky material between her legs.

She climbs higher on my lap, pinning my dick under her luscious ass. I slip two fingers under her panties and we groan at the same time.

Her lashes flutter closed and fan out on her skin and her lips part.

My teammates are loud as hell on the other side of the wall, partying and celebrating. Anyone in earshot could tell they're having a good time, but I wouldn't trade the feel of Sienna's slick, hot pussy squeezing my fingers for anything.

She rests her forehead on mine as her breaths come faster.

"Rhett," she whispers my name.

"Yeah, angel?" I drag the pad of my thumb along her clit.

She says my name again on a whimper and I seal my mouth to hers as she falls apart in my lap.

Chapter Twenty-Two

SIENNA

"Thanks for coming, everyone," I say to my yoga students as they pack up their mats and leave. I'm so tired. We got back three hours ago and I had to rush straight to class then here.

Maverick walks to the front, his black mat under one tattooed arm. "Good class today."

"You say that every day."

"And it's always true." He grins. "Going to the apartment?"

"Yeah. Am I that predictable?"

He laughs. "Want a ride?"

"That'd be great."

Maverick drives a shiny black SUV with leather seats and a sound system that makes my insides vibrate when the music starts.

"Sorry about that." He turns it down. "I think I killed the zen of the moment. Pick whatever you want."

"I'm easy to please."

"That's what Rhett said." He covers his mouth with a fist. "Sorry. It was right there."

"Hey now," I say as I laugh.

"I'm kidding, but for real, you're chill and I think that's good for Rhett. He's got a big heart."

"Thank you." I angle my legs toward him. "What *does* Rhett say about me?"

"Walked right into that, didn't I?"

"Pretty much."

Maverick leans back in his seat, one hand at the top of the steering wheel. "Not much, honestly, but to be fair, he's always been pretty quiet. Come on, you can't seriously be doubting that my boy is digging you. He was out of his mind when he saw that video of your accident."

"You know that point when you're spending all your time with someone and it's going great, but you're not sure if you're on the same page?"

"You're afraid you like him more than he likes you?"

"Yes. No. I don't know. The heart thing tends to freak guys out. It isn't a big deal when things are casual, but the second it's more—it becomes a real thing to them."

The more time I spend with Rhett, the harder I'm falling for him. I still worry he isn't ready for something serious and yet that's exactly how it's starting to feel. Last night I had a dream that I called him to make plans and he told me he was heading out on a date with Josie. Like, no big deal, just dating your friend.

Josie forced it out of me this morning when I couldn't look at her, then laughed in my face, hugged me, and promised she'd never do that to me, and I felt slightly better. But I don't need a psychology degree to figure out my subconscious is worried that I'm in over my head.

"I can't speak for Rhett, but I know that he's never seemed

happier since you two started hanging out. I don't think that's a coincidence." He parks the SUV in the apartment parking lot and turns off the engine. "I have exactly zero experience with serious relationships and I get that your heart condition adds complexity, but my advice? Tell him how you feel. Worst case, you're not on the same page. At least you'll know."

I hum a noncommittal response as I get out of the truck and round the front. "Maybe I don't want to know if it isn't the answer I want."

He drapes an arm around my shoulders. "You hiding from reality? Nah, you're too baller for that."

I lean my head on his shoulder. "Why haven't you had any serious relationships?"

"Oh no." He steps ahead of me to open the apartment door. "That's way more than you want to get into in an afternoon." His grin is playful and full of mystery which just makes me more curious, but Rhett's sitting in the living room playing Xbox when I step through the doorway.

"Hey." He presses pause on the game.

"Hey Sienna!" Adam calls from out on the back deck. The sliding glass door is open, and he sits in a lounge chair.

I wave, then look back to Rhett.

He stands. "I thought you were going to text before you came. I haven't showered yet."

My gaze travels over his bare chest "I'm sorry. Did you say something?"

Maverick chuckles. "And I'll be outside. Unless you two want to get into something freaky. I'm down for a shower. Or I could just entertain Sienna while—"

"No," Rhett says without waiting for Maverick to finish.

"So possessive of your girl." He winks at me and then laughs his way out to the back deck.

"Maybe I wanted to hear the rest of his offer," I say when we're alone.

"Well, by all means."

I make like I'm going to get him, and Rhett hauls me to him with his arms around my waist.

"I'm kidding." I slide my hands up his chest. "I've got my hands full with you."

"Shower and then movie? We may have to watch it out in the living room though because everyone got really excited when I told them you wanted to watch Mighty Ducks."

"Not want. Being forced."

"You can't not see it," he says in the same tone he'd used when I told him I'd never seen it before.

I chuckle at him. "Actually, I need to call Elias back. He has a competition tomorrow and I don't want to forget later. I tend to lose track of time around you."

One side of his mouth pulls up. "Sorry. Not sorry."

"Can I use your room?"

"Of course."

While Rhett showers, I sit on his unmade bed surrounded by his scent, feeling giddy and happy and not trusting either of those emotions.

Elias answers, his face filling the screen. "She's alive!"

"I'm sorry I keep missing you."

"It's fine." He runs a hand through his dark hair. "I figured you were off being happy-happy with your hockey hottie." His tone is too sarcastic and bitter for my friend.

"Uh-oh. What's wrong?"

"Nothing."

"Elias Mason Hummer."

He sighs. "I kissed Taylor."

"What?! When?" Those weren't the words I was expecting to come out of his mouth.

"Last night."

"How?"

"We were working late. It just happened. And now she's avoiding me. She was a no-show for practice this morning."

"Oh my god, E. Don't you leave for France tomorrow?"

"Yeah. The timing couldn't be worse. She won't even look at me and we need to skate our asses off for the judges in three days."

"Wow. What are you going to do?"

"Do? Nothing. Doing got me into this situation."

"You have to find her and talk this out before you leave."

"I'd rather catch up with my best girl. How the hell are you?"

I know he's deflecting, but lord knows I've done it enough times to him that I let it go for now. "I'm good. I finally fixed the footwork sequence that was giving me trouble and I think Coach is going to let me add the double lutz back in at my last competition."

"That's awesome. What day is it? Maybe I can come down."

"You can't run away from your partner."

"What? I never ask for time off. I'm sure Taylor can manage without me for a couple of days when we get back."

"You will do no such thing. You're so close. Talk with Taylor and get back to work. I'm only friends with you so I have a legit excuse to go to the winter games next year. Don't ruin this for me."

That makes him smile and I feel better. Because of Elias's crazy training and being away from home, he doesn't have a lot of friends and I feel bad that I've been preoccupied lately.

"Do you like her?"

"No, of course not. You know that I don't. She annoys the shit out of me on a regular basis. She does this weird thing when she kisses where she hums softly."

"Yeah, well, you wouldn't know that if you didn't go around kissing her."

"Touché."

After Rhett is done showering, we go back out to the living room to watch the movie. The entire group is over. Heath and Ginny are curled up on the opposite end of the couch as me and Rhett, Mav sits between us with Charli.

Dakota's in the armchair and Adam and Reagan laid a blanket on the floor and she sits in front of him, her back resting against his chest.

"I can't believe you've never seen this," Ginny says. "Doesn't your sister play hockey?"

"Yeah, but this movie was made like… thirty years before she was born. I have seen *Miracle* an obscene amount of times though."

"Ooooh, that's a good one too." Mav's eyes light up. "We should watch that one too."

Rhett yawns, making the group laugh.

"What?" he protests through a laugh. "You guys insisted on turning the lights out. You know how I get."

"Real talk," Heath says, looking to me. "Does this guy make you leave the lights on when you have sex?"

Ginny elbows him. "You can't ask people that."

"You wanted to know too," he says, tickling her sides.

"I have never fallen asleep on her," Rhett defends himself.

"That he remembers," I quip.

The movie starts and everyone quiets down and turns their attention to the TV. Rhett leans in to whisper in my ear, nipping the shell of my ear as he says, "I could never fall asleep while naked with you."

"I might make you prove that later."

"You're on." He sits forward. "Anyone else want a Monster drink?"

It's still early when the movie ends, but we both have to be up in the morning for practice, so we duck out and head to Rhett's room.

Despite the energy drink, my man is sleepy.

I'm undressing and grabbing a T-shirt from his drawer when he steps up behind me. His palms glide over my hips and stomach sending goose bumps racing over my skin.

I didn't see him drop his sweats, but his dick pokes into me from behind.

I fake a yawn. "Oh, I don't know. You seemed pretty tired earlier. Sure you can stay awake?"

"I'd bet my life on it."

I turn and wrap my arms around his neck. His blue eyes bore into me with such intensity my stomach flips. I take a small step back and let my arms fall to his chest, then give him a gentle push.

He falls back onto the bed, sitting up.

Kneeling in front of him, I stare up at him as I kiss the head of his cock.

"If you fall asleep on me," I warn.

"Angel, you don't have to have your mouth on my dick to have me captivated, but the fact that you do—there's no chance I'll be able to take my eyes off you."

His words mixed with the desire to be certain he doesn't doze off and mortify us both makes me bolder in my movements. His hand threads through my hair and holds the back of my head tenderly, slowly guiding me down his thick length.

"Need to be inside of you," he says, gripping me by the neck and pulling me to him.

Clothes are stripped and tossed and then it's just the two of us, naked and wrapped up in each other's arms.

His fingers brush along my skin tenderly, but his kiss is possessive and demanding. He lays me down and worships my body until I'm writhing and panting under him. I can't even make a witty comment about the glow-in-the-dark condom he covers himself with.

I have no idea how he can move so slowly when my heart races for more. I arch my hips to get more of him, but he chuckles and pulls back.

"There's no rush tonight, angel."

But every cell in my body wants to rush. I want him—all of him and I want him now.

His brow furrows as he keeps up the slow rhythm, feeding his cock into me and pulling back. I'm whimpering and tears prick my eyes. It's emotionally and physically overwhelming being with this man.

Finally, he gives me what I want. Picking up the speed, his kisses are harder and his moans match mine.

"Come for me, angel," he whispers. "Give me what I want."

And I do. I shatter underneath him.

"MY HEART IS STILL RACING," I SAY AFTER WE'VE CLEANED UP AND gotten ready for bed.

His arms tighten around me. "You good? Anything I can do?"

"I'll be fine. Just give me a minute."

"It's been a long week. Sleep. I'm going to grab some water and food in case you wake up later and need something."

"Thank you."

I doze off while he's gone, but stir when he slides back into bed behind me. His arm cradles me and he kisses my shoulder.

"'Night, Sienna."

I'm so tired I don't respond. I'm almost asleep again when his deep voice sounds again. "I think I'm in love with you."

I keep my breathing even, by some miracle, and stay silent.

"WHY DIDN'T YOU SAY ANYTHING BACK?" JOSIE ASKS ME THE NEXT morning when I fill her in before practice. We stretch in the tunnel outside of the locker room. I wasn't going to tell anyone about Rhett's late-night confession, but I needed to tell someone before I burst.

"He thought I was asleep. I didn't want to ruin the moment for him. Besides, he said *I think*. That's not the same thing."

Her blue eyes light up. "It's so sweet. I love this for you. I love *him* for you."

"Let's not get carried away," I mutter, more to myself than her.

The hockey team has a full day of practice, skills, film, and who knows what else so I don't hear from Rhett until I'm studying later in my room.

He sighs, laying back on the bed, the phone perched in his hand hovering above his face. He looks freshly showered. The ends of his hair are wet and he pushes the long top over to one side.

"I thought it was going to be a light practice."

"It was supposed to be until we started getting sloppy."

"Nerves, probably."

"Yeah, I guess. Hope we can work that shit out of our system before we leave."

"You will." I close the lid of my laptop. "What are you doing tonight?"

"Uh," he starts in a tone that makes me nervous. That one syllable sounds like guilt. "The guys wanted to have a chill night, just the four of us, at Prickly Pear. I could probably bail." He makes a face—an expression I can't read.

"Why would you do that? Go have a chill night with your boys. I have a quiz tomorrow anyway and I need to pack for the weekend. I should go to sleep early and rest. It's going to be a busy weekend." My body is tired. All of the traveling and practice, late nights with Rhett.

There's a beat of silence on his end. His brows raise.

"What?" I ask, finally.

"Sorry. I just realized this is what this feels like."

"What feels like?"

"One second," he calls away from the phone, then sits up. "I have to go before they leave my ass. I'll call you later, okay?"

"Yep. Have fun." I kiss the air and he winks before ending the call.

Chapter Twenty-Three

RHETT

"Just like that. Have fun. See you tomorrow." I wave my hand. "Fuck. I was speechless."

"I like Sienna," Adam says.

"We all like Sienna," Maverick adds. "Don't fuck this up."

"You know what the real mindfuck is?"

"What?" Heath asks.

We're having a low-key night at Prickly Pear before we head to the Frozen Four in two days. Just a couple of beers to clear our minds and help us sleep. The place makes me think of Sienna now and our speed dating adventure, but it's empty tonight, save a few locals sitting at the bar.

"Now all I want to do is go see her. Is this some sort of reverse psychology she's using on me?"

They laugh at me. Damn, it feels good. Phone tucked away, hanging with the guys, not a single worry to be found among the lot of us.

"And Carrie?"

I lift my beer and take a sip before answering. "I blocked her."

Adam is the first to speak after several seconds. "You blocked Carrie?"

"Yep."

"Well, damn. I'm speechless."

"It was time," I say by way of defending myself because in all honesty, it doesn't feel great. But neither did ignoring her calls and feeling like an ass every time Sienna was around.

We spend the next couple of hours hanging out at the deserted bar. We're slow to finish our beers, but it doesn't matter. We're all feeling good when Jordan shows up at the bar to give us a ride.

"I can't believe you assholes didn't invite me and then called me to drive you home."

"It was a roomie thing," Mav says, climbing into the passenger seat.

"Then why did you come?" I ask jokingly.

"Oh, Rauthruss, you're going to miss me next year. Don't even pretend otherwise."

"Someone's buying me chicken nuggets," Jordan says as he pulls away from the bar.

We make a stop for fast food and then Jordan takes us to the apartment. I catch the door before Maverick closes it. "I think I'm going to the dorms."

Heath makes a sound like a whip cracking.

"Oh please, like you have any room to talk." Adam shoves at his shoulder.

"See you guys in the morning."

"Don't be late for practice," Adam calls over his shoulder.

Sienna answers the door, eyes half open. "What are you doing here?"

"Surprising you."

"You look nice." Her eyes are slits. "And I look like this." She waves a hand in front of her baggy T-shirt and bare legs. Her hair is piled on top of her head, making her look a foot taller than she is.

"Nice shirt."

That gets a sleepy smile out of her. "I got it from this boy who gave me a black eye."

"Now, that sounds like an interesting story."

I close the door behind me and follow her to her bed on the left side of the room.

"Oh shit." I lower my voice to a whisper when I see Josie sleeping in the bed on the opposite wall.

"Don't worry. She sleeps like the dead."

I kick off my shoes and take off my jeans and T-shirt before climbing into her small bed.

"Now I understand why we always stay at my place," I say, moving closer to her.

I cuddle her against me, breathing her in. Damn. I had no idea it was possible to miss someone like this. Carrie and I were always apart and I still didn't miss her the way I missed Sienna today.

"How are you feeling?"

"Better," she says, grabbing my hand and pulling it up under her tits.

I was already sporting a semi just from being in the same room with her, but thanks to her soft, perky boobs I'm now jabbing her in the ass with my dick. And her ass is covered by some silky panties that are absolutely not helping the situation.

"Sorry, I didn't come here for that, but my dick doesn't care about my good intentions." I close my eyes and try to think of anything but sex, but when Sienna grinds back into me, I lose that battle completely.

"Neither do I."

THE NEXT AFTERNOON, I CORNER MAVERICK IN THE WEIGHT room. "I need your help with something."

Lying back on the bench press, he finishes his set before racking the barbell and sitting up. "Anything. What's up?"

After I've got Maverick on board, I head to campus to find Sienna. I wait outside of Moreno Hall where she has class. When she comes out, her head is downcast and her phone in hand.

Mine pings in my pocket and I retrieve it as I continue to watch her.

Sienna: Hey, handsome. Want to grab dinner? I'm starving.

Me: Sure do. You look good in red.

She stares down at the message for a long time, then her head pops up and she scans until she finds me. I push off the bike rack and meet her halfway.

"Stalker much?"

"I'm one of the friendly ones." I take her backpack and sling it over my shoulder. "I have a surprise."

"Does it include food? Because that wasn't a lame excuse to make plans. I really am starving."

"I've got you covered."

Chapter Twenty-Four

SIENNA

"Where are we going?" We've been in Maverick's SUV for thirty minutes and I have no idea where we are.

"You'll see," Rhett insists.

Everyone else is grinning. They're all in the know and I'm not.

"Have I mentioned that I don't like surprises?"

"You'll like this one." He leans over and presses a kiss to my lips. "Promise."

"We're here," Maverick calls from the front seat.

Eagerly, I peer out the front window. Color lights up the night sky as we're waved into a dirt lot to park.

"A carnival?" I can practically smell the popcorn and funnel cake from here.

Rhett holds my hand, swinging it lightly, as we walk toward the sound of rides and games intermixed with happy squeals of delight.

His friends push ahead of us to get tickets.

"Be right back." Rhett joins them and Ginny looks back and notices I'm alone.

"Are you excited?" She beams at me, and I want to be as excited as she wants me to be.

"Yeah. This is amazing."

"He really likes you," she says, looking over my shoulder. I follow her line of vision to Rhett. "And so do I."

She hugs me and then bounces off to Heath. Rhett's headed back with a Cheshire cat grin.

"Rhett, this is the nicest thing. I love it really. Thank you."

"It's not over until we ride all the rides, angel." He holds up a long string of tickets.

I scan the carnival. Tall rides that spin and rock. We're standing next to the octopus and a girl is screaming loudly while she holds her hads over her eyes. My stomach dips with unease.

"Let's do this," Maverick calls, heading off toward the rides.

"I think the Ferris wheel is about all I'm good for. Go with your friends. I'll watch."

"Are you kidding me? I'm not leaving you to ride shit with my friends."

"I can't—"

He stops me with a kiss. "Trust me."

"We'll meet up with you guys later," he tells Adam, and we head in the opposite direction. I'm not paying any attention to where we go. My stomach aches and I'm upset that I can't do the things he wants. That'll always be the case and there's nothing I can do about it.

"All right." He drops my hand and rubs his palms together. "What'll it be first, the roller coaster or the slide?"

I glance up to see we're standing in the kid's section. A roller coaster made out to look like a caterpillar and one of those slides you go down on a burlap sack.

I can't help but laugh and the knot in my stomach loosens. Rhett has a charming, knowing grin on his face.

"Rhett." My voice cracks.

He steps forward and cups my cheek. "I know it isn't the same, but I figured we could try it out anyway. It'll be good for a laugh."

"It isn't the same," I agree. "This is better because of you. And also because fifteen-year-old me wouldn't have had the balls to tell you that I'm so going to beat you down that slide."

"You wish." He scoffs as we rush to the line.

We climb up a tall staircase, smiling and laughing.

"On three," he says when we're in position.

I nod and he starts to count. "One, two—"

I push off, giving myself a head start. He roars behind me and then chases me down.

Giggling as I finish, I look over at Rhett expecting him to threaten a do-over, but he's smiling just as big.

We go on every single kiddie ride, which is particularly hilarious when Rhett tries to squeeze his long legs into the mini rollercoaster. He's so large we can't even sit together. He wins me an orange unicorn at the horse races, and I win a goldfish which I give to a little girl at the ping-pong toss.

I'm eating my second cotton candy of the night when we wander back over to meet up with his friends. I can't stop smiling.

"Thank you." I kiss him.

He wipes a hand over his mouth. "Sticky."

I kiss him again, but this time he captures me and holds me tight as he devours my mouth.

"Now we're both sticky."

He smooths a hand down my hair and pulls me farther onto him so my head rests in the center of his chest.

My heart flutters. *I think I love you too.*

THE DRIVE TO KANSAS CITY FOR THE FROZEN FOUR TAKES TWO days. Ginny's dad has to hate us by now. We've taken over his radio and the excitement for the upcoming games has us all loud and giggly.

When we pull into the hotel parking lot, he checks us in while we load up the luggage onto a trolley. We brought enough bags to stay a week instead of the three days the tournament runs. Mr. Scott lets out a long breath and stretches. "I'm assuming you girls have plans for dinner?"

"We're going to crash the team dinner," she says, holding her hand out for the room key.

"I'll be at the hotel bar if you need me. Tell Adam to stop by and see his old man later."

Ginny kisses his cheek. "Can you take up the bags? We're already late."

He shakes his head. "Have fun, girls."

The team is at a local restaurant next door to the hotel. Allison calls as we're about to walk in. There's a small waiting area between the doors and hostess stand.

I hang back. "It's my sister. I should answer. I'll meet you guys in there."

"I'll save you a seat," Dakota says.

"Hey," I answer, holding the phone in front of my face.

"Save me. Dad's decided to get in shape and wants me to run around the neighborhood with him while he listens to nineties music from a speaker which he carries while we run. Why can't he just use headphones like a normal person?"

"Because then you couldn't share the experience together." I laugh, but there's a little twinge of sadness. I haven't seen my family in a few months and that never seems to get easier.

"Where are you? Out to eat with your friends? You can call me later."

"Yes, but not in Valley."

"Where are you?"

"Okay, don't freak out, but I'm in Kansas City."

Her brow furrows. "What's in..." Her mouth falls open. "No!"

I nod. "Yes."

"Oh my gosh. I hate you. You're at the Frozen Four, really?" There's a whine to her tone. "What are you doing there?"

"I came with some friends."

"What aren't you telling me?" Her gaze narrows. "You don't like hockey that much."

"I'm dating a hockey player," I mumble.

"I'm sorry. What was that?" Allison has some serious sass when she wants to, and right now—she wants to.

"I'm dating a hockey player."

She's grinning. "Don't tell me. Let me guess which one." She puts a finger to her chin. "Adam Scott."

"No way."

"Okay, okay. Don't sound so offended. He's cute."

"He's dating one of my friends."

"Okay, then, Johnny Maverick?"

"Rhett Rauthruss," I say before she continues guessing.

"Oh, hey, he's from Minnesota."

"I know."

"Right," she says. "How long have you been dating him? And can he get me a last-minute ticket to the final game? If you're there, I bet Mom and Dad would let me come."

"Did you need something or were you just calling to catch up?"

"Both, but I'll cut to the chase since you have more exciting things to do." She stops. "The first game is starting soon."

"Valley doesn't play until later."

"You're not even watching the other teams?" She sighs. "You so do not deserve to be there."

"Noted. So what did you want to tell me? I'm standing outside of the restaurant where the team is having dinner."

"Jealous times one thousand," she mutters. "I was calling because I wanted to see if you were ready for your competition next weekend?"

"Oh." I expected her news to be something bigger. "Yeah. I'm so ready. I'm disappointed it's the last one, but I'm adding a double—"

"We're coming!" She grins and looks around, then leans closer to her screen. "Mom and Dad want to fly down and surprise you. Don't tell them I told you."

"Seriously?"

She nods. "Don't act like you know!"

"I won't. Thanks for the heads-up." Our parents are always trying to surprise us. They think it's the coolest thing, even though both their daughters are very anti-surprise. Especially on the day of a competition. It would be nice to see them, though. "Are you coming with them?"

"Unless they decide to start trusting me to stay home alone."

"Well, I hate to bet against your budding independence, but it would be good to see you." I hold up my hands where she can see I'm crossing my fingers. "So, here's hoping you're still untrustworthy."

She laughs. "I should get in the shower before dad puts in a workout DVD and makes me join him. Wish you were here. I miss you." She sticks out her bottom lip.

"Me too. Love you, Al."

"Don't forget—you don't know anything! They're going to wait until Friday when we're getting on the plane to tell you." She smiles big into the screen.

"I won't say a word," I promise.

"Why couldn't your competition have been a month ago. I won't even be able to see a hockey game while we're there." Her smile gives away her tease.

"Love you too."

"Call me during the game later. I just want to hear the noise of the game."

"Yeah, we'll see."

"Bye, S."

Inside the restaurant, the team is easy to find as they take up one entire side. A few other girlfriends and family members have crashed.

There's an empty chair pulled up next to Rhett's, but I skip it and sit on his lap so I can hug him. "Hey."

He chuckles softly. "Hey. Miss me?"

"Maybe." I squeeze him harder and then drop a kiss on his mouth. I'm well aware his teammates and coach are probably watching, but I don't care. He's at the Frozen Four! It's surreal and I want him to know how excited I am to be here with him.

"Wanna meet my parents?"

"What?" I jump up and look around. "I thought they weren't getting in until late tonight."

He stands and nods his head to a booth nearby. A man and a woman with a little boy sitting next to them stare back at us. "They got in earlier than planned. Come on, I'll introduce you."

"Oh, god. And they just saw..."

"You tackle hug me and shove your tongue down my throat." He nods. "Yep."

He chuckles when I cover my face with a hand.

"I'm so embarrassed and I just got really nervous."

"You'll be fine. They're cool." He pauses. "I told them you were my girlfriend."

I smirk. "*Am* I your girlfriend?"

"I could refer to you as my sidepiece or my old lady, but those didn't have the same ring to it."

I smack his arm playfully. "And you're not the president of a motorcycle club," I joke back as butterflies swarm in my stomach.

Rhett's mom has a friendly smile. Her eyes take in every detail of her son's body language, from his hand around my waist to how close we're standing.

"This is Sienna," he says. "Sienna, these are my parents and that is Ryder."

"It's nice to meet you." I lift a hand to wave.

"My brother is number twenty-three," Ryder says, staring at my shirt.

I glance down and my cheeks flame. Ginny made us matching

shirts with our boyfriends' jersey numbers on them for this weekend and I'd completely forgotten I was wearing mine to surprise Rhett. It reads, *Property of #23*.

"Are you excited to watch him play?" I ask the adorable mini-Rhett.

He shrugs. "Mom says I can have popcorn *and* a lemonade."

Rhett chuckles. "Who needs hockey when you have the snack bar?"

"Are you staying for the weekend, Sienna?" his mom asks.

"Yes, I came with the Scott family."

She smiles warmly. I can tell they're beyond nice, but there's still a beat of uncomfortable silence where none of us know what to say.

Rhett slides into the booth next to his mom and holds his arm out for me to sit next to him. There's only a sliver of space so I'm basically sitting on his lap again.

"Mom, I forgot to tell you that Sienna skates. She took second in her competition last weekend. She's really good."

I feel myself blushing at the attention.

"You do?" His mom moves forward to see around Rhett. "Oh, well, we'll have lots to talk about then."

"Mom skated in college too." Rhett nudges me.

"You never told me that."

"It was a *long* time ago," she says.

Coach Meyers announces that the boys have five minutes before they need to load up for the arena.

Mr. Rauthruss leans toward his youngest son. "Your brother is leaving. Do you want to give him your present?"

The little boy nods and holds his hand out, offering Rhett a shiny black rock.

"This is for me?" Rhett asks, taking and inspecting it.

"I found it at school. Sarah and Rachel wanted it, but I told them I was giving it to you for luck."

Rhett's chest shakes with a silent laugh. "Thank you."

Ryder smiles proudly.

I stand and Rhett slides back out of the booth. His parents and brother get up too to hug him and wish him luck.

"We hope to see more of you this weekend, Sienna," his mom says as Rhett and I start toward his teammates.

"Me too. Nice to meet you all."

We walk out with the team as they start to load up on the bus.

"You survived," Rhett says when we're outside.

"Shut up. I was so nervous. I've never met a guy's parents before."

"I've never introduced one before," he says. "They already knew Carrie."

"Right."

He wraps me up in his arms and hugs me. "Thanks for coming."

"Are you kidding? They have popcorn *and* lemonade."

He chuckles. "Are you going over to the arena for the first game?"

We break apart and he takes a step toward the bus stairs. "I don't know. I'm just along for the ride, but I imagine we're going wherever you guys are."

He nods and I realize he's starting to get nervous.

"You're going to be great. You have to be otherwise I'm going to get my ass kicked in this shirt."

He glances down at it and then fists it and hauls me to him for another kiss before getting on the bus.

Chapter Twenty-Five

RHETT

We win our first game, but it's close and we head back to the hotel with grim expressions and the final game looming over our heads. The morning of, Sienna and I have breakfast with my family at the hotel.

She has a jacket on over her property of number twenty-three T-shirt which makes me laugh. My mom is asking her about skating and it's nice. I knew they'd like her.

My knee bounces with anticipation as I half listen and finish my food. One more game. Win or lose, this is it.

"What time are you going over to the arena?" my mom asks, breaking my train of thought.

"Bus leaves in an hour," I say.

"Do you have my rock?" Ryder asks. His face is covered in chocolate from the donut he ate.

"Sure do." I pat my pocket. "Brought me luck last time."

"Can I see it?"

I hand it over and he inspects it, turning it over in his sticky hands. "Maybe we could share it? I could have it for this game."

A surge of panic shoots through me. I wouldn't say I'm overly superstitious, but when the stakes are high, I don't like to mess with something that's working. I kept the rock in my bag for the last game and touched it before every period. It probably wasn't the reason we won, but I'm not pumped about messing with probability today.

Still, I nod. "Yeah, we could do that. Hold on tight to it, okay?"

He grins.

I push back from the table. "I need to get ready. I'll see you guys there."

"Good luck," my mom says cheerily. I get a nod of luck from my dad and Ryder holds up the rock, then drops it. The chances of him holding on to that for the next four hours before we play seem slim.

"That was nice of you," Sienna says when the doors close on the elevator.

"And incredibly dumb."

"You don't really think that tiny rock is why you won the last game, do you?"

"No, of course not."

She's grinning.

"Maybe."

"You're adorable, and it makes the fact you let him keep it even sweeter."

I grumble quietly as we enter the room. Adam and Reagan are inside watching TV.

I get my bag ready, check and double-check it.

"Would you sit down," Adam says. "You're making me nervous."

"Yeah, well join the club." I sit on the bed and then stand. "I can't sit here. I need to move or do something."

Adam sits forward. "Come on, babe. Let's give them the room. We'll be back in thirty."

My brow furrows as my buddy and his girlfriend leave us.

"What just happened?"

Sienna climbs on my lap and threads her fingers through my hair. "I'm pretty sure they just left so we could have sex."

"What?" A rumble shakes my chest.

"Wild guess that's how your buddy releases his nerves before the game."

"Right." I shake my head. "Don't take this the wrong way, but I'm not even sure sex could calm me down right now. Today is my last game. It's the last time I'm ever going to play with these guys. I didn't realize how much I was going to miss it."

She massages my head and my scalp pricks with a chill that runs down my spine. My eyes fall closed. Now that my body is starting to relax, I'm very aware that her boobs are at nose level. I nuzzle in and she laughs. "I thought sex wouldn't calm you down."

"Might not, but it's worth a shot. Besides, it was the captain's orders."

WATERVILLE IS BIG AND PHYSICAL, AND THEY BOAST THE BEST record in division one hockey. They're also last year's national champ and that title gives them both the boost of confidence of being in this position before and the hunger to hold on to it.

"I think I'm gonna shit myself," Jordan says as we dress in the locker room. He jogs to the bathroom stall on the opposite side.

Maverick has music going on his phone and he dances around trying to keep the mood light, but the undercurrent of nerves is there for everyone.

When we take the ice, I swallow down a lump in my throat as I scan the crowd. I find my family and then Sienna and the girls, and then it's time to go to work.

"What do you say, men?" Adam says, skating through us.

"Men today, huh, instead of boys?"

"Between me and you, if we're going to win today, we're going to need to play like men instead of boys." He stops beside me. "Ready to do this thing?"

"Yeah." I shoot a puck into the net.

"Well, that's not very enthusiastic. Did you not work out your pregame nerves?"

"It isn't nerves. Well, not just nerves. This is all bizarre. I never cared about it all ending until now."

He fires at the net. "Yeah, I feel that too. The thing is, it won't be the same regardless. Next year it'll be a new group of guys starting out. Which means we might as well go out with a bang. Let's give them something to aspire to."

Chapter Twenty-Six

SIENNA

"Oh, come on!" Ginny yells when Heath takes a hard hit from the Waterville defense.

"Sit down," someone calls behind her and sweet Ginny turns and flips them off with such flair I have to bite back a laugh.

Mr. Scott places a hand on her shoulder and reluctantly Ginny sits back down.

"They're going to hurt him." She throws a hand up.

"He's tough," Reagan assures her.

"Is she always like this?" I ask Dakota.

"No, but I think seeing her all mini-psycho is adorable."

Waterville scores and our entire row groans.

"This is not good," I say to no one in particular. Rhett comes off the ice and tosses his water bottle to the back of the bench.

Dakota sighs. "I didn't want to have to do this."

She reaches into her bag and pulls out a T-shirt. It has Maverick's number on it.

"Did you make that?" I ask. It looks almost like mine, Ginny, and Reagan's but a little messier.

"No, of course not. Maverick did." She rolls her eyes. "He was feeling very left out."

"No property of?"

"I belong to no one, which I made very clear when he said he was going to make me one, but I promised him I'd wear his number it if things were looking bad." She pulls it on over her head. "It can't hurt, right?"

My gaze goes to the Valley bench. "No, it can't." I stand. "I'll be right back."

"Where are you going? The period is about to end."

"To get a good luck charm."

WAITING OUTSIDE OF THE LOCKER ROOM, I CAN HEAR COACH Meyers' voice bouncing off the walls inside. Silence finally falls and the head coach pushes out of the locker room. He lets out a breath, hands on hips, composing himself before he starts down the tunnel.

The team follows a minute later. The security guard that I begged to let me loiter in the tunnel, watches me closely. I smile at him again, giving him my best, *I'm not a stalker or a serial killer* smile that probably conveys the exact opposite.

Rhett appears and I push off the wall. "Rauthruss!"

His head lifts slowly and his brows scrunch together when he sees me. I stay put, as instructed by the guard and Rhett walks over.

"Is everything okay?"

"Yeah, no, I just wanted to give you this." I hold out my hand to give him the black rock his brother gave him yesterday and then took back this morning.

"How?"

"I sweet-talked a five-year-old boy, then bribed him with a foam finger. I'm not proud." But I knew how important it was to him. I could see his disappointment this morning.

"Thank you." His sweaty, heavily padded body steps forward and he hugs me.

"Now, go give someone a black eye."

The security guard clears his throat.

"I was joking. It was a joke. He gave me a black eye—" I stop when the guard's hard face remains impassive. I have not made a friend. I look back to Rhett who is still standing in front of me looking down at the rock in his hand like it's a diamond. "Go," I tell him.

"Thank you." He smiles and jogs after his teammates.

I get back to my seat as the second period is about to begin.

"There you are," Dakota says. "Everything okay?"

"Yeah." I take a seat and the four of us join hands. "They've got this, right?"

"They've got it," Reagan says with more confidence than I feel.

But as the second period begins and then ends, it seems like our optimism was on point. Valley fought back and now leads three to one, thanks to two goals by Maverick and some impressive saves from Ketcham.

"I'm so sweaty." Ginny fans her shirt away from her body. She looks to us. "Why am I the only one sweating?"

"You've been jumping up and down for the better part of two hours," Dakota says.

"I want this for them so bad." Ginny blows out a breath that puffs out her cheeks.

The third period is chaotic. Both teams are skating hard and hitting even harder. The coaches are red-faced, standing at their opposing benches shouting at their players. And every person in the arena is glued to the action on the ice.

It remains scoreless for the first fifteen minutes. Every time Watervillle has the puck, I hold my breath and hope they don't score. It's been close too many times and Ketcham deserves a freaking medal for the number of saves he makes.

At the two-minute mark, his luck runs out and the red and black shirts stand and cheer around the arena.

"It's just one goal. We're still ahead," Reagan says. "We've got this."

The words barely leave her mouth before Waterville gets a breakaway and scores again.

"Oh fuck," Reagan mutters. Her sudden worry and lack of conviction that we've still got this makes my chest ache.

"Should I take off the shirt?" Dakota asks. "Maybe I cursed them."

"You didn't curse them. They've got this," I say in my most convincing voice.

There isn't a butt in the chair all around the arena. It hums with energy as the two teams take a time-out. The four of us are a bundle of nerves, swaying, clasping hands, but no one speaks.

Rhett's line goes back in and I hold my breath for him.

Heath wins the face-off and Valley takes the puck down the ice, looking for a shot on goal. There are so many bodies in front of the net it's hard to see what's happening, but when a Waterville player skates hard in the other direction, my stomach drops. Rhett and another Valley jersey chase him and the Wolverines lose control allowing Rhett to knock the puck free.

It's Maverick that gets there first and Valley has a slight advantage as Waterville tries to reset to defend their goal. Mav passes to Heath who shoots. It's blocked but Maverick is there ready to knock it in. The goal post lights up and the roar of the arena is deafening.

With fifteen seconds left, Waterville tries to tie it up, but when the final buzzer sounds it's Valley by one. They did it. They won a national championship.

I call my sister and when she picks up, I can't even make out her hello, but I know she can hear the stadium and that she's smiling. I bounce around, hugging the girls, hugging strangers. Ginny's crying, Dakota's screaming so loud she's the only voice I can hear over all the others.

It's perfect.

ALMOST TWO HOURS GO BY BEFORE I FINALLY GET TO SEE RHETT and the team. There was the trophy ceremony, followed by cutting the net, and then whatever celebrating they did in the locker room.

Valley fans fill the lobby area waiting to see the team. When the first player walks out, the roaring applause and cheers starts up again.

Maverick comes out looking more humble and shy than I guy who scored three goals in a championship game. Dakota rushes from my side and jumps into his arms. "Who gets a hat trick at the Frozen Four?"

He drops his bag and hugs her back, finally laughing and looking more like the Maverick I expected.

The guys are swarmed as they come out. Rhett and Adam are the last two. I don't charge him like the other girls did. I let his family congratulate him first, hanging back and watching as he hugs his mom and dad and then picks up Ryder.

At last it's my time and he bear-hugs me, lifting me off the ground.

"Are you ready to celebrate, angel?" He spins me around. "Fuck, I love you."

Before I can say it back, he seals his mouth to mine and keeps spinning. I chuckle. "You're going to make me dizzy."

He's smiling when he puts me down. His parents watch on. His mother looks… not as happy as you'd expect for a mom whose son just won the Frozen Four.

When Rhett picks her up and spins her around, she finally breaks into a smile. "Put me down." She swats at him playfully.

"Me. Me," Ryder says.

Rhett spins him around even faster.

When he stops, Rhett sways. "Woah. Okay, maybe I need to eat something before I keep spinning people around."

He's grinning so big my chest feels like it might burst. I glance at my watch and take a few deep breaths.

"Are you okay?" Rhett's happy grin falls, and his gaze darkens.

"Yes. Just a lot of excitement."

He takes me in his arms and stills. "Breathe. Relax. We can have a chill celebration."

"Are you kidding?" I turn to face him. "I'll be fine. Just give me a minute."

And he does, holding me steady as we watch the team and their friends and family celebrate.

Everyone's phones are ringing and pinging with calls and texts to wish them congratulations. Rhett's is nowhere to be seen or heard.

Even his parents are blowing up. His dad has Ryder on his shoulders as he talks to his brother, Rhett's uncle, laughing and joking about how they nearly gave him a heart attack in the final period. Rhett shoots his dad daggers at that comment, since I'm currently feeling off-kilter thanks to my own heart, but I'm not bothered. Nothing could ruin this night. This moment. It's perfect.

His mom is trying to have a much more civilized conversation. She has a finger plugging one ear, phone pressed tightly to the other. She walks away from the commotion, presumably to hear better.

"Better? Want me to grab one of the trainers?"

"I'm okay." The lightheaded feeling is starting to pass, but I still lean into Rhett.

"All right, men. Let's load up." Coach Meyers stands next to the bus.

"I'll meet you there," I say, reluctantly stepping away from him.

He hugs a sleepy-eyed Ryder. "Thanks for letting me borrow this." Rhett hands him back the black stone.

"You can keep it." Ryder yawns. "It seems like you might need it more than me."

The three of us laugh.

"We're leaving early in the morning so I guess this is goodbye until graduation." His dad slaps his back as they hug again.

"Thanks for being here," Rhett says.

His mom finally finishes her call and comes over to say goodbye as well.

Rhett hugs her. "Thanks, Mom."

"We're going to follow the bus back to your hotel. There's something I want to talk to you about," she says.

"We can talk now," Rhett says. "It'll take the guys a few minutes to load."

"It's fine. We'll just follow you."

Rhett's features contort into confusion. "You're being weird. What is it?"

"That was Cory on the phone."

"Okay?"

"Who's Cory?" I ask when no one speaks.

"Carrie's mom," Rhett says. "It's cool, Mom. Sienna knows about Carrie."

His mom nods and gives me a small smile. Her eyes look a little teary and I'm so confused.

"What is it? She didn't drive down here, did she?" He looks around. "She can't seem to understand that it's really over."

"No, she's not here."

Rhett motions with his hand impatiently.

"She tried to come." His mom's voice breaks. "She left her dorm last night so she could be here today."

"Okay. Well, where is she?"

"She was in an accident near St. Joseph."

"Is she okay?"

His mom shakes her head slowly side to side and she starts to cry. My skin goes clammy and my heart rate accelerates.

"No, baby. She fell asleep and drove across a median. They took her to the hospital, but it was too late." She places a shaky hand to her mouth.

Rhett's dad puts a hand at his wife's back and stares at the ground.

Blood pounds in my ears and I'm warm all over.

"What?" Rhett asks like he's not sure he heard her right. His grip around my waist tightens.

"She didn't make it, baby. I'm so sorry."

My breathing gets shallow and my knees buckle.

"Shit, Sienna. Are you okay?" He turns his attention to me. There's no look of sadness on his face, but his eyes are hard and his jaw is set. "You're white as a sheet. Sit down. I'll be right back."

He helps me sit on the high curb and he takes off.

"I'm so sorry," I say to his parents, and then I close my eyes and focus on my breathing.

Chapter Twenty-Seven

RHETT

I'm fine, really," Sienna says, trying to stand.

"Let's give it a few more minutes." Jeff places a hand up to stop her and sits with her on the curb.

"There's no reason for everyone to wait. The bus should at least go back." She ducks her head. I'm standing in front of her, shielding her from anyone who might look, but I don't really think anyone is paying attention.

"My parents and I can give her a ride," I say to Jeff. I'm thankful our trainer was here. He came just to watch as a spectator, but I grabbed him the second Sienna went limp in my arms.

"Are you sure you don't want to go to the hospital, just as a precaution?" he asks her for the third or fourth time in the past thirty minutes.

"I'm sure. They'll only tell me what I already know. I need to rest."

"Okay." He stands and looks to me. "Text or call me if she needs anything."

"Thanks, man."

He pauses and lifts a hand to squeeze my shoulder. "And I'm sorry for your loss."

Swallowing the lump in my throat, I nod. Focusing on Sienna, I push out everything else. I can't go there right now. I'm on a teeter-totter with a nine-hundred-pound man. One second, I'm flying high, winning a national championship with my team and the woman I'm stupid in love with by my side, and the next I'm hitting the ground hard. Carrie's dead? Nah, it doesn't make any sense.

Dakota, Reagan, and Ginny move forward when Jeff leaves, hovering over Sienna like three mother hens.

"Give her some room," I instruct. Instructions that fall on deaf ears.

"I'm okay," Sienna says. Stubborn woman.

Adam appears at my side. "Hey, I just heard the news. Are you okay?"

"I'm fine. Listen, I'm going to stay with Sienna tonight. I already ran it by coach, and he said it was cool. Room's all yours."

He stares blankly.

"Dude," Mav says, joining us. We're a freaking circus act. He hugs me tightly, squeezing the air out of my lungs. "I am so sorry for your loss. What can I do?"

His tone is soft and sympathetic and I cannot handle it right now. I've gotta get the hell out of here. "I'm good."

"What's going on?" Reagan asks. The girls don't know yet, and I don't want to be around when more people find out.

I remove myself from Mav's hold and look to Sienna. "Angel, you ready? My parents will give us a ride. I'm going to stay with you tonight."

"Oh." She glances at the girls. "It's okay. Go be with your family."

"No chance."

She glances to Kota "I'm sharing a bed with Dakota."

"It's cool." She waves her off. "You two can have the bed and the room. These two won't be sleeping in our room, anyway." She points to Reagan and Ginny. "And I can find somewhere to crash."

"That's settled then." I scoop her up in my arms.

"I can walk, Rhett."

"I know, angel."

But having her in my arms makes me want to punch something a whole lot less.

"I'M SORRY." SIENNA SITS ON THE BED, HER BACK RESTING AGAINST the wall.

"It's fine. I don't really feel like celebrating." I toss my hat and run my fingers through my hair.

"I meant about Carrie. Are you okay?"

I ignore her question because I don't know the answer right now. I open the mini fridge. "Do you need anything? Water? Food?"

"Just for you to sit down. I'm okay. You don't need to worry about me."

With a sigh, I go and sit beside her on the bed. "You scared the shit out of me."

"I know." Her hands cup my face. "I'm so sorry."

"It doesn't feel real."

She smiles sadly. “If you want to be with your family or by yourself, I’ll understand.”

I kick off my shoes and drag my legs up so I’m beside her on the bed. “I’m exactly where I want to be.”

I thought I’d have trouble sleeping, but I drift off while Sienna runs her fingers through my hair, letting me stew in silence, and I don’t wake up until the sun shines through a crack in the curtains.

I ease out of bed carefully so I don’t wake her and pull the curtains together, shrouding the room in darkness.

Dakota lets herself in as I’m pulling on my jeans.

“Sorry,” she whispers. “I thought you two would be up.”

“She should sleep as long as she can. What time are you guys leaving?”

“Noon.”

I nod. “I need to go talk with my parents. You’ll be here?”

“Yes. I’ll keep an eye on her.” She walks forward and hooks an arm around my neck. “I’m really sorry about Carrie.”

“Thank you.” I grab my shoes and glance back at Sienna.

My parents are in the lobby when I walk down. My mom looks like she’s been crying all night and I don’t know why, but it sets off my barely-contained rage.

I grind my teeth as she hugs me.

“How’s Sienna?”

“Still sleeping. I just came to say goodbye. Are you guys headed out?"

"You're not coming with us?"

"Why would I come with you?"

"They haven't made arrangements yet, but they will soon. Cory said Tuesday, if they can get everything ready."

"I don't think I should go."

My mother rests a hand on my chest. "Oh, honey. Of course you should."

"We weren't together anymore," I say loudly, releasing some of my anger.

"If you want to go back to Valley with your team first, we'll get you a flight this week. Right, Julie?" My dad takes her hand. A united front like they've always been.

"If that's what you want," she says slowly.

I nod. Fuck. I know the right answer, but I'm not prepared to head back to Minnesota today. "I'll just ride with you guys. It makes more sense. Give me thirty minutes?"

I head back upstairs with breakfast. Sienna's coming out of the bathroom with a towel wrapped around her thin frame. She finger-combs her wet hair.

"I could only carry two plates." I set them on the TV stand.

Reagan and Ginny are back and packing their suitcases. They both shoot me sympathetic glances and take turns hugging me.

"How are you feeling this morning?" I ask Sienna.

"Better."

"You should eat something."

She graces me with a small grin that loosens the boulder on my chest. "I will."

I raise my brows.

She grabs half a bagel from the plate. "Are you going back to Valley or…"

Apparently everyone thought of the funeral except me. *Funeral?* What the fuck?

"Leaving with my parents."

"What day is the funeral?"

"Tuesday, I think."

"I could maybe come with you."

"No. That's okay. Thank you, but I know you have practice and school, and you need to rest up so that you're ready for your last competition. Will you still be able to compete?"

"Yeah, hopefully. I made a doctor's appointment for Wednesday."

I nod thoughtfully. "All right. Well, I guess I should get ready. Are the guys still here? I don't even know what time the bus is leaving."

"They're still here," Reagan answers for me. "I think Adam packed for you."

"I don't want to leave you like this," I say, hugging Sienna.

"I'm okay."

"You keep saying that." I close my eyes and inhale.

"One of these times you're going to believe me."

Chapter Twenty-Eight

RHETT

The guys and I hang at the back of the room. It's packed and so is the hallway outside. Most people I know, or at least recognize. Some I don't. The sheer volume of people that came should be comforting. It isn't.

I've been in this funeral home before, a bunch of times. Stood in this very spot, sometimes with Carrie, gone through the line, and offered muttered words meant to help, but that I'm sure didn't. None of those times felt anything like this. She was only twenty-one. It just doesn't make any sense.

Adam and Mav both insisted on making the trip to Minnesota despite my reassurances they didn't need to. They flew in this morning, and now that we're at the visitation, I'm glad they did. They're providing excellent cover and stopping people from approaching me to offer their sympathy.

As if this situation isn't awful enough, it's the first time I've been back home since Carrie and I broke up. Everyone is looking at me with these sad, pitying expressions. Clearly, they don't know that I no longer deserve those glances.

Along the back wall, three tables are pulled together. Collages with pictures of Carrie from when she was a baby to the present fill the poster boards. Many with me. Carrie and I started dating in high school. She was this beautiful, brave girl. She stomped around like nothing scared her, and I was in awe of that. Everyone was. It takes a special kind of person to walk through the halls of high school already knowing who you are and feeling confident enough to be only that. That was Carrie. Confident and fascinating.

"Woah! Is that you?" Mav asks, pointing to a picture of Carrie and me at a high school dance.

She's in a sparkly dress, her hair curled, arm looped through mine. We were juniors. I was all arms and legs. Scrawny, bad haircut, clothes that my mom probably picked out and forced me to wear so I'd look nice for the dance. I wasn't exactly shy. It was more that I didn't care about being cool or fitting in. And I never liked bringing attention to myself outside of hockey. Not that I really needed to worry. If people were looking my way any other time, it was to stare at Carrie.

That uncomfortable, hide-away feeling never really went away until I got to Valley and gained twenty pounds. I still don't give a fuck about fitting in, but I found my people regardless.

"Yeah, sure is." I shove both hands in my front pockets to keep myself from running them through my hair, which is styled with gel for a change.

Maverick covers his mouth with a fist as he laughs. "Oh man, are those pleats?"

"We can't all be as stylish as you were in high school. I've seen the photos of your nipple rings," Adam says and nudges him playfully with an elbow.

Mav scoffs. "Those were awesome, but you wouldn't have caught me at a school dance. Well, maybe in the parking lot passing around drinks and waiting for girls to get bored of the dance and come ditch with me."

"Of course," I say, a quiet chuckle escapes.

We fall silent again. My gaze keeps being drawn back to the front, where Carrie's family receives condolences. My own family hasn't arrived yet, but they'll be here. The whole town will stop by either tonight for the visitation or tomorrow for the funeral.

I shove my hands even deeper in my pockets. I'm gonna rip the seams before the night is over. Guilt seeps from my pores like yesterday's liquor, leaving my skin clammy. Carrie was on her way to see me, and I blocked her number so I didn't even know. Did she call? Could I have answered and stopped her?

I know that I couldn't have prevented the accident but maybe I could have stopped her from getting in the car altogether. Maybe I could have been a goddamn decent human and actually talked to her until she knew it was really over. Maybe I could have prevented the most awful thing to happen to her. Or that will ever happen to her. *Fuck. Fuck. Fuck.*

When my parents arrive, my mom wraps me in a big hug. Her eyes are teary, but she holds it together. My dad shakes my hand. Then the guys', all while wearing his best somber smile.

"Where's Ryder?"

"We left him with your aunt Leah," my mom says, then asks, "Have you been up yet?"

I shake my head.

"Come on. You can't hide back here forever."

She knows me well. I go with my parents, shuffling forward

with the line. Every step closer, my nerves fray a little more.

There's a large, framed picture of Carrie on a stand in front of the flowers. I can't bring myself to look at it or the casket next to it, but even out of my peripheral, I recognize the photo. Two years ago, she had headshots taken for her college newspaper, where she wrote a weekly column. She was so damn proud—her smile had been so big as she told me about it. She's not smiling in the picture, though. She wanted to keep it professional and serious. I'm glad it's not a smiley, happy photo. I don't know why. Not like it would make a difference.

I manage through tearful hugs from her mom, dad, and grandparents, and I'm thankful that my parents do most of the talking. And that her mother doesn't yell and scream at me for breaking her daughter's heart. I half expected that sort of reaction from her. She is so protective of Carrie. Was so protective. *Fuck.*

Actually it's her dad I should be worried about. Cam is ex-military and could break me like a twig if he wanted to. Age has only made him stronger and scarier. He doesn't though. No one seems to blame me. No one but myself.

My family and I step off to the side near the doorway to the hall.

"Your hair is too long. I can barely see your face." Mom smooths back the long strands hanging in my eyes. Hiding me. "Are you doing okay?"

"I'm fine," I say because I am. And because I'm not allowed to be anything but fine. *I* broke up with her. Sure, I still care about her. Cared now, I guess. *Fuck, fuck, fuck.* I don't know what to think, let alone say out loud.

I swallow around the lump in my throat. I don't feel like I

should be here mixing with all the people that were still a part of her life. People that hadn't brought pain to her recently or cast her aside. I'm an imposter. A has been. Maybe only by a couple of months, but I can't shake the uneasiness or desire to get out of here.

My mom pulls her purse strap higher on her shoulder. "We should get home. I'm making pies and casseroles for tomorrow, and I have a roast in the Crock-Pot. Will you be back for dinner?"

I can't even think about eating. "The guys and I will probably grab something before we head back."

"Okay." She leans forward and kisses my cheek. "Don't be too late."

Loosening my tie, I keep my head down as I walk back to my spot next to the guys. Even still, I'm stopped by a guy from high school. Jim or Jimmy, I think. He doesn't offer up his name as he leans forward and embraces me.

"I'm so sorry, man," he says. He smacks me on the back as he squeezes.

"Thank you." When I speak, my voice cracks.

He pulls back and checks my expression. I duck my head and walk away before he can say anything else. Maybe that's rude, but so is hugging someone without warning.

Mav hands me a bottle of water.

"I'm good."

He keeps his arm extended until I finally give in and take it from him. I unscrew the cap and take a long drink, then promptly cough because this isn't fucking water. Vodka burns my throat and heats my chest.

The guys huddle around me as people start to look in our direction.

"Little warning would have been good," I manage to get out. I glance around. Jim or Jimmy has broken the ice, and more people I went to high school with are looking my way like they might come say hello. I'd rather eat Tide pods. "Let's get out of here."

"You're sure?" Adam asks.

"Yeah, I'm sure."

"Rhett!" I look up as Carrie's mom, Cory, calls my name. She waves a hand in the air and holds her head up to see over the crowd.

"Go ahead. I'll meet you guys outside," I say to Mav and Adam.

Adam squeezes my shoulder as they leave.

Cory clutches a tissue in her hands. "You're welcome to stand up front with us. People are asking about you. They want to offer their condolences to you, too."

"Oh, uh, thank you, but I wouldn't feel right."

She tilts her head to the side. "Why not? You're like family." She reaches out and squeezes my arm. Her eyes fill with tears, and I flex my jaw to keep my composure. "She loved you so much. I can't imagine how hard this is for you. You'll come over tomorrow afternoon and be with us at least? We'll get through this together."

"DO YOU THINK THEY KNOW WE WERE BROKEN UP?" I STARE straight ahead at the bottles of liquor lined up behind the bar. My gaze keeps snagging on the coconut-flavored vodka. It was Carrie's favorite.

"I don't know," Adam says. "Was she close with them?"

"Yeah, pretty close. She talked to her mom every other day or so." Which means she'd definitely talked to her since we broke up.

Mav slides another shot along the bar in front of me. "So, what if she didn't mention you broke up. What's the big deal?"

I glance around. "Keep it down."

"What?"

"It's not that big of a town, and I'd rather Carrie's family not hear the news from the local gossip."

"Are you going to tell them?" Adam asks.

"I don't know. How do you bring that up?" I shake my head.

"Get through the weekend and then..." His words trail off.

And then what? Grow a new heart and brain? Forget this ever happened?

"Thank you guys for being here." I toss back the liquor. Logically I know I have to be drunk by now, but I feel nothing.

"Are you kidding? We fly together. Quack, quack, quack." Mav flaps his arms.

"Uhhh, what?" I'm not drunk enough to understand whatever he's communicating. Or too drunk, hard to say.

"Mighty Ducks!"

"No." Adam shakes his head. "Never refer to us as the Mighty Ducks again."

"Why not?" Mav looks crestfallen. "You can be Charlie."

"Who does that make you?" I ask.

"Please, I'm a bash brother, of course."

"Of course," I say, looking to Adam.

Adam's phone pings. I'm sure it's Reagan. I don't ask, just go back to staring down into my beer.

"Heard from Sienna?" Adam asks, setting his phone on the bar. It pings again, and this time I glance down to see Reagan's name flash across the screen.

"Yeah, she's been great." I wish she were here so badly, but maybe it's a good thing considering Carrie's parents might think we were still dating.

"I need to book my flight back tomorrow. What time you think?" Mav asks.

"You guys don't need to stay. I appreciate it, but there's nothing to do."

"There's an eleven o'clock or a five."

"Five puts us back at what time?" Adam asks.

They're checking airlines to find the best option and I'm wondering what the hell I'm even doing here.

"Let's do the eleven o'clock." I drain the rest of my glass and seriously consider ordering an entire bottle of Captain Morgan.

The heavy silence and sad eyes Mav gives me is the only reason I don't.

"Isn't the funeral at ten? We'll never make it on time." Adam finishes his beer. "You want another drink?"

"No, I'm good." It's my new favorite phrase. Succinct and total bullshit. "Book it. I've done what I came here for."

I stand and stumble over my own feet.

"Woah, there." Adam steadies me, Mav goes to the other side, and they hold me up.

"See?" Mav grins. He whispers, "Quack, quack, quack."

Chapter Twenty-Nine

SIENNA

Dakota and Reagan come to my late afternoon yoga class. Since the trip, we've been inseparable. They understand everything that's going on, which is nice, but I also just really enjoy being with them. Somewhere along the way, Rhett's friends have become mine.

"Is Rhett coming back today, too?" Reagan asks when everyone else is gone and it's just the three of us sitting on our mats.

"Yes. I wasn't expecting him until tomorrow, but I cannot wait to see him."

"How is he?" Dakota asks.

"Good. I think. It's hard to tell. Every time I ask him how he's doing, he turns it back on me." He sounds tired and a little off, but who could blame him?

"He cares about you a lot. You really scared him," Reagan says with a look that says that he's not the only one I scared.

"Do you still get to skate at your competition this weekend?" Dakota asks.

I nod enthusiastically. The one shining beacon in an otherwise crappy week. "Thank goodness."

"I switched my days working at the Hall of Fame so we can come," Dakota says.

"Really?" A smile splits my lips.

"Duh. We're not going to miss your last skating competition."

"My parents and little sister are coming, too. They haven't seen me skate all year." I glance down at my watch to check my heart rate.

Reagan leans back on one elbow. "Your heart condition, is it hereditary?"

"Sometimes, but in my case, it's not. My friend Elias is a third-generation though."

"The pairs skater?" Dakota asks.

"That's right."

"Does it freak you out or no? Also, feel free to tell me to mind my own damn business," Reagan says.

"I don't mind talking about it. And no, it doesn't really freak me out. Only when I can't do something that I want to, but for the most part I've adapted my life to a point that it doesn't feel like I'm missing out."

"Are your parents cool with you skating even with the risks?"

"Yeah. They have been great. The first year was hard and we fought a lot with me trying to keep living the same life and them always panicked that something would happen to me, but you can't live in a constant state of fear and anxiety. We went to therapy and we figured out what works for us. Namely, letting me do what I want." I grin. "I had to decide what was important to me and what things I was just holding on to because I thought I needed to drive my parents crazy. I don't care about binge drinking and I was pretty healthy even before I was diagnosed. The only thing I refused to give up is skating. Since I was already a skater, that helped too. Things that are outside of my routine seem to set me off more than anything."

"I think you're incredibly brave," Reagan says, flashing me her dimples.

I go back to their apartment with them. I haven't heard from Rhett since this morning, but I want to be there when he arrives.

Adam is standing outside of the apartment with a cocky grin when we walk up the stairs. Reagan takes off in a sprint, squealing.

"Is Rhett here too?" I ask.

"Yeah," Adam manages to say and motion with his head before Reagan occupies his mouth.

I go straight back to his room. He unzips the bag on the bed, looking up when I enter.

"You're back."

He stands tall. "I just got in. I was going to text you tomorrow. I'm so beat."

He faces me, and I can see the exhaustion. His normally smooth face is sporting scruff and his gray-blue eyes are hazy.

"Yeah, of course. I was with Dakota and Reagan and we ran into Adam." I linger in the doorway, then finally step forward to hug him. It's the first time I've breathed easy in two days. His scent and his strong arms wrap around me. "I missed you. I'm so glad you're home."

"Me too. I can't tell you how happy I am to have that behind me. How've you been feeling? And don't say fine."

"Better now." I squeeze harder.

I don't know how long we stand there embracing, but he lets

out a contented sigh. "I'm gonna shower and go to bed. Can you stay?"

"If you want me to." I wasn't sure if he'd want space after all he's been through, but I'm relieved when he looks at me like I'm ridiculous for considering any other option.

"Definitely. Maybe I'll be more fun after twelve hours of sleep."

"It's okay. I have some reading to do for class anyway."

He nods and then goes to shower.

True to his word, he showers and then climbs into bed and passes out. I read at his desk using my cell phone as a light, then crawl in beside him. When I wake up, he's wrapped around me like a human teddy bear.

And that's how the next couple of days go.

Rhett goes to classes, skates or lifts weights for several hours in the afternoon, and then comes back to his apartment exhausted and ready to sleep. We cuddle, we have sex, we watch movies, and sit together while we do schoolwork, but we barely leave his room outside of the previously mentioned activities.

When I ask him how he's doing, he says he's good and then kisses me. I don't know if it's a distraction technique, but it's effective.

Thursday evening we're sprawled out on his bed. He's watching a movie on his phone and I'm trying to read for class.

Heath yells from the other side of the door and then opens it a crack. "You guys want to play sardines?"

I look to Rhett.

"Nah, man. We're good. Thanks."

Heath glances to me, a flash of uncertainty in his gaze, and then nods.

"Are you sure? I'm just reading ahead so I can follow along better in class. I can be done if you want to play."

He shakes his head. "Not really feeling it."

"You could let me beat you at Mario Kart."

He snorts and then curls a finger around the front of my tank, pulling it down to show my cleavage. "I'm good right here."

Don't get me wrong, I love being with Rhett. I love being naked with Rhett, but his bedroom is starting to feel like our hideout.

"So, I heard that there's a party tomorrow night for the hockey team. Are you going?"

"Yeah, it's mandatory. The team is making an entrance. I promise we can duck out at a reasonable hour. I know you have the Valley Classic early Saturday."

"We, huh? I guess that means I'm invited."

"You go where I go." He leans forward and touches his lips to mine.

"A night out sounds fun, actually." I watch his expression carefully, but he's stoic. "And I don't have to be to the rink Saturday until ten so I'm good until at least midnight, when I turn into a pumpkin."

A small smile tips up one side of his mouth.

"I thought you'd be more excited about it."

"Excited about a night where I have to dress up and mingle with alumni and boosters?" He cocks a brow.

"A night celebrating with your friends. Since you didn't get to the night you won."

He doesn't respond and goes back to watching his phone.

I set my book aside and scoot closer to him. "Are you doing okay with all this? Really? I can't tell and I want to be here for you."

"You are here for me." He smiles and pokes me.

"Emotionally. You've barely said two words about Carrie or the funeral."

He drops his phone to his lap. "What do you want me to say?"

"Anything."

"It sucked and I feel awful about what happened. That help?"

"Does it help you?"

"No, which is why I haven't said anything. It's over and done, and I'm moving on. Talking about it is the opposite of what I want. Okay?"

I nod. "Okay."

"Being with you makes me feel better. You're here for me—physically and emotionally."

I kiss him. "I'm hungry. Want something to eat?"

"Mmmm." He hums, kisses me again and mumbles against my lips. "And mentally. I was just thinking about food. You read my mind."

"Want to go out?" I stretch my legs out.

"Nah, let's just order something."

Chapter Thirty

SIENNA

I'm worried about Rhett," I confess to Dakota the next night as we get ready for the party.

"Yeah, the guys are too."

"Really?"

She nods. "I wasn't sure if I should say anything."

The pit in my stomach grows. "I don't know what to do. He doesn't want to talk about it, and he isn't doing anything wrong. He just wants to stay in his room and make out."

Dakota laughs. "Most girls wouldn't consider that a problem."

"I know. I know. The last thing I want to complain about is my boyfriend wanting to have sex too often, but I just have this terrible feeling that he hasn't dealt with the loss at all."

"Maybe it isn't something he can just deal with in a week. I know they were broken up, but he was with her for a really long time. My mom died when I was fifteen, and it took me years to really deal with all the emotions I was feeling."

"Oh my gosh, Kota, I had no idea. I'm so sorry."

"Thanks. I got through it, but there's still moments where I miss her so much I can't breathe."

"I've never lost anyone that close to me."

"He'll be okay," she promises. "Give him time."

She stands from the vanity in Reagan's room. "How do I look?"

"Hot. The shoes are a nice touch, too."

She kicks up one leg behind her, showing off the red Converse. Somehow paired with a short black dress, it works. Very Dakota.

"Reagan, hurry up in there!" Dakota yells toward the bathroom.

"My hair is not cooperating." She emerges, spraying hairspray as she walks. "Is Ginny here yet?"

Dakota shakes her head. Her red hair is at full volume, framing her face in big curls. She plays with a strand, twisting it around her finger. "No, she's meeting us there. Somehow she got roped into helping set up."

"All right, then, I think we're ready," Reagan says and smiles, looking from me to Dakota. "We are some serious eye candy. Let's take a photo."

We cram together, cheesing at the camera, as Reagan snaps a dozen photos of us.

The party is thrown in front of University Hall. A large open tent is set up with a buffet line and bar. The Valley U dance team and cheerleaders are in attendance, as well as the roadrunner mascot. It has a whole *Friday Night Lights* vibe that I have to wonder isn't more about the alumni and boosters than the team that just won a national championship.

The guys are set to make a grand entrance so Reagan, Dakota and I grab a drink from the bar and stand as far away from the cheering and dancing section as we can.

Servers in white tux jackets bring out hors d'oeuvres on shiny platters. Old guys stand in groups laughing and talking loudly.

"This is…" I start, not easily coming up with the word.

"Excessive," Dakota says. "I feel like I made a wrong turn into a fortieth reunion class."

"You guys." Reagan stands taller in her red heels. She and Dakota nearly match with their red shoes and black dresses, but their styles are so different, no one would ever notice. "They won a national championship. They deserve excessive."

"What they wanted was a kegger with drunk girls in skimpy outfits, not shrimp cocktail with old dudes." Dakota downs her champagne.

"We should do that for them, then," I say quickly but the more I think about it the more I like the idea. A do-over for Rhett to celebrate with his friends. I know it won't change what happened, but maybe he'll at least feel like he got one last hurrah in with his teammates.

"There they are," Reagan says.

The three of us watch, along with everyone else, as they walk in. Music plays and the cheerleaders and dancers move into action making a path for them to a podium with a microphone.

"That's Maverick's dad," Dakota whispers when a man steps up and welcomes everyone. "Or, I guess he's Maverick Senior. Mr. Maverick. Weird."

We chuckle together.

"How do you know?" I ask. "Have you met him?"

"Are you kidding? Just look at him."

The man introduces Coach Meyers and then Dakota's assumption is confirmed when Coach comes forward and thanks John Maverick for hosting the party tonight.

As he goes on thanking everyone, Ginny steps up beside us. "I thought they'd at least be in their jerseys."

"You made it." Reagan hugs her.

"I was on confetti duty."

"Confetti?"

"You'll see," she says as the first pop sounds. Each of the cheerleaders has a confetti cannon in their hands and they go off each time a player is introduced.

"Look at Maverick. Holy crap," Ginny says as his name is called. They're all dressed similarly in dress pants and shirts, but Maverick is striking in a white button-up with rolled sleeves showing off some of his tattoos. His dark hair is styled, and he has a hard set to his jaw. Sophisticated and pissed is a good look for him, even if it makes me sad to see a unsmiling Maverick. His dad squeezes his shoulder with a proud look on his face.

"He does not want to be here," Reagan says.

"Who could blame him," Dakota says. "The first time his parents come to Valley and they've made a spectacle."

"Wow." That's all I get out before Rhett waves and comes into view. Unlike Maverick, he didn't bother styling his hair, but it doesn't matter. He's still the hottest guy I've ever seen. He runs a hand through that messy hair and all I can think about is how I can't wait to spend the evening with him. It isn't exactly the celebration we would have had after the Frozen Four, but he's here and I'm here and that's celebration enough.

After several more speeches, the guys are released. They mingle into the crowd and by the time we get to them, Rhett already has two beers in hand, one stacked on top of another.

"Hey," I say cheerily as I step to his side.

"Hey." He wraps an arm around my waist, chugs the top beer and then tosses it and pops the tab on the second.

"I'm surprised they have beer here," I say.

"They don't," Heath says. "We had to bring our own cheap booze."

Maverick takes out a bottle of Mad Dog, takes a long swallow and passes it to Rhett who does the same.

He offers it to me.

"No thanks. Kind of early for shots."

He shrugs and passes it back to Mav.

Our little group is interrupted by alumni and important people from the university approaching the guys to personally congratulate them. Rhett never lets go of me as he thanks each and every one of them, but his grip on me tightens to the point I feel like I'm the anchor keeping him from floating away.

"How long do you have to stay?" I ask quietly.

"Coach said three hours, but I doubt anyone is going to miss me. Do you need to get back?"

I don't. Not really. I have everything ready for tomorrow and it isn't like I'd be sleeping even if I were at home, but something tells me he needs to leave. I can feel it. The pain and frustration radiates off him.

"We can stay if you want."

"Nah, you've gotta skate tomorrow. What's Coach going to do? Kick me off the team?"

We say hushed goodbyes to our friends and then sneak out and walk back to his apartment. Rhett grabs another beer from the fridge and sits on the couch. He doesn't speak, but at least we aren't confined to his room for a change.

I get a text from my sister saying they made it to the hotel. "My family is in town. They'll be at the arena tomorrow if you're up for meeting them."

"Yeah, of course. I'm looking forward to it."

"Good, because my sister is so excited. She knows all your stats and she's totally going to fangirl."

He laughs like I'm kidding, but she totally will.

"I thought tomorrow night we could take her out somewhere or have a small party here?"

"Saturday night... it won't be hard to find people drinking and hanging out somewhere."

Rhett turns on the TV and I text my sister, making plans to meet up with them in the morning.

The rest of Rhett's roommates and their girlfriends aren't far behind us. First Ginny and Heath appear, followed by Adam, Kota, and Reagan.

"Where's Maverick?" I ask, looking at Dakota.

"He went to let Charli out. I'm sure he'll be up soon." Adam sits between me and Rhett on the couch and my boyfriend passes him a controller. "Hey, buddy. Doing okay? You haven't said much since we got back from Minnesota."

"Not a lot to say, I guess."

"Was your mom pissed we left early?"

My ears perk up. "What do you mean you left early?"

There's a flash of guilt on Rhett's face before he shrugs. "We missed the funeral so we could catch the early flight back to Valley."

My mouth gapes.

"She chastised me a little," Rhett admits. "I don't see what the big deal is. I paid my respects to Carrie's family at the visitation.

Staying wasn't going to bring her back to life."

A heavy silence falls over the apartment.

"As long as you got the closure you need." Adam is the first to speak.

Rhett scoffs and lifts the controller in his hand. "Sure, man. Whatever. Are we going to play or what?"

I'm on edge after that trying to process this information. He didn't go to the funeral?

Mav enters, still wearing his dress clothes, but the shirt is unbuttoned and untucked. He's got a box under one arm and carries a bottle of Mad Dog in the other hand.

"Did anyone make it the full three hours?" Rhett asks.

"We told the freshmen if they left before midnight, we'd fill their dorms with that fucking confetti." Mav grins. He sets the box on the kitchen counter and opens the bottle of Mad Dog. The second, or maybe third of the night. "Rauthruss, that box is for you. Delivery guy fucked up and left it outside my place by mistake."

Rhett glances up to the box. "For me? Who's it from?"

"Someone in Minnie-soda." He picks it up with one hand and tosses it across the room.

Rhett stands to catch it. He stares down at the label and his face pales.

"What's wrong?" Adam asks, picking up on the change in him.

"It's from Carrie's family." He sits and sets it on the coffee table, glaring hard at the small box.

"Are you going to open it?" Heath asks.

"It's probably just pictures or something. I'll open it later."

"We're all here and the booze is freshly stocked. Might as well open it now and get it over with." Mav sits on the arm of the chair across from him.

We're all staring at him, so he proceeds. He rips off the tape and opens the flaps. His throat works before he reaches in.

My pulse thrums quickly as he sets the contents on the coffee table.

"My first college goal." He holds up a hockey puck.

"No way, let me see." Mav grabs it.

"I remember that game," Adam says.

I have to admit I feel a pinch of jealousy for all the years I missed. For the history I'll never have with him. I could never admit that out loud, not now, but before all of this happened I was jealous of Carrie and the time she had with Rhett. But as I watch him pull out mementos from their time together, I realize how stupid I was. He wouldn't be who he is now without her. He'll carry pieces of her with him forever, and I'll be thankful that he is who he is no matter how he got here.

Among the other items he removes from the box is a Bruins hat that looks nearly identical to the one he always wears, a few newspaper clippings highlighting Rhett's high school hockey days, and the last item is some sort of collage or photo cube.

"Oh, hand that over." Adam grabs it. "I need to show Sienna what your Gumby ass looked like at sixteen."

The pictures of them together are heart breaking, as are the words cut out from magazines to say things like *perfect couple*, *true love*, and *forever*. But the real punch to the gut is the sound that comes from it. At first there's a hint of confusion on Adam's face when a female voice giggles. "I love you, Rhett."

But when Rhett's voice repeats the sentiment back, we all stare at him and then the cube where the sound is coming.

"Oh my god." The words tumble from my lips and I put a hand to my chest. They recorded it together, who knows how long ago. It doesn't matter. The look on Rhett's face is gut wrenching.

He doesn't say anything for too long.

Adam holds the cube with two hands in his lap. "Hey, man. I'm so sorry. I didn't know."

Rhett stands and his phone on the coffee table in front of him rings. I feel like I'm watching everything unfold in slow motion. I hold my breath as he picks it up, curls his fingers around it, and launches it at the wall above the TV. It ricochets and falls to the ground with a thud, screen up and very much shattered.

Adam pushes to his feet and places a hand on Rhett's shoulder.

"Save it." Rhett swipes a hand through the air and shrugs out of his embrace. "You didn't even like her. None of you did."

"Rhett, we didn't really know her." Mav's voice is calm and steady.

A bitter laugh erupts from him, and he tips his head back. "Fuck all of you and your weak ass attempts to be understanding now. Little too late, don't you think?"

He storms off to his room.

Adam looks to me. "I'm sorry."

I go after him. He's changing clothes and packing his hockey bag.

"Rhett?" I ask tentatively.

"Not now, Sienna. I know that had to suck for you, and I'm sorry, but just… not now."

I stay in place until he's walking toward me to exit his room.

"Where are you going?"

"The rink. I need to clear my head."

Silent tears slide down my cheeks. I want to hug him or go with him, but he doesn't ask as he pushes past me. He's finally out of his room and now I just want him to come back.

Chapter Thirty-One

RHETT

Anger vibrates through me as I stand under the hot water. Closing my eyes and unclenching my hands, I try to find release from the giant weight sitting on my chest.

I thought I'd feel better after a couple of hours on the ice. Fuck, I thought that about coming back to Valley, too. That's really why I skipped the funeral. I wanted to get back to school and back to normal. Back to Sienna.

Instead, every day I just wake up and feel shitty all over again. I turn off the shower and wrap a towel around my waist. The locker room is empty and dark. I didn't bother turning any lights on when I came in.

Adam sits in his stall, leaning back.

"Fuck off. I'm perfectly capable of dressing myself."

He says nothing. I really wish he'd tell me to shut the fuck up or clock me. Maybe that would make me feel better. It certainly couldn't make me feel worse.

I ignore my buddy as I get dressed, hoping he'll get the hint and leave. I'm in no mood to have a heart-to-heart. I'm in no mood to do anything but go back to the apartment where I can shut myself in my room and not speak to anyone.

But Adam didn't come all the way here in the middle of the night to let me be a broody asshole.

"Well?" I ask, antsy to get this over with. "Say whatever it is you came to say."

He sighs. "I love you like a brother. You're my best friend in the whole world. I just want to be here for you."

"You didn't even like Carrie," I say again. It's petty as hell, but it's true. Adam never liked Carrie. No one was happier than him when we finally broke up for good.

"Because I know that she fucking cheated on you," he screeches, voice low. Immediately, his features morph, and he lets out an exasperated sigh. "Fuck. I'm sorry."

Well, shit.

"How long have you known?" I ask, then, "*How* do you know?"

"I overheard you on the phone one day. I wanted to ask you about it, but I figured you'd tell me when you were ready to talk about it."

"Yeah, that never would have happened." I didn't tell a soul the real reason me and Carrie broke up. Until Sienna. Besides, it may have been the last straw, but we were heading that way for a while. We drifted apart, became different people, wanted different things. I guess I didn't want to give my friends any more reasons not to like her.

"So, yeah, I wasn't her biggest fan. Because I'm *your* biggest fan and I will always have your best interests in mind. I didn't think you should be with her, but I didn't hate her. I'm not glad she's gone."

"I know." I rough a hand through my hair. "Fuck, I know. I'm so goddamn angry, and I don't know why."

"Because you're hurting. You still cared about her."

"It doesn't make any sense. I can't wrap my brain around it."

We're quiet for a beat.

"Sienna went back to her dorm."

The knife in my gut twists, but I nod. "Good. I'm shit company."

"You need to talk to her."

"And say what?"

"Look, Rhett, I can't imagine what you're going through, but we all just want to be here for you. Sienna included. It wasn't your fault."

"I know," I grit out.

"Do you?" He lets me get by without answering. "Are you ready to head back to the apartment?"

"Maybe you're right. I should go see Sienna. What time is it anyway?" I pat my pocket for my phone and then remember I destroyed it.

"After two in the morning."

"Or tomorrow."

"She'll be up," he says and claps a hand on my shoulder. "Text me if you need anything."

Despite Adam's encouragement, I don't go see Sienna. I wander to her dorm and then walk home slowly. She has to skate tomorrow and as much as I want to see her, I know it's selfish of me.

I send her an email. One quick line, *Good luck tomorrow.*

Then I pass the fuck out and hope that tomorrow is better.

I'M UP EARLY DESPITE HAVING GONE TO BED SO LATE. BEFORE I even open my eyes, the events of last night make my head throb. But worst of all, Sienna's not here.

I check the time and hop into the shower. I have a lot of people to apologize to in a short amount of time if I'm going to catch Sienna before she skates today.

Heath and Ginny are in the living room.

"Rhett," Ginny says, sitting up. She looks hesitant and I fucking hate that. I've known Ginny for years, since she was a junior high kid dropping off her brother at college. Now she looks afraid of me.

"I'm really sorry about last night."

She gets up and hugs me.

Heath tips his head. "Feeling better?"

I shrug. "A little, I guess. Don't feel like throwing anything."

He chuckles. "Good because these thin ass walls can't handle it."

I glance up to the small hole in the wall where my phone hit. "I'll fix it. Seen Adam?"

"Out back," Ginny says, letting me go.

Adam and Reagan are sitting on a lounge chair together, talking and laughing. So happy. I want that.

He looks up when I step outside. "Hey, you're awake."

Reagan turns and smiles at me. "I should go get ready for Sienna's competition."

She kisses Adam and leaves us alone.

"I'm sorry for everything," I say. "I lost my head. It's no excuse."

"Don't worry about it. Already forgotten."

"Thank you for checking on me even when I don't want you to."

He chuckles. "I'm gonna remember you said that for next time."

"God, I hope there's not a next time like this."

His expression sobers. "Are you on your way to the arena?"

"Soon. I have a few things I need to take care of first."

"I meant what I said last night. I always want whatever is best for you. I like Sienna. She's sweet and caring, and I've never seen you so happy. That must be hard, considering everything else."

"She's incredible. I love her. I love her in ways I never thought I could love a person. I thought it would be enough."

Enough to move on and to not feel the agony of losing a girl I'd known my whole life.

Adam nods. "I should have made you stay for the funeral. I didn't know what you needed. I still don't, but I'm here."

"I know that, and I appreciate it. I should have stayed, but that's on me."

He stands and hugs me. "Whatever you need. I'm here."

"In that case, can I borrow your phone?" I hold up what's left of mine.

He laughs. "Yeah, of course."

Chapter Thirty-Two

SIENNA

I'm sitting in the tunnel talking with Elias trying to calm my nerves. The competition starts in just a few minutes. I'm not set to skate until later this afternoon, but with everything going on, I'm a jittery mess.

"I'm back in the good ole USA." He tilts the phone to show me his new weight room. He and Taylor are training at her home gym in South Dakota for the next month.

"Too bad her home gym wasn't in Arizona. You're so close."

He snorts. "Just a twenty-four-hour drive. I checked. Looked at flights too but our training is crazy. And it's a two hour drive just to the airport. There isn't even a McDonald's in this town."

"Oh man, you really are roughing it," I tease.

"So… the doctor cleared you for today?" he asks.

"Yeah, once I told him I'd taken out all the difficult jumps, he and coach were both good with it. I've been feeling stronger every day."

"Was changing the routine your idea?"

"Yeah. It isn't worth the risk for a showcase event."

He grins. "Look at you, growing and shit."

I roll my eyes, but I guess he's right. A few months ago, I would have been tempted to push through even when I knew my body was weak. My phone pings with a text from my sister telling me they're walking in the building.

"I gotta go. My family is here."

"Hey, wait." His face gets closer to the screen. "Forget about everything going on with Rufus. Today is your day to shine."

My chest aches at the mention of Rhett.

"Kill it." He makes a cross over his heart and I mimic. "Good luck."

"I never understood why you two do that." A deep voice echoes in the quiet hallway as I end the call.

"Rhett." I scramble to my feet and hug him. I wasn't sure he'd come and wasn't sure how I'd feel about it if he did. I want to be angry that he ran last night, but I'm too happy to see him.

"Hey, angel." He wraps me in his arms and smooths a hand down the back of my head.

"I wasn't sure you were still coming." I tilt my face up to him and he places a kiss on my forehead.

"I'm sorry about last night, but I wouldn't miss it. You've got a whole fan club out there. Dakota and Reagan even brought signs."

I smile. I knew Dakota and Reagan were planning to come, but hearing it confirmed makes my heart squeeze.

"I'm so glad you're here. Today is going to be amazing. By the way, how do you feel about Italian for dinner? My dad has his heart set on some restaurant he saw driving through town."

He smiles. "About that..."

"Too much? Do you not want to hang out with my family?"

"It isn't that." He blows out a breath. "I'm leaving Valley, Sienna."

"What do you mean? For the night or… the weekend?"

"For… I don't know. School is almost done. I talked to my advisor this morning and he said I could finish my classes online and still graduate next month. I'm flying out this afternoon."

All the air is knocked from my lungs. "I don't understand. Can't you wait one more month to finish out the school year?"

"I need to go home and deal with my shit. It isn't fair for me to keep clinging to you like a life raft. I'll take us both down if I keep going this way."

"I want to be your life raft or at least your arm floaties."

I get a small smile but can tell he's already decided he's leaving, and I can't stop him.

"What about us?"

"I hope you can understand, but I get it if you can't. The last thing I want is to hurt you or bring more stress on your life."

"I'm stronger than you think." My phone pings again. "My family is waiting for me. Do you still want to meet them?"

"If you still want me to, yeah. I'd love to."

My family adores Rhett. No surprise there. My sister grins so big when he asks her about her team's hockey season, and seeing my sister so excited wins over my mom. My dad is the last one to crumble, but when he finds out Rhett is from Minnesota, my dad welcomes him like a fellow neighbor.

"I have to go get ready and warm up. I'll see you guys after the competition." I get hugs from all of my family members, and then Rhett walks with me toward the locker room.

"Will I see you after?"

"My flight is at four."

So, no.

"Will I hear from you?"

"Yeah." He hugs me. "My phone is destroyed so it might take a few days to get a new one."

"Okay."

His mouth covers mine and I live in the seconds before he pulls away. "Later, angel."

With a broken heart, I walk into the locker room. Josie is sitting on the bench lacing her skates.

"Hey." Her face falls when she gets a good look at me. "What's wrong?"

Instead of answering, I sit next to her and lean my head on her shoulder. "Life isn't fair."

"No, it definitely isn't. Anything I can do? Do I need to dick punch someone to even the karma scales?"

My laugh is short and clipped. "No, sadly it doesn't have a revenge solution."

"Pity." She smiles. "Skate it out?"

"Absolutely."

And that's what I do. Those moments just before I skate always go by in a blur. Music, applause, the chill in the air. It isn't until my name is called that I snap to attention. I take the ice and I skate for Rhett. I skate for my family.

But most of all, I skate for me.

SPENDING TIME WITH MY FAMILY IS NICE, BUT MY MIND continually returns to Rhett. I replay the past week wondering if there are things I could have done differently to have changed the outcome.

They don't ask why Rhett doesn't come with us, but my sister notices I'm not my usual self.

"Do you still want to go out later? If you're not up for it—"

"Of course." I force some enthusiasm into my smile. "Rhett's roommates are having people over and we can crash in his room."

"Okay." She squeals.

"But, no drinking. I promised mom and dad."

Allison rolls her eyes. "I don't drink. Beer is gross."

It's a chill night at the apartment. Some of the hockey team is over playing Xbox and the rest of us are sitting outside on the deck.

Allison is quiet, but the giant grin on her face hasn't faltered since we walked in.

Maverick, who miraculously still has his shirt on, sits next to me and throws an arm over my shoulder.

"It's weird, right? Rhett not being here."

"Very," I admit.

"He'll be back. He has to come back."

"I don't know. There's only a few weeks of school left."

"Yeah, but you two are in love. He won't be able to stay away for that long."

I feel my face heat and I look down to my lap.

"You are in love, yeah?" Mav drops his arm. "Please tell me you didn't drop kick the poor bastard's heart on his way out the door."

"No, of course not. It's just… I haven't told him that I love him."

"Oh. Well, fuck." He backtracks when I shoot him a panicked look. "I'm sure he knows how you feel."

I want to kick myself. "I should have told him. Now I may never get a chance."

"Cheer up. You'll get your chance. I know it." He stands. "Allie, you look like a ringer. Wanna be on my team for washers?"

My sister nods enthusiastically, not even bothering to correct the shortening of her name which she usually hates. "Sure."

THE NEXT MORNING, I SAY GOODBYE TO MY FAMILY OUTSIDE OF my dorm.

"We'll see you in a month for graduation," my dad says, hugging me. "Try not to flunk out before then."

"Funny."

My mom always tears up when we say goodbye and this time is no different. "Love you, mom. I'll talk to you soon."

"I made up your old bedroom in case you want to stay with us after graduation while you get settled into the new job."

"Thank you. I'll think about it." I've given such little thought to the job. I haven't even looked at apartments. It doesn't seem nearly as important as everything else going on.

"Thank you for letting me tag along last night," Allison says when it's finally her turn. "Will you give Maverick my number?"

"Definitely not."

She smiles. "Bye, S."

I've barely gotten back to my room and crawled into bed where

I fully intend to spend the day feeling sorry for myself when there's a knock at the door. My stupid, hopeful heart convinces me that it's Rhett.

It's another hockey player standing outside with coffee. "Mav?"

"Gooooood morning. Coffee?" He extends the cup in his left hand. "It's decaf."

"What are you doing here?"

"I thought about it all night and I decided we should do it."

"Do what?"

"Make the big gesture."

I take a sip of the coffee while I give my brain a chance to work through the puzzle that is Maverick. "What?"

"We're going to drive to Minnesota and you're going to make the big gesture."

"That sounds…"

"Awesome," he says as I say, "Like a terrible idea."

"Come on. I live for this shit. The look on his face will be worth the two-day drive."

"I can't ask him to come back."

"Then don't, but you have to tell him how you feel."

I can't believe I'm considering it.

"Minnie-soda bound?" He asks, dancing in place.

Chapter Thirty-Three

SIENNA

Road-tripping with Maverick is as fun as you'd imagine. He has the best playlists, at every gas stop he loads up on tons of candy and junk food, and he doesn't let me get too in my head and convince myself that this was all a terrible idea and we should turn around.

Okay, he doesn't stop that last thing from happening, but he does laugh and make me feel better when I voice all the really awful thoughts churning in my brain.

On the morning of our second day, I see a sign for South Dakota. "Do you think we could make a stop?"

"Yeah, we're about three hours away from Rhett. You want to have brunch and talk about the epic way you're going to confess your love?"

I stare at him unblinking. "No, but now I'm worried just saying the words is going to be really lame."

He chuckles. "Where do you want to stop?"

"Elias is training nearby. I've never met him and we're so close." Also, I think I need a pep talk from my best friend because my stomach is in knots.

Maverick hands me his phone. "Punch in the address."

"Thank you for doing this. All of it. Talking me into it and driving. Elias is going to lose his mind."

"How'd you meet Elias?"

"YouTube." I grin. "He was documenting his journey, living and skating with long QT. I stumbled onto it right after I was diagnosed and we exchanged some messages, that led to texts, which led to us talking every day, sometimes multiple times a day. He's kind of my best friend."

"Always strictly friends?" He studies me carefully.

"Always. You'll understand when you meet him. He's impossible not to like. Kind of like you."

"Throwing me off with a compliment or is that sincere?" He shakes his head. "Doesn't matter, I accept."

When we get to the arena where Elias is training, I end up having to call him so we can get in. Auburn, South Dakota may be a small, nameless city, but the arena is big and grand and heavily monitored.

"What? How?" He stops six feet away and then rushes forward and crushes me in a hug. "You're real."

"That would have been some impressive catfishing." We gawk at each other for a few minutes. His dark hair curls around his ears and his brown eyes are a shade lighter than they'd seemed through the phone. He's tall, which I knew, and has that lanky but strong build of a typical male figure skater.

He's the same in person, and any weirdness I felt at finally meeting him in person is quickly dissolved when I discover it's just as easy to be with him in person as it is on the phone.

I angle my body to introduce the guy at my side. "This is Johnny Maverick."

"Traded up already?" Elias lifts a brow.

Mav cackles. "Traded up. That's hilarious, and thanks for saying up instead of down."

"The other one is currently on my shit list, so it isn't hard to look better than him right now."

"Elias!" I slap his arm.

"I know. I know. His ex died. It's awful, but I'm still pissed he took off."

The guys shake hands and then Elias takes us on a quick tour of the building. It's impressive and I find myself already missing the hours I've been lucky enough to spend on the ice the last four years. Oh, how I'm going to miss skating every day.

"I have to get back. How long are you staying? Can we skate together?"

"I would love that." I look to Mav. "Do we have time?"

"Yeah, I wouldn't mind checking out that ice myself."

"Awesome." Elias grins. "Sit wherever, don't talk to the mean-looking lady with the flaming red hair, and I'll be done in about two hours."

"Mean-looking lady with the flaming red—Ah! Found her." Mav leads the way to a row about midway up.

I snort. "That's his coach and she's amazing."

There are two other pairs on the ice, but it's Elias and Taylor I focus on. I've seen videos online of their competitions and some clips that Elias has sent, but they're even better in person. Taylor has this presence about her and Elias is a great partner, syncing with her and making every movement seem so connected and like it's all about her.

"What are you doing over there?" I ask Mav a while later. We've barely spoken since we sat down since I've been so enthralled with watching. He's leaned back smiling at his phone.

"Sexting Kota."

"What?!" Well, that definitely has my attention. "No way. Let me see."

He sits up and shows me a picture of Dakota holding Charli. "O-kay. I was expecting something a little... sexier."

"She's watching her for me while I'm gone."

"That's nice, but how is that sexting?"

"Trust me. I invented this move."

"What move?"

"Sending chicks I'm interested in pictures of my dog to get their attention. It's a signal and way more effective than nudes."

"Wait a minute." I pull out my phone and scroll up toward the beginning of mine and Rhett's text history, then show Mav.

He covers his mouth with a fist. "Worked, didn't it?"

"OF COURSE YOU TRAVELED WITH YOUR SKATES," ELIAS SAYS AS I step onto the ice.

"Mav did too." I nod my head to where he's skating around, hockey stick in hand.

"This place is incredible." I look up and take in the view from down here. "And here I was feeling sorry for you being in small-town hell."

"It's pretty nice," he admits. His gaze goes to Taylor. "How are *things*?"

"Good. We decided to give dating a shot."

I stop. "Dating?"

"Yeah, it isn't a big deal. We figured the only way to keep things from being weird was just to date, give in to the chemistry."

I laugh. The first time I've really, truly genuinely laughed in a week. So hard I can't stop for a full minute.

"I'm sorry," I say, clutching my stomach. "I don't mean to laugh. Do you really think this is the less weird route?"

He flashes a sheepish grin. "Probably not, but she kisses like a damn goddess about to be struck down by Zeus."

"Is that good?"

"It's..." He holds his hands together in front of his face. "So good."

"I'm happy for you then."

"It'll be good while it lasts," he says with forced lightness in his tone. I hope for his sake that it ends as casually as it started. He's so close to reaching his gold-medal dreams.

"So..." He starts. "What's the plan? You're going to just show up at Rhett's house and then what?"

"I don't know," I admit. "I just need to tell him to his face that I love him. Maybe he already knows, but until I've said the words out loud I'm going to feel like I didn't do everything I could."

"You *still* haven't told him?"

"You're *dating* your partner?"

He flashes a sheepish grin.

"It probably won't matter. He loves me and that wasn't enough. I think he wants to protect me."

"From?"

"My *broken* heart."

"Did he say that?" Elias looks pissed at the prospect.

"No, not exactly, but he said that the last thing he wanted to do was hurt me or bring more stress into my life."

He gives me a small smile.

"I guess I can't blame him for thinking I can't handle it considering I nearly fainted when we found out Carrie had died." I hate so much that he has any question that I'm capable of being there for him. And I hate even more that I let him down when he needed me most.

"Honey, you're not broken. He knows that. Or he should. Don't even try to play the woe-is-me card. You're the strongest person I know. You're a motherfucking badass. He said it for the same reason you haven't told him you love him."

"I just haven't found the right time. Sorry your ex-girlfriend died, but hey, consolation prize, I love you."

"You're no one's consolation prize."

"I know." I sigh. "And I know he doesn't think that. But what if..." I place my hand over my heart.

"What if he can't deal with being with someone who could drop dead at any minute?"

"It is a lot. Especially now."

"We're all ticking time bombs. You're scared. He's scared. Life is fucking scary."

"People don't like to be reminded of their mortality."

"True."

Elias and I don't get the luxury of believing we're untouchable. We know better, but anyone that gets close to us has to accept that too and that can be a really hard thing to admit.

"What if he can't get over this? What if he doesn't come back?"

"Then Rickie really is a dumb hockey player." Elias takes my hand. It's so weird being here with him, skating, like we've done it a million times before. "Do you want to meet Taylor?"

"Oh my gosh, really? Is it weird if I ask her for an autograph?"

He laughs under his breath. "Oh, she's going to love this."

Mav and I climb back into his SUV. We're only a few hours from Rhett's house and the nerves and anticipation slam into me.

"This was an awful plan. How did I let you talk me into this?" I ask Mav when we're on the freeway.

"It's a great plan and I talked you into it."

All too soon the signs for Rochestertown start appearing indicating we're close.

"Maybe we should wait until tomorrow. He could still be busy or, I don't know, out with friends."

"Really?" Mav asks with a chuckle. "No can do. I've gotta be north of the city for dinner. I have just enough time to drop you, say hey to Rhett, and get back on the road."

"You're leaving me?"

"Relax. I'll be back later tonight."

"What's north of the city?"

"The Wildcats. My team." He taps the Wildcats hat resting on the dash. "Forgot I was a big shot pro hockey player, didn't you?" He winks.

"I don't think you get to call yourself a big shot pro hockey player until you play an actual pro game."

He grins.

"Do they let you drop in and practice during the Valley off-season?"

"Nah, just have a meeting with the coach and my agent."

I'm too worried about seeing Rhett to pry, but a few minutes later Mav asks, "Wanna know a secret?"

I nod.

"I'm not going back to Valley next year."

"Why not?"

He shrugs a big shoulder. "It's time. We won a national championship. There's no topping that."

"Wow. Does anyone else know?"

He shakes his head. "It's our little secret."

I blow out a shaky breath as he exits the freeway.

He takes his eyes off the road for a second to look at me. "You're gonna be fine."

"What if he isn't excited to see me?"

"That's what you're worried about?"

"I hate surprises. They never go as planned." Something Elias said earlier keeps replaying in my mind. "Stop. Pull over."

Mav's brow furrows but he pulls into a coffeehouse parking lot just off the freeway. "Are you okay?"

"Yeah, I'm fine, but I can't do this."

"Sie—"

"Not because I'm afraid he doesn't want to see me." I turn to face him. "I'm a motherfucking badass."

Mav's body shakes with laughter. "Yeah, you are."

"He asked this one thing of me. I can't roll up and try to convince him not to do it."

"What about telling him you love him?"

"I will, but for now, I think I have to believe in what we have. If I show up there, I'm basically proving that I can't handle whatever life throws at us. I can. I'm strong enough. If he wants to run, that's on him. But I'm here or I was there. I was strong enough but he wasn't."

"I'm not sure I follow," Mav says.

I open the door, phone in the other hand. "Give me five?"

"Stay. I'll grab some coffee."

"Thanks." I shut the door and Maverick gets out of the vehicle.

I have no idea what I'm going to say, but my finger hovers over Rhett's number when a text pops up.

Rhett: Hey, angel. Back in MN and have a new phone.

A second one pops up while I'm rereading the first for a third time.

Rhett: This is just something I have to do. I can't explain it. I know it's the worst possible timing with school ending, but I can't come back until I'm sure... Fuck, I don't even know what I need to be sure of.

Rhett: I'm sure that I miss you.

I type out a dozen responses. I want to tell him how I feel and beg him to come back. Of course, I do. I miss him. But if he doesn't want to lean on me right now, I can't force him to.

Me: I miss you too. I get it. Do what you have to do, but I'm here if you need anything.

I power off my phone so I don't crack and tell him I love him over text message. He'll come back. He has to.

Mav climbs back into the driver's seat, hands me a cup, and sets his in the middle console. "Well?"

"I'm sorry that I dragged you fifteen hundred miles from school for nothing, but I have to let him do this his way."

He nods slowly. "You're sure?"

"Positive."

"All right." He slides on his sunglasses. "Wanna meet my new team?"

Chapter Thirty-Four

SIENNA

Mav and I get back to Valley Wednesday night and the rest of the week I'm playing catch up on my classes. It has been a crazy month but luckily my professors are as eager for the semester to be over as I am and I didn't miss any quizzes or major assignments.

And without Rhett or skating to occupy my time, by Friday evening I'm caught up and bored. I finally meet up with the girls at the dining hall. I knew they'd have a million questions and I'm not disappointed. The second we sit down at a table, they start asking me questions about Rhett.

"You went all that way there and then didn't even go see him?" Ginny asks.

"I couldn't. I wanted to, but I just couldn't."

"Have you heard from him?" Reagan smiles sadly.

"Just a couple texts." I shake my head. "Hopefully he's dealing or doing whatever he needs to."

"It's only been a week," Dakota says.

A week that has felt like an eternity. I hoped that from afar maybe he'd open up more, but it's been radio silence while he deals with this on his own.

"Yeah." I sit taller. "I know. I just miss him."

"I can't believe you drove all that way," Reagan says.

"It wasn't a total loss. I got to meet Elias finally, and the Wildcats roster. I'm not sure which was more exciting."

Dakota leans forward. "I know Elias is your best friend and all, but the locker room of men. One man is never better than a hockey roster full of them."

"Except when it's the right one," Reagan says.

With a roll of her eyes, Dakota says, "Well, until then…" She waves her hand. "I need details."

I tell them everything I can remember about Maverick's new team and the giant arena where they practice. I leave out that he's going to be playing for them sooner rather than later. As far as I know, Maverick hasn't told anyone else about his decision to leave Valley and go pro next year.

Eventually Reagan and Ginny leave us to sit with their boyfriends.

"Are you aware that Mav thinks you were sexting him while we were gone," I tell Dakota as we leave the dining hall.

"Umm… what?"

"The picture you sent him with Charli. He has this whole theory on how sending a picture with his dog is better than sending dick pics."

She stares blankly.

"As in, more effective at getting him laid."

"So that's why he keeps sending me photos of him and Charli."

We both laugh.

"What's your night like?" Dakota asks. "Wanna hang out?"

"I'd love to, but I had to trade some classes while I was gone. Tonight I'm teaching two beginner-level yoga classes."

"I'll come with you. I was going to run at the track, but the last class I took with you kicked my ass. How long have you been doing it?"

"Yoga or teaching it?"

"Both."

"My mom was always doing yoga around the house when I was growing up. I would do a pose or two with her, then get bored and go do something else. Then when I got to Valley I took a more advanced yoga class. It was so hard, but I loved the challenge, and it really helps with skating." I swipe my card on the door reader to let us in the locked room. "And I started teaching when I realized I could get paid for doing something I was planning on doing anyway."

She laughs. "It doesn't suck the joy out of it for you being a job?"

"There are days I dread coming, but once class starts, no, I love it."

"That's really cool, and you're good at it so it works out well for everyone."

I start the music and sit on the floor to stretch out. "What are you going to do this summer?"

She lets her shoulders sag forward and the end of her red ponytail falls over one arm. "I have applied for so many internships, but so far they're either unpaid or the salary is so low I couldn't afford to feed myself."

"What kind of internship are you looking for?" I ask.

While we wait for people to join the class, Dakota tells me she wants to do public relations or marketing and she's hoping to find something this summer to get some experience for her resume.

"It looks like it's going to be another summer working at the Hall of Fame. It's so quiet over the summer. The only people that come in for tours are alumni wanting to relive their glory years."

"Oh, that sounds kind of nice." A few people have joined us and are rolling out their mats and getting ready.

"It really isn't. Never fails, I get stuck listening to an hour's worth of stories about how much harder they partied back then or how much better the team was."

I laugh at the visual.

"I'm whining. I'm sorry. It's a wonderful job and I love it, but I'm starting to seriously stress about graduating and getting a real job."

"I feel that. I've spent many nights lying awake wondering if I should just get another degree and keep doing this for another couple of years."

"Working out and getting paid? I could get down with that too."

Dakota is athletic and in great shape, but after the first class, she falls back onto her mat and declares that she is done.

"That was beginner?" She places a forearm over her eyes.

"You didn't have to do the modified versions."

"I was trying to keep up with you. I failed."

"Thanks for coming. It was good to chat and get my mind off everything."

"Any time. I was thinking..." She bites the corner of her lip.

"Uh-oh."

"I think you could do this as a job after college."

"The pay is crap. I'd be living in cheap apartments with twelve roommates."

"What if it wasn't?"

"Then sign me up, but I've looked around. It's crappy pay and no benefits."

"I have an idea. Can I stay and record the next class?"

"You want to record the class?"

"Well, no. I want to record you."

Maverick walks in and raises a hand in greeting before he joins us.

"Staying for class or just finishing up?" he asks Dakota.

"Both." She looks to me. "I'll only record you. I won't get anyone else so you don't have to worry about getting waivers or permission or whatever."

"Record her for what?"

"I want to show Sienna how great she could be teaching yoga online."

I'm sorry, what?!

"You'd be great at that," he says definitively. "You can get me in the shots. I make yoga sexy."

Dakota rolls her eyes.

"Don't deprive the world of my mad yoga skills."

"What do you say?" she asks me, grinning hopefully.

It's time to start class and I don't have time to think through everything she's throwing at me right now. "Fine. Yes to recording, but try to make it look casual so it doesn't disrupt the class and only me and Maverick."

"Yay!" She does a little happy shimmy.

"And no posting anything until I see it."

"Of course. It's going to be amazing. I promise."

"Mhmmm. I'll believe that when I see it."

My class doesn't seem to notice Dakota filming from her mat, but I do. I spend the first five minutes stiff and robotic in my movements and instruction. Soon enough though I'm able to get into the flow and mostly forget that someone has a camera aimed at me.

When class is over, I cringe as she approaches with her phone.

"It's okay. I don't need to see it to know how awkward that was."

Mav stands beside her staring at her screen.

"It's a little shaky at the beginning. I had trouble finding the right angle, but there's some good stuff here."

"Look at that perfect form." Mav grins.

"I hate to admit this, but the camera loves you," she says to him.

His smile couldn't be any bigger as he throws an arm around her shoulders.

"Is the room free? Can we try a couple of things?"

"You don't have to do this," I say.

"I want to."

"Why?"

"Because, as your friend, I see potential in you that you cannot see."

"There are so many yoga videos out there already." Most of them crap, admittedly.

When I'm not convinced she adds, "You have a story. That makes people want to like and follow you. And you're a really good yoga teacher."

"Plus, you're hot," Mav says.

I laugh, but Dakota nods. "He isn't wrong. That helps too."

"Let me take some video and play around with formats. You're right, there are a ton of yoga videos out there, but they don't have you."

"Fine. Okay. What else do I have going on tonight?"

"That's the spirit," she says with a laugh.

OVER THE NEXT WEEK, THINGS GET EASIER. I MISS RHETT something fierce but I keep busy with classes and Dakota's new obsession of turning me into a yoga influencer. I cringe every time she says the word influencer.

We film videos, take photos in the studio and all around campus. I have to say, even if I never get the courage to post any of it, it was worth all the time and energy in distracting me.

"Let's go out tonight," Dakota says Thursday afternoon.

We're video chatting as I walk back to my dorm from classes.

"I can tell by that look on your face you were planning to stay in and sulk."

"I'm not sulking. I just don't feel like being overly happy."

She laughs at me. "Noted. I will make sure you only have a decent time then. Nothing too fun."

"Okay. I'm in. I'm going to ask Josie and Olivia, too." They've also been pestering me about going out so I can please everyone at once.

"Cool. I'll see if I can pry Reagan and Ginny away from their men."

We meet up at Dakota and Reagan's apartment. They've bought enough wine and mixed drinks to keep the whole group of us drunk for a week, and Dakota has dance music pumping in their living room.

"We have sparkling water, Gatorade, and Diet Coke," Reagan says as I enter the kitchen to survey the drink options.

"Thank you."

She shakes her ass as she walks away, cup in hand. "Meet you on the dance floor."

For almost an hour that's exactly where we stay. We have a dance party in the middle of their living room, belting out every lyric and jumping around. It feels good to get lost in the music and the moment with my friends.

We move outside to take a break. Josie sits beside me and rests her head on my shoulder. "I can't believe you're graduating and leaving me all alone."

"Hey!" Olivia nudges her from the other side.

"We should throw a party to celebrate," Josie says, sitting tall. "We could do it at Kate's house."

"You guys don't need to do that. This is perfect. Just my girls."

"We'll be there too," she says. "And maybe some hockey boys."

"They tend to follow these two around," Dakota says and points to Ginny and Reagan.

"Please??" Josie asks. "It'll be so fun. Let us send you off with a proper goodbye." She kisses the air.

I smile. "Sure. That sounds great. Thank you."

But my chest aches when I realize the only hockey boy I want won't be there.

The next morning, I wake up early. My body refuses to accept that I no longer need to be up and at practice in the mornings. So, I get dressed and head there anyway.

I warm up and then fall into my old routine. It's weird to think that there will be no more new programs. I'm not sad about giving up competing or shows. I could do both of those things if I really wanted. And I know I'll still skate. I'll make time for it because I love it. But this... just being on the ice with nowhere else to be. I will miss it being such a big part of my daily routine.

The lights are still dimmed and I'm the only person here. With both the hockey teams and our season being done, I can finally have a little bit of that solitude on the ice I've been wanting all semester long.

Admittedly, it isn't as great as I thought it would be. I was used to keeping people at arm's length before Rhett. I used a lot of things as an excuse. Needing to skate, my heart condition, and probably a million other things, but he changed me. I don't think I can ever go back to believing that I'm better off on my own.

I'm strong enough to skate, to love, to give someone all of my heart—every imperfect piece. I just hope that when he comes out on the other side of this, he can accept it and accept me.

Every imperfect piece.

Chapter Thirty-Five

RHETT

It's quiet at the rink. Summer camps haven't started, and few people come in before late afternoon when school is done for the day.

"Probably feels small after all the big arenas you've been skating in the past four years." My mom appears at the gate.

"Still my favorite." I stop in front of her. "Anything you need me to do? I could help with one of the classes later?"

"We've got it covered."

"I know you do, but I'm here, I might as well help."

"You're not on the payroll for another month."

"Mom, come on. Let me help. I heard you and dad complaining about the coach for Ryder's class. I can jump in there."

"I know that you're eager to be useful while you're here, but that's not why you came, and I don't want to have to replace you if you decide to go back. If you want to help today, fine. But just for today."

"I'm not going to up and leave you high and dry. I love this place."

"And it will be here in a month or two when you're ready."

It's exasperating not having a purpose to the day. For years it's been school or hockey, and now I wake up each day, do whatever classwork I need to finish and submit so I can still graduate, and then come to the rink. I'm here when it opens and usually when it closes, but my mom has been adamant that I take this time for myself.

Officially, my role will be teaching private hockey lessons and working the camps. I'm excited to start. I have all sorts of plans for expanding the rink and making it better, but she's probably right. I used Sienna as a crutch in Valley and here I'm doing the same trying to keep so busy I don't have to really deal with it. I've been home for almost two weeks and still I don't know what the hell I'm doing.

"Have you gone to see Cory and Cam yet?"

I hang my head and give it a shake. The look she gives me says more than her words ever could.

"Oh, shoot is that the time?" She glances over my head to the clock on the wall. "The repair guy still hasn't shown up and I have to get your brother in ten minutes."

"I'll get him."

She gives me that look again.

"Fine, then at least let me call the repair guy, and I will call Cory tomorrow. I promise."

She's out of choices and she knows it. "Invite them to dinner this week."

"Mom, you don't have to—"

"It's going to be hard. Don't make it harder than it needs to be." She straightens. "That locker room door has to be fixed today.

We have a peewee hockey game here tomorrow morning and I need a working door. If they try to put you off, call someone else."

"I will manage. Go."

I give up after I get three answering services and one person who says they can do it, but can't get out until the week after next. Digging through the maintenance closet, I find tools and head off to the boy's locker room.

The mammoth solid wood door is heavy as fuck. I'm sweating and swearing as I try to remove it from the hinges.

"Anyone here?" someone calls from the front doors.

"Hang a right," I call and rest the door against the wall, thankful the repair guy finally decided to show his ass up. It's probably going to take two of us to get it back on.

I wipe my hands on a rag as he steps into view. His jeans are far too clean to be the repair guy and there's no toolbox in sight.

"Rhett?" He juts his chin.

"Yeah. Who are you?"

He grins. A cocky smirk that flickers recognition in my brain. "Elias."

"TO WHAT DO I OWE THE PLEASURE? WAIT, DOES SIENNA KNOW you're here? She'll be so pissed I met you before she did."

"No, she doesn't know, but actually I met our girl last week."

"Really?" I smile, picturing Sienna's face meeting her best friend after all this time.

He nods. I get the sense he's not going to give me more details unless I pry.

"How is she?"

"Oh no. You won't get any info out of me."

I chuckle. "Fair enough. Wanna tell me why you're here then?"

"In time, Robbie."

"Kind of far from Toronto to swing by."

"We're training in Auburn for the next two months. It's my partner, Taylor's hometown rink."

"Well, if you're not going to tell me why you're here, wanna grab a side? This door is sticking. A little kid couldn't get out last night. Major catastrophe."

Elias snickers. "I'll bet."

We work together to replace the warped hinge and then get the door back on.

"Thank fuck," I say when we test it out and the door swings open without issue.

I toss him a dirty rag to wipe his hands and then grab a couple of stray chairs and motion for him to sit while I do the same.

"Place isn't half bad." He sits and glances around the arena.

"It's been in my family for four generations. Skating and hockey camps in the summer, classes year-round, and we rent it out for teams." I have a lot of plans to expand and bring in more revenue opportunities, but in time.

"Reminds me of the rink I grew up skating at." His gaze continues to roam. "She almost came to see you."

"She did?" My heart kicks up a notch at just the idea.

"She talked herself out of it. Decided you needed to work out your shit on your own."

I nod. I guess I did say that, and I meant it, but in the time we've been apart, I just feel like I'm slogging through mud. I'm slowly losing my mind, or what's left of it, anyway.

"I miss her."

"But?"

"I don't want to drag her down with me while I work through my shit."

"Because you don't think she can handle it physically?"

I stare at him.

"Her heart condition? It's cool, man, I get it. I can't tell you how many people have walked away because it's more than they can deal with. If you and Sienna have any chance together, you're going to have to lean on her. You're going to have to trust that she's strong enough."

"Of course, she's fucking strong enough. I didn't leave because I don't think she's healthy enough to deal. Fuck. Is that what she thinks? I'm angry and sad, and she doesn't deserve any of that. She's an angel." My angel.

"Do you want to know what makes me and Sienna so close? What makes any two people close, I'd wager?"

I don't respond, but he keeps going. "Going through challenging shit together. Being vulnerable and letting the other person see all your fucked-up-ness. For Sienna and me, it's our heart condition. We get to say things to one another—scary shit—that we can't admit to anyone else."

"Cross my heart, hope to die." I do the X over my heart I've seen them do a dozen times.

"Exactly."

"This is different."

"It really isn't. She just wants to be there for you—whatever you need. You said it was coming here so she let you go. She's a tough chick. She'll always give you what you need, but is that really being thousands of miles away from her? You've been through some shit and I'm sorry for that, man. Truly. But girls like Sienna don't come around very often. I suggest you get your shit together, Rhett, and go get our girl before I have to see her sad face one more time when I call. I've got my own problems I need her to focus on."

I chuckle knowing that's exactly how Sienna and his relationship goes. She helps him. She's his rock.

He stands and offers me his hand. "I have to get going, but I'm glad I stopped by. You're not half bad, hockey player. Don't make me regret liking you."

THE FOLLOWING NIGHT, CARRIE'S PARENTS COME OVER FOR dinner. When we're finished, we all go outside. My mom and Cory walk around admiring the new garden mom put in this year. Dad and Ryder are playing catch in the yard, and that leaves me with Carrie's dad, Cam, sitting on the porch. I'm just waiting for him to dig into me for missing the funeral.

"School already done for the year?"

"No. Two more weeks to go. My professors are letting me turn in assignments remotely."

He nods thoughtfully. "Planning on going to graduation or are you going to skip that too?" He gives me a look as he lifts the bottle to his lips. Cam was in the military, a sergeant, and he has this glare that makes a man want to piss himself.

"I don't know," I say honestly. I wipe a sweaty palm on my thigh. "I'm sorry that I left. I should have been there. That's why I came back. I know it doesn't change anything, but I felt like I needed to be here."

"How many lefts are you going to take to try to make it right?"

"I'm still going to graduate even if I'm not there. I don't need to wear the cap and gown. I don't even need the degree." Not really. I've always known I wanted to work at the rink and someday take it over completely.

"And you don't need to go to a funeral to grieve. If you're looking for absolution from me, you won't find it. Hell, you don't need it. I know how much you cared about my daughter and that's enough for me."

I swallow. "Thank you, sir."

Knowing he doesn't hate me, is a relief but it doesn't make me feel as good as I hoped.

He asks about the rink, hockey, school. We bullshit and keep the conversation light until my mom and Cory wander back over.

"We should probably get home," Cory says to Cam. She smiles at me. "It was good to see you. Stop by the house sometime, huh?"

"I will." I get up to walk them out.

Cory hugs me, a little teary-eyed.

At the front door, my parents follow Cory out to her car, still chatting away, and Cam hangs back to shake my hand.

"You know, most celebrations in life aren't really about the person you're supposed to be celebrating. Funerals, baby showers, *graduations*."

"Your point?"

"There are few things I was looking forward to more than

watching my baby girl walk across the stage and get her college diploma." He squeezes my hand a little harder. "Understand what I'm saying?"

I glance at my mom and dad. "Yes, sir."

He hugs me. I think it's the first in all the time I've known him that he's ever embraced me. It's not his style, or mine, but something tells me he isn't hugging me right now. He's hugging the closest thing to his kid he's got left. So I hug him back and then I go inside and pack my bags.

Chapter Thirty-Six

RHETT

The early afternoon sun soaks up the dew on the grass and birds chirp in the distance. The soil underneath my feet is still new and the grass hasn't had a chance to grow yet.

"I thought I'd know what to say by now," I whisper to Carrie's headstone. "I guess… I'm sorry. I'm sorry that I didn't know how to be your friend after everything we'd been through. I'm sorry that I hurt you because that's never what I wanted."

I let out a sigh and look up at the blue sky. "I'm mad at you, Carrie. I'm so mad at you for getting in the car. I know that doesn't make any sense. I hoped someday we could be friends. Maybe that was wishful thinking. I don't know."

"It doesn't make any sense to me. Why you? Why now? You were going to do such incredible things. That much I know for a fact."

"Your parents are going to be okay. Don't worry about them. I'll look after them. I wasn't always a good friend, I probably wasn't always a good boyfriend either, but you're the first girl I ever loved and I'll never forget you."

I back away from the grave and then turn to get in the car.

"Are you okay?" my mom asks when I'm seated in the passenger side.

"Yeah. I'm okay."

She hugs me. She's been doing that a lot lately. I think Carrie dying hit us all in different ways and I don't know when we'll feel normal again. Not today, that's for sure.

My mom starts for the airport and I swivel in my seat to face Ryder. Ever since I announced I was leaving last night, he hasn't spoken to me.

"I'm going to miss you, Ry, but I'll see you in two weeks for my graduation, and then I'll be back for good."

The only acknowledgment I get that he heard me, is him turning his head farther away from me to look out the window.

"I was wondering if you wanted this?" I pull the Bruins hat out of my bag. "I bought it for someone a long time ago, but she didn't really like it." I lean closer to him. "She wasn't really a fan of the Bruins, can you imagine?"

"You never could resist teasing her about the Bruins winning the Cup that year." Mom smiles at the memory. Yeah, I guess I had bought it as a joke, but she held on to it and giving it to Ryder just feels right. He didn't know Carrie that well, but I think she would have wanted him to have it.

He squirms and eyes the hat in my hands. "It's like yours, but cleaner."

"Yep." I hold it out to him, but he still doesn't take it.

"I'll tell you what. I'll set it here and if you don't want it, just put it back in my room later, okay?"

Finally he looks at me. "Are you going away like Carrie did or are you really coming back?"

I can't speak for a few seconds as I swallow the lump in my throat. "I'm really coming back."

He doesn't look convinced so I unbuckle and crawl through the opening between the seats to the back.

"What in the world?" My mother laughs as I try to squeeze through. It is not easy.

"You're too big." Ryder giggles as I struggle to sit beside him.

And I laugh too. It feels good. I put the hat on his head and then hit the brim of mine against his. "I'll see you soon."

I GET BACK TO VALLEY LATE SUNDAY EVENING. ADAM PICKED ME up and I had him bring me straight to the arena. I knew she'd be here. I could feel her and every step closer to the ice feels like I'm rushing to the finish line. She's it for me. She's my endgame.

When I see her, it takes my breath away. Hiding in the shadows, I put on my skates and watch her glide around the ice. My heart hammers in my chest, and my stomach is in knots. It's crossed my mind that she might not be nearly as excited to see me as I am her.

She stops in the center of the ice. Her chest rises and falls as she catches her breath. She places her hands on top of her head and scans the arena like she's memorizing it.

Fuck, I missed her. I missed the way everything feels better when she's nearby. I thought I was relying too much on her, like she was a drug that I couldn't live without. I was so scared that staying would destroy us both. But the truth is, I can live without her. And she can live without me.

We were both doing just fine on our own two months ago. I don't want to be fine. I want to know that I have a partner that will let me lean on her when life kicks me in the teeth. And the same for her. I want to be her person and kick life in the teeth when it tries to mess with her.

Slowly, I walk toward the plexiglass. Seconds or minutes pass as she stands there center ice taking it all in.

The click of the gate catches her attention and her eyes widen slightly when I step out. It's the only indication that I've caught her by surprise.

"Rhett." My name out of her mouth sets every part of me on fire.

"I thought I'd find you here."

"Habit." She still hasn't moved. "You're back."

I go to her. "Yeah, I'm back."

"How are you? I mean… did you do what you needed to?"

"Truthfully? I'm not sure. I'm still a little lost."

"I get that."

"Some days I feel like I dreamed the whole thing. I feel guilty and sad. I'm pissed at myself and at the world. I'm even pissed at Carrie which I realize makes me sound like the worst possible asshole."

"You're not an asshole."

"I'm going to try my hardest not to be, but I'm still figuring out how to move forward. Basically, I'm a mess but I want to be here with you."

"But you said—"

"I was wrong. You were trying to tell me that it was okay to unload on you and I couldn't bring myself to believe it. Everything is better with you. And that isn't me not dealing, that's just the honest truth."

"I know you think I'm broken, that my heart makes me weak, but it doesn't. I can handle it."

"I don't think that. I never thought that. I didn't leave because I thought you weren't strong enough. I left because I wasn't sure I was. You are the strongest chick I know. The strongest person I know. Your heart isn't broken. *You're* not broken. I hate that I ever made you question that."

"When people get close to me they realize one of two things: that there's a good chance that I might die or they internalize it and realize they're not bulletproof either. Which are you?"

"I'm both. I can survive a lot of things, but not living without you."

She blows out a breath and a small smile curves her mouth. "Wow. You should disappear more often."

"I had some help getting there," I say, then add. "Elias came to see me."

"He did?"

"He's a good friend. I'm glad you have him. You're his rock. Turns out, you're mine too."

"I don't know what to say. You caught me off guard." She wraps her arms around her middle, keeping her distance.

It stings even though I knew it was a real possibility she'd tell me to eat mud. I was hoping her response would be an enthusiastic yes and then lots of kissing. I've missed kissing her and holding her.

"This is all so sudden. Maybe I could have some time to think about it?"

Damn. I really fucked this up. I nod slowly. "Of course. I know how much you hate surprises, but I needed to see you as soon as I got back."

"I'll text you."

"Okay, yeah, uh, you have my number." I give her finger guns and then a little piece of me dies that I'm fucking this up so badly.

I turn and skate off the ice as fast as I can go. When I get to the gate, she calls after me, "Hey, Rauthruss."

I compose myself, ball my hands into fists, and turn. *No finger guns, asshole*. "Yeah?"

She skates to me, stopping short and spraying me with ice. Amusement twinkles in her green eyes. "I'll skate you for it."

A thousand pounds lifts off my shoulders and I bite back a smile "You want to race me?"

"If you win, then you get my heart."

"And if I lose?"

She launches herself forward and hugs me. Air fills my lungs and I breathe in all of her.

"I love you so much. I'm so sorry I left. Never again. I'll prove it however you want me to, as many times as you want me to."

"You already own my heart. I don't know when it happened, but I am madly in love with you too."

I smash my lips to hers. We stumble around on the ice, kissing and hugging. It's impossible to get close enough. I need her. I want her. Forever.

"We might need to get out of here because I have a feeling getting my balls stuck to the ice would fucking hurt."

She laughs into my mouth. "Take me to bed then, Rauthruss, or the bathroom maybe." She pulls back and gives me finger guns.

I groan. "I'm never living that down, am I?"

"Definitely not in this lifetime."

And that's exactly how long I intend to keep her. This lifetime and all the others, too.

Chapter Thirty-Seven

RHETT

"Do you guys want to watch a movie or something?" Adam asks from the doorway while giving me finger guns.

I flip him off for mocking me. I'm the dumbass that told him and I really regret it. The guys mock me with it hourly. Whatever. I got the girl, so what if I had to make an ass of myself to do it? I'm sure it won't be the last time.

"Nah, I have to watch some creepy ass documentary."

A pillow hits me on the side of the head. "You said you wanted to watch it."

"I said I wanted to spend the night in bed naked. Not the same thing."

"This." She holds up her laptop. "Leads to this." She waves a hand in front of her.

Adam grins at Sienna and then nods. "I'll leave you guys to it then."

"Oh wait." Sienna stops him before he leaves. "Did Reagan tell you about the party Friday?"

"Yeah, she mentioned it. She said you wanted me to spread the word."

"Yes, please. All the hockey players."

"Thinking of trading me in?" I ask with the lift of a brow.

"No, but where the hockey team goes, others follow, and Josie wants this party to be epic."

My buddy taps the doorframe. "We'll be there. It'll be my final order as captain."

"Thank you." Sienna beams at him. Her smile makes me smile—a big, dopey grin that is basically the equivalent of finger guns.

We lie in bed, Sienna between my legs, her back resting against my chest as we watch the documentary. It's about a serial killer who targeted people in their homes at night and it is creepy as fuck. She doesn't seem fazed. Of course she doesn't. I close my eyes for a second, but I must doze off because the next thing I know I'm being woken up by a half-naked woman and a fully erect dick.

"Did you like the documentary?" she purrs.

"Mhmmm." My voice is gravel. "I especially liked the end part where you got naked."

"You fell asleep."

"I'm awake now." I slide my arms around her and press her into me while tilting my hips up.

Her mouth covers mine in a sweet and slow kiss. She pulls back and green eyes stare at me for a long beat.

"What's wrong? Heart beating too fast?" I reach for my phone and pull up the tracking app. "Seems normal. Chest hurt?"

She gapes at the screen. "Oh my god, Rhett Rauthruss, did you sync my watch to your phone?"

"Damn right I did, angel."

"I can't decide if that's serial killer creepy or sweet."

"Definitely sweet." I put my phone back and flip us so I'm on top.

She's shaking her head but grinning at me in that way that makes *my* heart feel all fluttery. "I love you."

"I love you too, angel." I hop up and lock my bedroom door.

"Afraid someone is going to walk in on us?"

"No, I'm afraid I'm going to be murdered in my sleep."

Her sweet laughter fills the room. "I'll save you, baby."

She has no idea how much she already has.

Friday night, we head over to Kate's house for Sienna's party. I don't think Adam had to do much convincing to get all the guys here. Sienna said free keg and they all perked right up.

My girl is looking extra fine in a short skirt that I intend to have my head under before the end of the night.

"Did you tell your parents?" I ask as we walk up the sidewalk toward the house.

"Yep. My dad was a little bummed, but I promised him that if I failed miserably, I'd reconsider working at his company."

"You won't fail."

Dakota took a bunch of photos and videos of Sienna doing yoga and it blew up. There's this one where she's doing some pose on the ice and it is fire. She's working on making a paid site where users can gain membership to online classes and uploaded videos. I'm excited for her.

I'm also excited that I was able to convince her she could do that just as easily living with me.

"I have a surprise." Sienna stops short of the door.

"But you hate surprises."

"This is a good one. I promise." She pulls me through the house to the backyard. My teammates are all standing around in their jerseys. And, damn, there's a lot of people here. People really do follow wherever we go.

"Surprise!"

"I don't understand. I thought this was a party for you?"

"It is. Kind of. They wanted to throw me a party and I figured out a way to celebrate both of us. I know things are still hard, but you have a lot to celebrate too. You won a national championship and you have a great job lined up. Plus, you got me."

She pulls a wad of blue material from her purse and holds it up. It's my hockey jersey, or a really good replica.

"How'd you pull this off?" I ask, pulling my jersey down over my head. Man, I never thought I'd get to wear it again. I swear I've got goose bumps.

A mischievous grin pulls at her lips. "I can't say, but if they aren't returned by noon tomorrow, I might not graduate."

"You're incredible. Thank you."

"You haven't seen the best part." She steps back and picks up a confetti cannon.

A deep chuckle rumbles from my chest. Swiping it from her, I fire it into the air above us. It rains down as I kiss her. Now *this* feels like something worth celebrating.

Epilogue

SIENNA

The girl sitting in front of me shoots me a glare and plugs her right ear. I keep right on screaming, though, as Rhett walks across the stage with his diploma. He catches my eye and holds it up. I do the same.

We did it!

He comes down the side aisle, and I abandon my seat to meet him at the back of the gymnasium. I leap into his arms, tassels dangling between us. "We graduated!"

"Thank fuck." He picks me up and twirls. "Ready to party, angel?"

We have an early dinner with our parents. Our fathers have become best buds overnight. They both love their time on the lake, football, and their families. And I think our mothers have planned a vacation together this summer.

"Good thing I don't plan on getting rid of you anytime soon," Rhett whispers in my ear. "Because our families would be devastated."

"Get rid of me?" I rest my hand high up on his thigh,

dangerously close to his balls, and squeeze.

"I said I *don't* plan on getting rid of you anytime soon."

"Maybe I plan on getting rid of you."

"Oh no, you're stuck with me for at least the next year."

I smile at the mention of our lease agreement. I still can't believe it. We found the cutest condo not too far from his family's rink and it has a lake view that is going to be amazing for recording yoga videos until I get a studio of my own.

I can't believe this is my life.

"Can we steal Allison for the night?" I ask as we're hugging our families goodbye. "I promise to return her before you need to leave for the airport in the morning."

"No drinking," my father says immediately, like my master plan was to take my fifteen-year-old sister out and get her plastered. Cleaning up puke is not on the agenda tonight.

We head straight to the arena.

"What are we doing here?" Allison asks as I hold open the door for her.

Our friends are waiting in the tunnel.

Allison goes a little starry-eyed when she sees all the guys in their skates with sticks.

"We're going to play a little hockey," I tell her and loop my arm through hers. "You're on my team."

"Seriously?" Her voice squeaks.

"Seriously." Mav steps forward and hands her a stick. "Let's see if we can find you some skates in the equipment closet."

The rest of us walk out onto the ice. Reagan's clutching Adam's hand and Dakota is holding her arms out, yelling at anyone that gets within three feet of her.

“I’ve got this,” she demands. “Just give me a second.”

“I’m going to miss this,” I say, watching our friends as Rhett and I skate together holding hands.

“Me too. It hit me when we stepped out here, I’m never going to play another game of hockey.” He looks up into the empty stands. “I mean, I knew it. It’s been more than a month since our last game, but it finally hit me.”

In the weeks since Rhett’s been back at Valley, there have been times he’s battled his emotions. Sometimes he’ll take my hand or hug me a little tighter and I know that he’s struggling a little more in those moments. And I’m just there. Right now, it’s my turn to be the rock, but I know there will be times I’ll need him to be mine too.

When we skate around to the benches, I reach in and grab two hockey sticks.

“You’ll play. You will. You’ve got beer league written all over you.”

He grins and lifts the hem of his T-shirt showing off his six-pack.

“Top tier.” I hand him a stick. “Plus, you’ll need to keep sharp if you’re going to beat me.”

“Yeah?” One brow lifts. “You think you can take me, angel?”

“Oh, I know it. It’s all in the butt.”

His gaze is glued to mine as I turn and stick it out and take a shot. The ding of the puck hitting the post finally makes him look up and he lights up. Admiration burns in his eyes. It really is the best sound in the world. Or maybe it’s the way he’s looking at me like I’m his everything.

He skates in a circle around me. “Been practicing?”

"No, I got lucky." I fist his T-shirt in my palm to drag him closer. I got really, really lucky the day Rhett collided into me. And every day since.

Epilogue

RHETT

Three years later

"Twenty-three, huh?" I ask Ryder as he walks out to the bench wearing his game jersey.

He shrugs it off like it's no big deal, but I love that my little bro is carrying on the Rauthruss number.

"Are you ready for today?" I ask, taking a seat on the bench. It's the Mighty Cubs first game of the season.

I get another lift and fall of his shoulders. I might be more nervous than any of my players. It's my first time coaching and even though it's just a bunch of local kids looking to have fun and play hockey, I feel the pressure like I did going into big college games.

"How much longer?" My brother stands impatiently near the gate ready to take the ice.

"They're almost done," I assure him and find my wife at the other end of the rink teaching a group of three and four-year-olds. They march forward toward a pile of toys in the center of the ice.

Sienna marches in front of them in tennis shoes, showing how it's done and encouraging them to lift their legs higher. Her pregnant bump leads the way and pride, excitement, and more than a little nerves spreads through my chest. She's thirty-six weeks and hasn't been able to skate since we found out she was pregnant around nine weeks in, but she refused to give up teaching. She's good at it too. Particularly with the younger kids. They love her.

She started coaching figure skating the summer after we graduated. It began as a way to make money while she built her yoga business, and now she splits her days between the rink and her studio.

"I came up with a few more names for the baby," Ryder says, pulling my attention back to him.

"Let's hear them." I cross my arms over my chest.

"I was thinking Peter or Parker."

The corner of my lips twitch with amusement. "Spider-Man?"

He grins and nods. "Or Bruce for the Hulk, Clark for Superman, there are so many good options and how cool would it be if the baby was named after someone awesome?"

Sienna's class has finished, the kids clutch their toys in their hands, and she corrals them off the ice. "I'll run them by the boss."

"Okay." He stands, anxious to get out there. "Cool."

"Stay out of the way as dad cleans the ice, all right?" I head toward Sienna as he rushes out with his hockey stick and a handful of pucks.

"Hey, angel." I palm her stomach and drop a kiss on her cheek.

She whimpers and places a hand on her lower back. "This kid of yours is misbehaving today."

Smiling, I place my other hand on her stomach. "Don't worry, little angel, I'll protect you from your mom."

I don't know a lot about being a dad yet, but I know this kid already has me wrapped around its finger. Only two more weeks until I get to meet him. Because of her heart condition, the doctor recommended a C-section. And because my girl hates surprises, she was all for having a date on the calendar.

"Are you staying for the game?" I ask.

"Of course. I picked out a seat right next to the bench so I can heckle the hottie coach."

"I'm nervous," I admit.

"You're going to be great. Ryder's ready to carry you to victory." She nods her head where he's skating backward in front of the Zamboni like it's a defender. I start to yell at him to move, but our dad's grinning from the driver's seat.

"Good luck, Coach."

When the rest of our team arrives, I give the world's worst pep talk while sweating bullets and then send them out to play. Some of these kids have been playing together since they were in preschool, which means they pick up the slack of my novice coaching. Ryder's incredible. At eight he's already a great hockey player.

By the start of the third period, I've relaxed. We're up by five and I'm rotating my players through to give everyone a chance to play together.

A tug at my elbow makes my gaze snap to the left. Sienna stands outside of the bench in the walkway to the tunnel.

"Angel. Come to kiss the coach?" I lean against the half wall and stare out at my players.

"I've come to steal him away," she says. "It's time."

"Time for what?" I'm still staring at the game as we talk.

"It's *time*."

I give her my attention and her words sink in. "It's time?"

She nods.

"Oh my gosh. It's time!"

My dad's right behind her and steps into the bench. He grabs my shoulder and squeezes. "I've got it from here, Coach. We'll meet you at the hospital."

"Thank you," I rush out, taking Sienna's hand.

I don't remember the drive to the hospital or getting her signed in. It isn't until they shoo me out of the room to administer the epidural that all of my worries and anxiety about being a dad and Sienna going through delivery hit me at once.

I pace the hallway. My mom arrives and tries to calm me down, but I don't breathe easy until I'm back in the room.

I rush to her bed and let out a shaky breath.

"Easy there, Dad," the nurse says as my knees buckle. "Would you like to sit down?"

Sienna smirks, but then another contraction hits and her face contorts with the pain.

"No, I'm good." I take Sienna's hand and let her squeeze it until the bones feel like they'll break. "I'm here, angel. Just breathe."

Her pain gives me something to focus on. "I thought the epidural stopped the pain."

"It'll take a few minutes to kick in," the nurse says while Sienna continues to crush my fingers.

When it's time, I'm given scrubs to put on over my clothes and a hairnet and little booties. I stay right by the side of her bed as they wheel her into the surgical room.

She looks over to me with tears in her eyes. "What's wrong?

Does it still hurt?" I'm ready to throw down in here until I find someone who can stop the pain.

"What if something goes wrong?"

I swallow thickly. "Everything is going to be fine."

"What if I'm a terrible mother?"

"No chance, angel."

"I'm so scared. Distract me."

I lean over her until my mouth hovers next to her ear. Then I sing. The same song I sang the first time she dragged me to a real karaoke night and the same song I sang to her as we had our first dance at our wedding. Mister Bryan Adams has come through for me in some clutch moments.

She closes her eyes and smiles as I sing "Heaven". That's exactly what she is. My heaven. My angel.

"Here he is," the nurse says with a soft smile as our baby cries out.

We look up as they place our son on Sienna's chest briefly. He's got her dark hair, but the rest I don't make out through the tears in my eyes. My heart swells and I feel more pride and love than I ever have.

"He's perfect." Sienna puts her nose to his head and inhales.

I kiss her temple. "Absolutely perfect."

THE NEXT MORNING WE'RE BLEARY-EYED FROM LACK OF SLEEP but deliriously happy. Mom stayed most of the night with us, but had to leave to see to the rink. Dad brings Ryder by just as the baby is waking up.

He walks in with slow, hesitant steps.

"Do you want to meet your nephew?" Sienna asks him.

Dad takes a seat next to me, and Ryder goes to stand next to the hospital bed.

"Mom wouldn't tell me what you named him. Did you go with one of my suggestions?"

"About that." I stand and step up beside him. "We talked about it, and Sienna and I decided you were right. He should be named after someone awesome."

Ryder grins.

"Which is why we named him after you," Sienna says. "Meet Ryan Ryder Rauthruss."

My brother's eyes widen and his mouth pulls up into a smile. "Cool."

The four of us chuckle and stare at Ryan. Dad hands me a little blue teddy bear. "From Cory and Cam."

I take the soft stuffed animal in my hands and feel a twinge of sadness for all the moments like this that they won't have. I've done my best to keep my promise to Carrie. I talked Cam into helping with our middle school hockey camps in the summer and I have coffee with Cory every Sunday morning. It doesn't change anything. I get that. Somewhere along the line, my promise to look after them became a way to remember her instead.

Ryder grins from ear to ear as he sits on the bed next to Sienna and she carefully places Ryan in his arms.

"I can't wait to teach him to play hockey."

"Maybe he wants to be a figure skater." Sienna nudges him playfully.

Ryder scrunches up his nose.

Sienna's phone rings from the table and she lifts it with a smile. I know that smile. It's reserved for Elias. They still talk almost every day and a few months ago he and Taylor spent a month with us while they prepared for a competition.

The day continues with family and friends calling and stopping by to see us. Adam calls and I give him every detail from Ryan's dark hair to his tiny, perfect toes. Maverick texts congrats and makes plans to come see us as soon as he can. Even Heath gets the news and sends congratulations and best wishes from him and Ginny.

When night falls and the hospital quietens, it's just the three of us. My little family. I crowd in next to Sienna on her small bed and Ryan sleeps in the bassinet beside us. The TV is on mute as we watch the Wildcats game.

"Maverick's having a great game," Sienna whispers with her head resting on my chest.

"He asked if he could be Ryan's godfather if he got a hat trick tonight."

She lifts her head an inch. "What did you say?"

"I said hell yes."

She laughs quietly and then yawns. "I don't think I've ever been so tired. Or so happy."

"Me either, angel." I close my eyes. "Get some sleep."

"He'll be up again soon."

"Mhmmm." I think it's the first time I've ever looked forward to being woken up by someone crying or screaming. I probably won't even sleep long enough to dream. Doesn't matter. Even the wildest dreams couldn't compare with this.

ACKNOWLEDGMENTS

Thanks to Anelise and Katie for always being my cheerleaders, and to my editors Becca and Ellie. You ladies make my books so much better with your insight and eagle eyes!

Thank you to my readers. Your messages and emails mean more to me than you know.

And lastly, thanks to Bianca for answering all my questions and sharing your struggles with me. You are a mother f-ing badass!

ABOUT THE AUTHOR

Rebecca Jenshak is a new adult romance author, caffeine-addict, and lover of all sports.

Be sure not to miss new releases and sales from Rebecca – sign up to receive her newsletter *www.subscribepage.com/rebeccajenshaknewsletter*

www.rebeccajenshak.com

Made in the USA
Coppell, TX
29 May 2023

17470091R00177